Ac
Psychic

"An invigorating   /
realm. . . . I cannot wait for the next book."
                              —Roundtable Reviews

"Well written and unpredictable. Everything about
this book is highly original . . . a fun protagonist
with just enough bravado to keep her going."
                              —*Romantic Times*

"The characters are all realistically drawn and the
situations go from interesting, to amusing, to laugh-
out-loud funny. The best thing a person can do to
while away the cold winter is to cuddle up in front
of a fire with this wonderful book."
                              —The Best Reviews

"A fresh, exciting addition to the amateur sleuth
genre."   —J. A. Konrath, author of *Dirty Martini*

"A fun, light read, and a promising beginning to
an original series."
                    —The Romance Readers Connection

"Victoria Laurie has crafted a fantastic tale in this
latest Psychic Eye Mystery. There are few things
in life that upset Abby Cooper, but ghosts and her
parents feature high on her list. . . . [A] few real
frights and a lot of laughs."   —Fresh Fiction

"A great new series . . . plenty of action!"
                              —*Midwest Book Review*

Other Psychic Eye Mysteries

Abby Cooper, Psychic Eye
Better Read Than Dead
A Vision of Murder
Killer Insight

CRIME SEEN

A Psychic Eye Mystery

Victoria Laurie

AN OBSIDIAN MYSTERY

OBSIDIAN
Published by New American Library, a division of
Penguin Group (USA) Inc., 375 Hudson Street,
New York, New York 10014, USA
Penguin Group (Canada), 90 Eglinton Avenue East, Suite 700, Toronto,
Ontario M4P 2Y3, Canada (a division of Pearson Penguin Canada Inc.)
Penguin Books Ltd., 80 Strand, London WC2R 0RL, England
Penguin Ireland, 25 St. Stephen's Green, Dublin 2,
Ireland (a division of Penguin Books Ltd.)
Penguin Group (Australia), 250 Camberwell Road, Camberwell, Victoria 3124,
Australia (a division of Pearson Australia Group Pty. Ltd.)
Penguin Books India Pvt. Ltd., 11 Community Centre, Panchsheel Park,
New Delhi - 110 017, India
Penguin Group (NZ), 67 Apollo Drive, Rosedale, North Shore 0632,
New Zealand (a division of Pearson New Zealand Ltd.)
Penguin Books (South Africa) (Pty.) Ltd., 24 Sturdee Avenue,
Rosebank, Johannesburg 2196, South Africa

Penguin Books Ltd., Registered Offices:
80 Strand, London WC2R 0RL, England

First published by Obsidian, an imprint of New American Library,
a division of Penguin Group (USA) Inc.

First Printing, September 2007
10 9 8 7 6 5 4

For two women of iconic beauty, brains, and class—
my aunts, Mary Jane Humphreys and
Elizabeth Laurie

Acknowledgments

It is great to love what you do. It is even better when you love who you work with and the people that make up your world. I've been really lucky on that front, with an amazing team devoted to helping me take Abby on all sorts of adventures, whether they're in New York, slaving away behind the scenes, or cheering me on in other parts of the country and inspiring characters and plotlines. Here's where I get to tell them how much I appreciate all they do for me, how incredibly thankful I am that they work so hard on my behalf, and how I don't let a day go by without thanking the Big Guy that they're in my life.

First up, I'd like to thank my amazing editor, Molly Boyle. Again, I have to say good-bye to someone with such talent and class; I'm a little crushed by the prospect of not having this woman marking up my manuscripts with her ever-vigilant red pencil. Instead, she's off to make a whole new group of authors look good—lucky, lucky them.

I'll miss you more than you could know, Molly.

You've been simply wonderful to work with. Thank you so much for everything you've taught me. Your enthusiasm, your grace, and your calm demeanor will forever make me a fan. I wish you the very best of luck on your new adventure. You will be missed . . . every . . . single . . . day.

Kristen Weber—well, it looks like I lucked out again! I was handed over the last time into the very best of care, and so the handoff falls again in my favor. If you have to let go of someone you adore, it's so nice to be given to someone with such an amazing reputation and gracious manner. I'm truly excited and thrilled to be working with you. Thank you so much for agreeing to take me on.

Jim McCarthy, my agent and dear, dear friend. I've said it all before, so here's the shorthand version . . . mush, mush, gush, gush, and all that. You're fabulous. You rule. You're the best. Da bomb diggity. The shizzle. ☺ I love you and thank you so much for . . . well . . . *all* of it!

Sandy Upham, sistah girl. How extraordinary you are. You dazzle me, you know that? Truly, truly. I can't believe such a phenomenal woman shares my blood, my eyes, and my love of water parks. Thank you for always being there, for sharing, for your honesty, and yes . . . sigh . . . even for those "ors." Now get your butt down here and come visit me. I miss you somethin' fierce!

Yohan and Naoko Upham. My little bro and sister-in-law. What an amazing couple you two are. A *powerhouse* of love. What a team you make, and what great cheerleaders you've been. I'm so grateful for your love and support. Rock on, "dudes." (Yohan—that was for you!)

The two women this book is lovingly dedicated to:

Mary Jane Humphreys and Betty Laurie. For forty years you two have been my icons of beauty, class, and women dedicated to living an adventurous life. I am forever in awe of you. Thank you for being my connection to the past, for the revelations, and for the hilarious stories. Here's to Italy this autumn!

Michael Torres. God, you are a beautiful man, do you know that? How amazing you've been to me, how gracious and kind. Thank you for coming into my life, and enriching it with your wonderful friendship.

Karen Ditmars, Leanne Tierney, Nora Brosseau, Tess Rodriguez, Jaa Nawtaisong, Kristy Robinett, Silas Hudson, Thomas Robinson, and *so* many others—I am forever blessed and enriched by your friendships. Everywhere I travel, I always meet the most extraordinary people—many of whom I've been lucky enough to befriend. Thank you, thank you, thank you. I love you all.

Chapter One

The way I see it, there are two kinds of people in this world: cat people and dog people. And as a general rule, you'd be better off mixing oil and water.

Or so I thought as I lay on the couch in my boyfriend's house, recovering from a bullet wound to the chest I'd received three months earlier. My sweetheart, Dutch, owns a big, fat, annoying, allergy-producing tomcat named Virgil. I own a cute, cuddly, adorable, hypoallergenic dachshund named Eggy. I guess you can see which side of the dog-versus-cat smack down I fall on. Yes, I'm biased—so sue me.

On this particular Sunday, however, as Eggy and I were snuggling on the couch and easing into a really good nap, my nose wrinkled. Something smelled off . . . *really* off. "Ugh," I said as I took a whiff. "What *is* that?"

"Abby?" I heard Dutch call from his study. "Did you say something?"

I sat up on the couch and Eggy gave me an annoyed

grunt. "There is really something foul around here," I said, sniffing the air again.

"What?" he asked, coming into the living room. "Did you need something?"

"What's that smell?" I asked him, looking around as I caught Virgil trotting over from behind an end table to twirl figure eights around Dutch's leg. It was then that I spotted something brown and smelly on my purse, lying close to where Virgil had been. "Oh, no! You *didn't*!" I said angrily.

"What's the matter?" Dutch asked me.

I pointed with a growl and snapped, "Your cat just pooped on my purse!"

Dutch turned to look where I was pointing, and I could swear I caught a smirk on his face before he turned back to me and said in a calm, soothing voice, "I'm sure he didn't do it intentionally."

"Of course he didn't do it intentionally!" I spat as I got up off the couch and headed into the kitchen for some paper towels. "Just like he didn't *intend* to pee on my side of the bed the other night, or hurl his hairballs on top of my clean laundry, or use my backpack for a scratching post. I'm sure it's all just a big, fat, furry *coincidence*!"

"Edgar," Dutch said, using his favorite nickname for me, after famed psychic Edgar Cayce. "Come on, he's just a cat. He doesn't have a malicious bone in his body."

"Tell that to the dead chipmunk he showed up with yesterday," I groused as I came back into the living room and scrunched up my face to wipe off my purse. "I'm sure those two had loads of laughs before Virgil *ate him*."

"Try and look at it from Virgil's perspective, Abs.

He was king of the roost until you and Eggy moved in, so he's had to make a pretty big adjustment."

I glared at my boyfriend and raised the wadded-up paper towel in my hand, letting him know just what I thought of Virgil and his "adjustment." "Eggy's had to make some concessions too, you know, and you don't see him walking around here pooping on everything."

Dutch sighed and picked Virgil up protectively. "Can we not fight about this?" he asked me.

I rolled my eyes and stomped into the kitchen. Normally, I like cats. I mean, I like them as long as they keep to themselves and don't defecate on my things. But ever since I'd come here to recover, Virgil had been the bane of my existence, and Dutch refused to believe his feline was out to get me.

I strolled back into the living room, about to continue the argument, but the phone rang. Dutch gave me a "saved by the bell" smile and moved toward it. Glancing at the caller ID before he picked it up, he said, "It's Candice. That's the third call this week. Think you'd better talk to her this time?"

I sat down heavily on the couch. I wasn't ready for this.

I make my living as a professional psychic, and three months ago I'd had a booming practice. All that changed one winter morning when I'd very nearly died after being shot at close range. Okay, scratch that—I technically *had* died, but only for a minute or two.

So ever since then, I'd been laid up here in my boyfriend's home, tucked away in the lovely little city we both live in, Royal Oak, Michigan. For the first month I'd done little more than sleep. My doctor advised me that when you're recovering from a major trauma, like being shot, your body slows down considerably, and mine was no exception.

But over the past two months I'd steadily gotten stronger, and I'd been able to do more physically. Mentally, though, I just could not seem to get a grip. The prospect of going back to work actually terrified me, and even though my bank statements continued to show a decline in my liquid assets, I couldn't motivate myself to get up off the couch and venture back to the office. I reasoned that I'd probably already lost most of my clients anyway. As a psychic, if you stop tuning in, you stop eating.

Dutch, who's an FBI agent, recognized what I was going through. He had labeled it post-traumatic stress disorder, which sounded to me like a tidy way of calling me a loo-loo.

Now here I sat, not having done a single reading in three months, and one of my best clients was on the phone. Again.

I looked up at Dutch and gave him a winning smile. "Can you tell her I'm out and take a message?"

Dutch smirked and answered the phone. "Hi, Candice. You looking for Abby?" I breathed a sigh of relief and sat back on the couch, thinking that I had a great boyfriend after all. "Sure, sure," he said, nodding his head. "She's right here. Hang on," he said casually and extended the phone to me.

I mouthed, "I'll get you for this," and took the receiver. "Hi, Candice!" I said breezily. "Long time no talk."

"Abby!" she sang. "Man, girlfriend! It is so great to finally hear your voice. How're you feeling?"

Dutch was still hovering nearby, and I cut him a look of death but continued to keep my voice light.

"Oh, you know, taking it slow and easy. I still get a little tired, but what can you do?"

Candice clucked into the phone and said, "You poor thing. I bet you haven't gone back to work yet, have you?"

"No," I said, fiddling uncomfortably with the tassel on one of the couch cushions. "I'm easing into the idea. I don't want to push it."

"That's got to be a real drain on your finances," she said. "It must be hard to maintain your mortgage and the rent on your office."

I wasn't sure where Candice was going with this. She and I had never really had a normal psychic/client relationship. Candice was a private detective at a decent-sized firm in Kalamazoo, about 140 miles west of Royal Oak. On occasion she would call me and drive over to get my feelings on a case she was working on. We'd made a great team on the few cases we'd worked together, and I'd come to consider her a friend as well as a client. "Yeah, but I've got some pennies saved, so I should be okay for a while."

I couldn't see Candice's reaction, but I could have sworn I heard a hint of disappointment when she said, "I see."

There was a bit of a pause before I asked her straight out, "Want to tell me what's up?"

Candice giggled. "I never could be subtle with you. Here's the deal, Abs. I've decided to hang my own shingle."

"Really?" I said with a smirk. "Gee, now where have I heard that idea before?"

Candice's giggle turned into a laugh. "Yes, I know, you were right—again!" I had given her a reading about six months before, and in that reading, I'd told her that she was going to entertain the idea of starting her own PI firm, and that it was worth considering. "But here's the catch . . ." she added.

"Yes?" I asked when she paused.

"I need to find cheap office space to work out of."

"Have you tried the classifieds? I'm sure there's plenty available in Kalamazoo."

"No, not in Kalamazoo," she said. "I'm moving in with my grandmother, so I'll need to find a space close to her."

"You're moving here?" I asked. I'd met Candice's rather eccentric grandmother, Madame Dubois, a few months before. She also lived in Royal Oak.

"Yes. Just like you, I need to watch my pennies, and when Nana offered a room in that big house of hers, I couldn't pass it up."

That was when the lightbulb went on in my head. "And you were thinking I could sublet you some office space."

"I know, I know," she said quickly. "I shouldn't have asked. It's just that I know you have that extra room in your suite, and I heard you'd all but quit the business, so I thought I could help you out until you got back on your feet, as well as give myself a little head start."

"It's a terrific idea," I said as the right side of my body went light and airy, which is my sign for yeppers.

"Really?" she said. "Oh, Abby, that's awesome!"

"Absolutely." I grinned. It had been a long time since I'd shared my office with anyone. The extra room in my suite had once been rented by my best friend and gifted psychic medium, Theresa, who had moved to California almost exactly a year ago. I'd entertained the idea of a suitemate since then, but no one had ever seemed quite right. Until now. "When would you like to move in?"

"I'm moving to Nana's on Tuesday, so I'd really like to get a jump on getting things squared away with you too—if that's okay."

"That's fine," I said. "Come on over when you get into town and I'll give you the spare key. We can talk rent then if you'd like."

"Perfect. Thanks again, Abby. And I'm so glad you're feeling better."

I clicked off with Candice and poked my head into the study in search of Dutch, who had stopped his eavesdropping around the time I'd agreed to sublet some space to Candice. "That was a dirty trick you pulled," I said as I handed him back the phone.

"Needed to be done," he said gravely. "Now, have a seat. I want to talk to you."

"Sounds serious," I said. I plopped down in one of the leather chairs across from his desk.

He looked at me for a long moment and, as always, I felt my breath catch at the beauty of the man. Dutch Rivers is tall, blond, and incredibly handsome. But the most riveting thing about him is his eyes. They're midnight blue in color, and whenever they bore right into mine, the way they were doing then, I knew I was in for a lecture. "I'm worried about you," he began.

"Here we go," I said. Dutch was big on worry, but usually only where I was concerned.

"I'm not kidding," he said. "It's time for you to think about getting your feet wet again."

"But I took a shower this morning," I said lightly.

"Edgar." He sighed. "You know what I mean."

"I'm not ready," I said as I looked down at my hands.

Dutch didn't say anything for a long minute. Finally, he made a startling suggestion. "Not even if it's to help me?"

"Pardon?" I asked, lifting my eyes to his. "This is a new twist, Agent Rivers."

Dutch picked up three folders on his desk and waved them at me. "When you were in there talking to Candice, it gave me an idea. These are the three cases I've been working this month, and I'm at a roadblock on all three. I need a break, Abby, and I was thinking you could do for me what you usually do for Candice."

My jaw dropped. Dutch had *never* asked me for help on a case. In fact, he'd all but fought me off every time I'd tried to assist with an investigation. For him to ask me this favor meant he'd turned a corner of sorts, and the sneaky bastard had done so knowing full well I could hardly turn him down. Still, I was a bit doubtful that he was for real. "Are you fooling with me? Because if you are, that would be a low move on your part."

"I'm dead serious," he said, holding my gaze.

"I see," I said, weighing my decision. Half of me really wanted to help. After all, my boyfriend was legendary for his skepticism. I'd seen him run to the aid of a female ghost who'd disappeared before his very eyes, and he still tried to deny what he'd seen. He was also the type of guy who liked to be the hero, and asking for help wasn't something he'd ever been comfortable with.

But if I were honest with myself, I'd have to admit that the trouble wasn't so much on his end as on mine. I hadn't used my radar to any real extent in nearly ninety days, which was an all-time record for me. In fact, I'd worked hard not to use it. The truth of it was, my intuition had failed me at the moment in my life when I'd needed it the most. I'd been sucker punched in the chest by a bullet that I'd had no idea was coming.

And that was what was really eating away at me—the fact that when I'd relied most heavily on my intuition, it had failed me. What if it failed me when I was sitting with a client? I just wasn't ready for that hypothetical yet.

So Dutch was really throwing me a curveball with an offer that would allow me to step back into the ballpark with no risk of injury. I could give some remote impressions about a case in which I would never meet the actual players involved, and if I was wrong—so what? The FBI would continue to investigate, and hopefully the case would eventually be solved through good solid detective work, not dependent on whether or not my radar was having a good day.

"Okay," I said grimly. "I'll help, but only on the condition that you continue to investigate the case outside of my impressions. Don't rely solely on me to get it right."

Dutch smiled and extended his hand. "Deal," he said, and we shook on it.

"By the way," I added, "you really need a haircut."

Dutch grinned and ran his hand through his unruly hair. "I know, I know," he said. "I've been swamped and haven't had time for it."

"You should make time," I said.

"Glad to know you're keeping me aesthetically on track," he shot back.

"I'm your girlfriend," I said, getting up. "It's my job to keep you socially acceptable. I mean, at least try some gel or something until you can get to the salon."

Dutch gave me a withering look. "I don't go to the *salon*—I go to the barber. And does it really look that bad?"

I softened at Dutch's suddenly self-conscious expression. "No, babe," I said and came around to stand in front of him. "You could look like Cousin Itt and still do it for me," I murmured, leaning in to kiss him just as Virgil jumped in his lap and slapped his shaggy tail in my face. "Plah!" I said and backed away.

"Oops," Dutch said as he set Virgil on the ground. "Now, you were about to kiss me?"

I rolled my eyes. "Sorry, cowboy. The moment has passed."

"Aw, come on, Abs. Don't be like that."

I walked toward the door. "Try me later," I said, cranky about the cat again.

"I'll go get my hair cut!" Dutch called as I left the room.

"Promises, promises," I replied over my shoulder, knowing full well that the stack of work on Dutch's desk was preventing him from doing any of his errands. "Ah, well," I said as I took my seat on the couch and snuggled up to Eggy. "Where were we?" I added, closing my eyes for one heck of a good power nap.

Later that evening, while we were eating dinner, there was a knock on Dutch's door. "Expecting company?" I asked.

"It's probably Milo," Dutch said. He got up from the table and headed to the front door.

Sure enough, when he returned, he had his best friend and former partner in tow. "Hey there, Abs," Milo said jovially.

I smiled broadly in greeting. Milo was one of my favorite people. Tall and elegant, with mocha skin and an easy smile, he was a handsome, stylish man. He and Dutch worked the local detective beat together before Dutch landed at the FBI. "Hey there," I said and waved him to an empty chair at the table. "Want some food?"

Milo took in the delicious scent of pork tenderloin filling the kitchen. "Who cooked, you or Dutch?" he asked.

I gave him a dirty look. "Dutch," I said.

"I'm in," he answered and headed over to the cabinet to extract a plate.

Dutch chuckled and returned to his seat. "The man knows what's good," he said, giving me a wink.

"That's it," I said, tossing my napkin at him. "I'm taking a cooking class."

· Both Milo and Dutch burst into gales of laughter. "What?" I demanded. "What's so funny?"

Milo wheezed his funny laugh a few times before saying, "I don't know who we should feel more sorry for, the instructor or the fire department!"

"So I've filled the kitchen with smoke a few times," I said defensively. "Dutch's oven runs hot."

Dutch sputtered several more times, trying to regain his composure. "Maybe you should just stick to the crystal ball thing, Edgar, and leave the cooking to me."

"Speaking of which," Milo said as he took his seat at the table, "Dutch tells me you're going to help him out on a couple case files."

I squirmed in my chair. "I was thinking about it," I said, poking at my dinner and suddenly feeling pressured. "Jeez, Dutch, I didn't realize you were going to tell the whole world I was helping you."

Out of the corner of my eye I saw Dutch glare at his friend. "I only told Milo, Abs."

"I think it's a great idea," Milo said helpfully. "After you work on some of his cases, would you mind looking at a few of mine?"

Dutch cleared his throat and said quickly, "Abby's taking it slow and easy, buddy. Let's just see how comfortable she is looking at my stuff first, okay?"

Milo shrugged and changed the subject. "So, you ready for the hearing next Wednesday?"

"Almost. Did you bring me the file?"

"It's in my car. I'll bring it in after dinner and we can talk about which way to play it."

"What hearing?" I asked, relieved that the attention was off me.

"There's a parole hearing next week that Milo and I have to attend."

"Who's coming up for parole?"

"Bruce Lutz," Dutch said, and I couldn't help but notice the even tone of his voice when he spoke the name.

"Bad guy?" I asked.

"The baddest," Milo said. "He murdered my partner nine years ago."

I sucked in a breath of surprise. I'd never thought of Milo having a partner before Dutch. "I'm sorry," I said. "I didn't know."

Milo shrugged again and gave me a smile, but I could tell the memory still bothered him. "Walter was a great guy," he said quietly. "I was a rookie detective when I came up here from walking a beat in Detroit. Walter had been on the Royal Oak payroll for almost twenty-five years. He was a real fixture around here. He used to go to the middle schools and high schools and talk to the kids about staying out of trouble. Everybody loved him." Milo shook his head and took a breath before continuing.

"He was one of the best detectives in the biz. When he worked a case, he treated it like it was his only case. He really cared about people. That's what made him such a great detective—he wanted to give closure to people and he wanted to get the scum off the streets. I only worked with him for about a year, but everything I learned from him, I still use today, almost ten years later."

I looked at Dutch, who had been listening quietly while Milo talked. "Did you know him too?"

Dutch shook his head no. "Not really. I met him once at a police conference where he'd given a lecture. But I remember how impressive the guy was. He was smart, he knew his stuff, and his reputation was legendary."

Milo chuckled. "Yeah, he was a legend, all right. Riding patrol with him was like riding around with a superhero. Everybody knew him."

"So what happened?" I asked quietly.

Dutch looked at Milo, and I noticed how quickly Milo's eyes went from amused to angry. "He was shot execution style one night in August, nine years ago."

"Did you see it happen?" I asked.

"No," Milo said bitterly. "I was in the hospital passing a kidney stone. Walter and I had been working a case against a guy named Dick Wolfe, a real SOB. We were scheduled to go on a stakeout that night in front of Dick's girlfriend's house, but I'd started having really bad abdominal pain around noon. Walter convinced me to go to the hospital, and the next day I walk into the precinct and the captain tells me Walter's been murdered."

"How does this guy who's up for parole—what's his name?"

"Bruce Lutz," Dutch said.

"Yeah, how does he fit into the picture?"

Dutch said, "He was working for Wolfe at the time, and word had it that Wolfe wasn't very impressed with his track record and was about to cut him loose. He knew that Milo and Walter were sticking their nose into his boss's business, so to impress Wolfe and secure his position in the ranks, he murdered Walter."

I noticed Milo had stopped eating. "Thank God you weren't with him," I said to him.

"No," Milo said. "I could have stopped it. Walter didn't have anyone watching his back, and that's why he died."

My left side felt thick and heavy, my sign for "nope." "I doubt that, Milo. It seems to me that if a smart and experienced detective could be ambushed, then his not-very-seasoned sidekick wasn't exactly going to see it coming. You'd have been the second casualty."

Milo pushed his plate to the middle of the table. "There's no way to know for sure," he muttered. "Anyway, let me go out and get that file."

After I heard the front door close, I turned to Dutch and said, "It wasn't his fault."

"I know," Dutch said. "But that doesn't mean he won't feel guilty about it for the rest of his life."

I nodded soberly, then asked, "So how do you figure into this?"

"When Walter was murdered, it opened up a vacancy. I'd been working undercover vice in Detroit for a couple of years, and needed a change of pace. I applied for the job up here and got it."

"And that's how you and Milo met," I said.

"Yep. The first case we worked together was Walter's murder."

"Must have been a good feeling to put away the guy who did it."

"Bittersweet," Dutch said as he put his hand over mine and gave it a squeeze. "Walter had a wife, three kids, and four grandkids."

"How is it that Lutz is up for parole after only a few years?" I asked. "I'd think someone like that would go away for a long, long time."

"We never got a chance to go to trial with it. The son of a bitch DA offered Lutz a plea bargain and the coward took it. He got twenty years, eligible for parole after eight."

"And you and Milo are going to make sure he serves his full sentence."

"That's the plan," Dutch said, nudging my leg with his.

Just then, we heard the front door open and Milo called from the living room, "I got the file."

I stood up and grabbed a few dishes. "You two go do your strategizing. I'll clean up in here."

Dutch got up and came around the table, pausing to kiss me on the neck before he went into the living room to join Milo. As I worked in the kitchen, I could hear the two of them talking, their tones low and serious. I thought about the change in Milo that came over him when he talked about his former partner, and worried that he was carrying around so much guilt. It wasn't his fault he'd had a kidney stone, after all. The poor guy.

Putting the dishes into the dishwasher, I wondered if there was something I could do to help Milo realize that he wasn't to blame. That was when I got the bright idea to ask Dutch later on if he wanted me to tune in on the case file—maybe I could come up with another bit of evidence that would help them at the parole hearing.

Looking back, I think I would have been better off minding my own beeswax.

Chapter Two

Dutch was off to work early Tuesday morning, with promises to take me out to dinner that night. I had agreed to look into his three FBI cases and give him some feedback over dinner. I'd been too busy getting my office cleaned up and ready for Candice's arrival to offer my services before now. I also made a mental note to bring the Lutz case up at dinner that evening.

Since Candice was coming into town later in the morning, I decided to get up right after Dutch left and take a gander at the files. I was walking groggily down the stairs with Eggy in tow, trying to shake off sleep, when I felt something furry brush against my legs. In the next instant, I was tumbling down the rest of the stairs. I landed at the bottom with a hard thud and lay there for several long seconds, not daring to move until I could determine if I'd broken something. With a groan, I rolled over to a face full of wet, slobbery kisses as Eggy came to my rescue.

"Owwww," I said to him, reaching up to feel a bump forming on the back of my head.

I heard a meow above me and opened my eyes to see Virgil purring on the staircase in the exact location where I'd lost my footing. "You son of a feline," I snarled at him.

He purred back, and with a flip of his tail, he sauntered up the rest of the staircase like he was all that and a bag of chips. I remained on the floor a while longer, wondering how guilty I'd feel if I were to take Virgil for a little ride in the country and drop him off in some lovely cornfield upstate.

As I was about to push myself to a sitting position, I heard a knock on the door. "Hang on," I called, getting to my feet. It appeared nothing was broken, but I knew a few places were definitely bruised.

I opened the door to a welcome sight. Dave, my hippie-looking handyman and business partner, stood on the front porch, wearing a big, fat smile that faded the instant he took notice of me. "Your lip is bleeding," he said and pushed the door open. "What happened?"

"Dutch's stupid cat is trying to kill me," I said, motioning him into the kitchen.

"He scratched you?"

"No, he got underfoot as I was coming down the stairs."

"Well, you should watch where you're going," Dave said simply.

"It wouldn't matter," I groused as I got a baggie and some ice from the freezer. "He'd find a way."

Dave smiled at me and I put the ice to my lip. Just then, Virgil strolled into the kitchen and shimmied up to rub against Dave's leg. "Seems like a friendly enough cat to me," he said.

"Oh, he's quite the charmer," I agreed. "Until he decides to mark you as his next victim, that is. Then all bets are off."

"His *next* victim?" Dave asked, thoroughly amused.

"Yeah, yesterday Mr. Chipmunk got the ax. Today it's me."

"You don't say," Dave said, giving me a quizzical look. "Say, you're not still taking those pain meds, are you?"

I rolled my eyes at him. "I'm not imagining this, Dave. He's out to get me."

"Sure, sure," he said. He picked up Eggy, who had nudged Virgil out of the way to dance around Dave's legs. "Say, you got any coffee?"

"Yeah, I made it in my sleep," I muttered as I pushed away from the counter I'd been leaning against and walked over to the coffeemaker. "What brings you by at, oh, seven a.m., anyway?"

"We got an offer on the Fern Street property," he said.

"No kidding?" I said, turning around to face him. "This morning?"

"No, the Realtor left me a message last night, and I didn't get it until I was on my way to work."

"Where are you working these days?"

"Milo's place," Dave said.

"Really?" I asked as I measured out the coffee.

"Yep. Putting in a new bath for the missus. Have you ever met her?"

"I have. She's a gorgeous woman, wouldn't you say?" Milo was married to an exotic beauty named Noel.

"Definitely," Dave agreed. "He's a lucky guy, if you ask me."

"So, is it a good offer?" I said, referring back to the Fern Street house that Dave and I co-owned.

"It's a little under the asking price, so, yeah, it's a good offer."

"We'll have to run it by Cat," I said. I pressed the button on the coffeemaker and headed over to the table to sit down.

Dave groaned. Cat was my sister and the third partner in our real estate development firm. She was as sharp a businesswoman as ever there was. "She'll think it's too low," he said.

"Let me do the talking," I advised. "She might be happy to be rid of it." The three of us had invested in a rather dilapidated property in early January, and the place had proven to be a nightmare on many fronts. I knew that Dave had been working to unload the house for several months, and I could only imagine how nervous he was that Cat was going to ruin his chances of getting his name off the title once and for all.

"Just remind her that we're still making a profit," he said. "That's really all that matters in the end."

I smiled wryly. "Unless you're my sister, in which case it's not about making a profit as much as it's about maximizing one."

Dave groaned again. "We're never going to dump this thing," he complained.

"Leave it to me," I said, getting up to pour our coffee. "I'll just tell her that my intuition is saying we should definitely accept the offer."

Dave seemed to brighten. "It is?"

I walked back to the table with our coffee and cautioned, "No. I mean, I don't know. I haven't checked on it yet."

"Well, what are you waiting for?" he asked, taking the mug from me. "Ask your squad what they think."

I smiled at his reference. I called the spirit guides who worked so hard to assist me with my readings my "crew." Dave could never remember the term, so he substituted any and every nickname for them he could think of. "I will," I said with a wave of my hand, and took a sip of the coffee.

"What'd they say?" he asked me after a moment.

"What'd who say?"

"Your team. Your squad, you know . . . *them*."

I gave him a quizzical look. "Again, I don't know. I haven't asked them."

"Oh," he said, looking a little dejected. "I thought that's what you were doing."

I sighed heavily and changed the subject. "You and your wife got any big plans for Memorial Day?"

Dave shuffled his feet and looked down at the ground. "Uh, no," he said uncomfortably. "No plans."

I cocked my head at him, puzzled by his sudden change in demeanor. "What's happened?" I asked him.

Dave cleared his throat and set his mug down. "Nothing," he said dismissively. "Listen, I gotta get to Milo's and get back to work on that bathroom. Call me after you talk to Cat." And with that he was out of the kitchen and walking quickly toward the door.

"Dave?" I called after him, completely thrown by his quick retreat.

"I'm late," he said over his shoulder as he pulled the door open. "Call me later." And then he was gone.

I stared blinking at the front door for a bit, then shrugged my shoulders and decided to worry about it later. Still holding the ice to my lip, I went into

Dutch's study and scooted his big leather office chair up to the mahogany desk. I loved the energy in Dutch's study. It was a beautiful blend of rugged masculinity and perfect comfort, reflecting his personality to a T.

I felt just a hint of guilt about being in here without him—after all, he was a private guy and this was his space. But the files were in here and he'd left me a pad of paper with a note thanking me for my efforts, so obviously he didn't mind. Still, as I got comfortable, I resolved not to disturb anything and to leave the room as soon as I'd finished with my impressions.

I picked up the stack of files and casually eyed them for a moment. They were bound with a rubber band, and the front cover of each file had a large FBI embossment on it. Briefly, I wondered what Dutch's boss would think about having his field agent's psychic girlfriend look into a classified case file, but then I figured that was Dutch's battle to fight if it ever came up.

With a sigh, I put the files back on the desk and closed my eyes. I had a little bit of prep work to do before I could focus my intuition on the cases in front of me.

There are lots of people who think that psychics have all the answers. The very fact that we're able to sense things that may not be obvious or even known makes us seem omnipotent. Nothing could be farther from the truth. Most of the intuitives that I know are just as lost as the rest of the world. And that was because intuition can be a tricky thing.

It's a complex language of metaphors and subtleties. An intuitive message can be crystal clear or completely muddled. And, as a rule, just when you think you've got the message figured out, you'll discover that what you first thought wasn't really it at all. To use intuition professionally, like I do, requires a whole lot of patience, skill, and concentration. To use intuition professionally also dictates that I be very careful about how I relate my interpretations. A psychic can be just as hurtful to a client as helpful. Go into a reading with the wrong intentions, and you can do some real damage—and unfortunately, there are some out there who use their intuitive gifts to take advantage of the vulnerable.

However, more and more of us legitimate professionals are emerging to reverse the bad reputation that a few shameful charlatans have given psychics.

The idea of responsibility swirled around in the back of my mind as I sat quietly in Dutch's chair and got ready to turn my radar on. I didn't want to screw up, especially on these case files, so my focus was especially critical this morning. I began by getting centered, which is simply the act of breathing deeply and really feeling each inhalation and exhalation. Once I was centered, I ran through all of my chakras—those energy points that line up along the spine—then called in the crew.

My crew is made up of roughly five spirit guides. I'm not sure why I have five as opposed to two or three. Maybe the universe thought I needed a few more babysitters than most, and given my ability to get into trouble, five didn't seem unreasonable at all.

My master guide, or my primary contact, is an energy that identifies himself as Samuel. He's a terrific guy as far as spirit guides go. Great sense of humor . . . usually at my expense, but who can blame him? Today, as I felt his energy come forward, I greeted him and asked for his assistance. His response was something along the lines of *Hello, Abigail. It's been a while. . . .*

I smirked and did a mental eye roll. "Yeah, yeah," I said. "Maybe if you had given me a little heads-up before I got *shot*, I'd be checking in more often."

His reply surprised me. *The direction of your path needed to be decided. You could not have chosen if you had not been called to the other side. . . .*

I mulled that over for a minute. He seemed to be telling me that I'd needed to die in order to choose to live. Sometimes I hated how complicated this whole big-picture thing was. "Okay," I said to him. "I'll take your word for it, but just so you know—next time just have me choke on a cough drop or something, 'cuz taking a bullet hurts like a son of a bitch."

There was laughter in my head, and it wasn't just from Samuel. *We are here to assist, Abigail, whenever you're ready.*

Without opening my eyes, I reached my hands out to the folders on the desk and picked them up one by one, trying to decide in which order to proceed. The middle file called my attention first, so I set the other two aside and laid it flat on the desk, placing both palms down on top of it. In my mind's eye, I saw a row of slot machines. "Gambling," I mumbled and opened my eyes to reach for the pad of paper and a pencil. I scribbled that thought down and waited while my radar and my crew did their thing. A series of images flashed in my mind's eye; one of them was truly confounding.

In my mind I saw a long pipe and some water running through it. The pipe let out into a large pool of water, and at the bottom of the pool were thousands of poker chips. I watched as the water trickled into the pool, and then my attention moved to a plug at the deep end.

A hand appeared in my vision. It was a man's hand,

beefy and hairy-knuckled, and my eye traveled to its
pinkie ring, which seemed to catch the light as it glim-
mered. The hand was tossing poker chips into the
water and as the poker chips sank to the bottom of
the pool, the hand then reached down and pulled at
the plug. I followed the hand up to see who had pulled
the plug, and I got a very quick flash of a man in his
fifties with salt-and-pepper hair and a very large nose.
He had dark eyes and I sensed that he was very
sneaky.

I wrote the vision down on the notepad and left a
space at the bottom of the page. This I headed with
the word "Interpretation" and paused as I read back
through what I'd already written. Finally I wrote:

> *My sense is that there is a large pool of money
> belonging to some sort of fund, like a pension
> fund for the waterworks department or some sort
> of utility's pension fund. There is a central figure
> here with access to the management of this fund,
> and he has been stealing from it to supply his
> gambling addiction. Lately, he has been losing,
> and if he's not caught he will dispense with all of
> the money in short order. The man is of medium
> height and stocky or portly build. He has salt-
> and-pepper hair, dark-colored eyes, and a very
> large nose. There is also a pinkie ring on his right
> hand in the shape of a horseshoe.*

After writing all that down, I tore off the page and
paper-clipped it to the front of the file. Next I closed
my eyes again, feeling around the desk for the other
two files. My right hand hovered over one of them
and I felt it pause just above the cover. I heard an
alarm go off in my head and pulled the file close,

laying both hands on top of it just as I'd done with
the first file. In my mind's eye I saw a big, black, ugly
dog. The thing was sinister and had long white fangs
that dripped blood. I could feel the goose bumps rise
along my arms as the hair on the back of my neck
stood on end. This dog was evil and very, very dangerous.

I asked my crew to move past the dog and give me
something else, and that was when I saw a pigeon
flying around the dog. The dog snapped at the pigeon,
but it flew through a window to the safety of a birdcage. Once the pigeon was inside the cage, the door
slammed shut and the pigeon paced the floor of the
cage nervously.

None of this made sense to me, so I reached out
to my crew. "Guys, I need more than these animal
metaphors. Show me something that makes sense."
The image quickly changed, and I saw a car parked
in front of a large warehouse. The red flash of a strobe
light blinked distractedly against the gray brick of
the building.

I noticed there was a man inside the car. He too
appeared to be in his mid-fifties, with a receding hairline and bushy red eyebrows. He seemed to be staring
at the building in front of him, his attention on the
blinking strobe lights. Then he suddenly glanced out
the window to his left and became frightened. The big
black dog appeared next to the car, and the man
reached over to the seat next to him. He held up a
juicy raw steak and tossed it out the window, but the
dog ignored it and snapped at the man. A moment
later, the car was surrounded by a pack of other dogs,
all menacingly snarling, with their hackles raised.

The pack drew near the car as the man inside
looked panic-stricken. Then a sheep walked up to the

car, though the dogs seemed not to notice it. The man seemed to relax when he saw the sheep, which was bleating earnestly at him. He nodded at the sheep and got out of the car. The moment I saw the door open, I knew it meant trouble, and suddenly, the dogs leaped to attack the man.

My eyes flew open and I yelled, "Stop!" to the empty room. I was breathing hard and shaking. The image had been so vivid and terrifying, and I swore I could almost hear the howls of pleasure as the dogs had torn the man to pieces. I looked down at the file my hands were resting on and noticed that it wasn't one of the blue FBI folders. This one was manila and the tab read, LUTZ.

"Oh, shit!" I said as I realized what I'd just tuned in on. Quickly, I grabbed the pad of paper and began frantically scribbling everything I'd seen in the vision. When I was done, I sat back and circled a line here and there. I stared at the space at the bottom of the page, where I would need to write my interpretation of the vision I'd been shown, and my hand hesitated. I knew in my heart that Bruce Lutz had taken the fall for a crime he had not committed, and further, I knew that Dick Wolfe had not only ordered the hit but had been there when it went down. What I didn't know was why. My gut was telling me there was more to it than just the fact that Walter and Milo had been nosing around in Wolfe's business.

There was something key in the vision, something I'd seen about the crime, that was troubling me. It was the sheep, I realized. Obviously it represented someone Walter had known and possibly trusted, but who was it? Who could have lured Walter out of the car when he knew he was surrounded by danger?

I sat there for a long time, trying to decide what to

do. If I took this to Dutch, he would likely dismiss my interpretation. And even I had to admit, as I read back through the description of my vision that a pigeon being snapped at by a big dog and ending up trapped in a birdcage didn't exactly look like it should clear Lutz of the murder. But this was how my intuition worked. It was partly visual and partly just knowing when I was right on target. I *knew* I was right about Lutz. But I also knew that in order to convince my boyfriend, I'd need a lot more than descriptions of big dogs, a sheep, and a pigeon. If I went to him with only that, he was likely to ask me if I'd also seen a partridge in a pear tree.

I tore the page from the notepad and folded it, then tucked it securely in my back pocket. I had no idea what I was going to do with it, but I could decide on that later. For now, I was so drained that what I really needed was a nap. I got up from the desk and headed into the living room, where I sank down onto Dutch's soft leather couch and fell almost immediately to sleep.

"Abs." I heard a deep baritone whisper in my ear and I felt a tug on my arm. "Come on, honey, wake up."

"Huh?" I said, my eyes snapping open. "What's going on?"

Dutch laughed as he stroked my hair. "You've been out cold since I walked in."

"Ohmigod!" I said, sitting up straight. "Is it after six?"

"No, babe. It's noon. I came home for lunch to see what you'd come up with on my files."

I rubbed my eyes and shook my head, trying to clear the fog from my tired mind. "I only got through one of the files," I said. "It really wore me out."

"Well," he said, holding up the folder with the paper attached, "looks like you hit pay dirt here."

"Yeah?" I asked.

Dutch nodded and stood up. He took my hand and pulled me up from the couch. "Come on. I'll make us some lunch and fill you in."

We ate hot dogs and potato chips as Dutch told me about the county waterworks pension fund. "Two weeks ago we got a tip from a retired waterworks employee that he'd noticed a small change in the pension's monthly yield, but the corresponding rate assigned to the fund should have netted a little more cash."

"How much more?"

Dutch smiled. "Five dollars and sixty-seven cents."

"Someone's watching their pennies," I said.

"Hey, he's retired. What else is there for him to do?"

"Good point."

"Anyway, the file could have been tabled for a while, but this guy's son-in-law happens to work at the Bureau, and he made enough noise to get one of our accountants to look into it. Sure enough, the old guy is right. The yield is off, and it's been off for three of the past six months."

"How many people receive pensions from that fund?"

"About six thousand," Dutch said.

I whistled. "Times five and a half dollars every month—that's big money over the long haul."

"Exactly," he said with a wink at me. "Which is why the case ended up with me. I've been going through all the people who have both direct and indirect access to the fund, but whoever's been pulling from it has been doing a great job of covering their tracks. The guy you describe here sounds exactly like Max Goodyear. I interviewed him early on and thought he seemed a little nervous—but most people do get nervous when they're sitting across from me."

"Oh, the things you do to people," I said and fanned myself.

Dutch threw a potato chip at me. "Goodyear's one of the financial advisers assigned to the pension fund," he continued. "But his personal bank records keep coming back clean. There's been no spike in activity, either up or down. The guy owns a modest house, drives a Volvo, pays his bills on time, and doesn't cheat on his wife.

"Also, as far as we can tell, he doesn't have direct access to the fund, which would mean that if you're right, and he's been gambling it away, he's got to have an accomplice."

I smirked. "*If* I'm right," I repeated.

Dutch stood and picked up our plates from the table. "I'd love to sound more confident, Edgar, but we've been all over his personal finances and there's nothing out of the ordinary."

I felt a little buzz in the back of my mind as my radar kicked back on. "Does Goodyear have any family besides his wife? Like children?"

"Nope. Just him and the missus," Dutch said, setting the dishes in the sink.

"Huh," I said, puzzling that one over. "You sure?"

Dutch turned around, leaned against the sink, and crossed his arms. "Yeah. At least, that's what I remember. You thinking I should double-check?"

"Yes. There's something off. He's got a kid, Dutch, and that's your missing link."

"Okay, I'll look into it. In the meantime, if you get any thoughts on Goodyear's accomplice, jot 'em down, okay?"

"Gotcha," I said and grinned at him. Just then my cell went off. I answered after glancing at the caller ID "Hey, Candice."

"Afternoon!" she said jovially. "Are you ready to swing by your office and talk figures?"

"I'll be there in ten," I said and clicked off.

Dutch came over to me and wrapped me in his arms for a quick snuggle. "I need to get back to work too," he said as he kissed the top of my head. "Thanks for your help, sweethot," he added in his best Humphrey Bogart voice.

I squeezed him and let go. "You can pay me back by taking me shoe shopping this weekend," I said. "Right after we get you that haircut."

"Can't I just give you my credit card and tell you to keep it under fifty dollars?"

I laughed. "Where do you think I shop for shoes? Bucky's Bargain Barn of Flip-flops?"

"I like flip-flops," he said as he hung an arm over my shoulder and walked me to the door. "They're sexy."

"Ah," I said. We paused on the front step. "Well, then, if you get excited over flip-flops, just wait till you see me in a pair of Jimmy Choos."

"You're turning into your sister," he said, and gave me another smooch on the cheek. "Which reminds me—she called while you were napping."

"Thanks," I said, getting into my SUV. Before closing the door, I added, "I'll call her back tonight and she can give me some pointers on what styles are in this season."

I drove across town to the big tan professional

building that houses my office. The structure used to be one of the largest in downtown Royal Oak, but in the past few years so much new development had cropped up that the Washington Square Office Plaza now found itself in rather mixed company—much like a middle-aged swinging single at a trendy twentysome-thing nightclub. Still, I loved the old guy. It had char-acter and personality. It also had a terrific landlord who'd hardly made a fuss about all the recent trouble originating in suite 222. There had been serial killers and blood, Mafia types and more blood, psychopaths and yes . . . a little more blood, and through all of it my rent had gone up only fifty bucks.

I parked in my usual slot in the parking garage across the street and hurried to the front lobby, glanc-ing at my watch as I pushed through the doors. I headed up the two flights of stairs to my floor, then down the polished marble hallway to the second suite on the right. Candice was already there. "Hey!" she said with a wave. "God, Abs! You look fabulous for a girl who's been shot."

I smiled tightly and pulled at the collar of my blouse. Physically, I remained pretty much the same as the last time she'd seen me—five-foot-six, one-twenty give or take, with very long brown hair and blue eyes. The only real change was a nasty scar on the right side of my chest that was sore to the touch and ugly as hell. "No worse for wear," I said, giving her a hug. "But you look completely different," I added as I took in her longer hair and its slightly darker color. "Your hair looks fantastic."

Candice was taller than me by a few inches and her look was sleek and trendy. She had a sense of style that made people notice her. And in all the time I'd known her, I'd never seen any color on her but white, black, and gray. That is, except for today. "And what's with the new duds?" I asked as I turned to unlock my office door.

"I know—right?" she said, running her hand along her pink sleeve. "I've been on this new kick lately. I'm trying to soften my look."

"It's good on you," I said, waving her in.

"So is this office," she said as she paused in my tiny front lobby and did a three-sixty turn. "Abby, this is wonderful!"

I'd had some trouble with a local psychopath a few months earlier, and he'd completely trashed my office. Luckily, I had insurance up the yin-yang and I'd been able to upgrade a lot of my furniture. The front lobby now held two red suede chairs and modern, dark-wood side tables, and a painting of colored patches hung just above the chairs, giving warmth to the space.

"Come see the rest," I coaxed, walking her into my reading room.

"Wow," she said as she entered. "This is completely different!" The room had previously been painted a Moroccan blue, with two cream-colored chairs, a lovely cherry oak credenza, and a blue-and-green-mosaic mirror on the wall. Crystals, both small and large, had dotted nearly every surface, and a huge, soothing waterfall had stood prominently in one of the far corners. I'd been truly crushed by the devastation that the wacko had wreaked on such a precious space and I couldn't stand the thought of trying to re-create it, so I'd opted for a completely different look.

The room was now a very soft mocha brown, and I'd spent long hours painting the molding light cream. Two espresso-colored leather chairs faced each other in the center of the room, and a short chestnut book-case had replaced the ruined credenza. The waterfall had been too expensive to replace, so I'd settled for a large terra-cotta pot filled with five-foot-tall bamboo shoots, and to the side of that, I'd actually made a new mosaic mirror out of shards of stained glass, which turned out much better than expected. I'd also hung sheer cream curtains along the window. The overall effect was more like a living room than a psychic's parlor.

"You like?" I asked.

"No," Candice said as she wrapped an arm over my shoulders and gave me a squeeze. "This, I *love*." She pointed to the mirror. "And where did you get that? It's like your other one, only bigger, right?"

"I made it," I said.

"Get out of here!" she exclaimed. "I didn't know you did art."

I laughed. "A friend of mine taught me years ago. It's really easy. I've kind of taken over Dutch's garage making these recently."

"Can you make me one?" she asked, then said quickly, "I mean, I'd pay for it."

"Hell, Candice, I've got a whole friggin' garage full of these things. My physical therapist said it would be good to help me regain the motor skills in my right arm. I think I've got a dozen of them lying around. Come by anytime and pick whichever one you like. There's no price tag. They're cheap to make and I like to do it."

"Thanks, Abs," Candice said and gave me another squeeze before settling into one of the leather chairs. "Now, let's get down to business. How much were you thinking to charge me for Theresa's old room?"

I opened my mouth to suggest the price I had in mind when my intuitive radar gave me a buzz. Moving over to sit in the chair opposite Candice, I hesitated for a moment before answering her as I pulled the thought close. "Actually," I began, sending a mental thank-you to my guides, "I was wondering if, for the first month, we could do a trade?"

"Trade?" she asked. "What did you have in mind?"

I reached into my back pocket and pulled out the folded piece of paper on which I'd written out my impressions about Walter's murder. "I've come across something that I could really use your professional opinion on."

Candice cocked an eyebrow. "Just my opinion?"

"And maybe a little legwork," I added.

"Opinion and legwork?"

"Okay, so maybe there will be some interviewing and background checking and other private eye stuff too."

Candice chuckled. "This deal just went from fantastic to are you serious?"

"I see your point," I said, looking at the paper in my hand. "Make that the first two months' rent." My crew was making me feel like I was definitely going to need Candice's help on this one, and I knew I had to pin her down quickly before her caseload built up.

"How much legwork, background checking, and other private eye stuff are we talking about?"

"Depends."

"On?"

"On what we find out initially."

Candice sat back in her seat and eyed me critically. "Want to elaborate a little just so I know what I'm getting myself into?"

I looked up and met her eyes. I'd really wanted to avoid the whole getting-into-the-details end of the case. As I saw it, this Wolfe guy was one bad dude, and if Candice had heard of him prior to committing to me and found ~~out~~ he was involved, well, that would be a good reason for her to turn me down. "It involves an old case of Dutch's," I began.

"Did he finally wise up to the gold mine he has for a girlfriend and ask you to tune in on some cold cases?"

"In a manner of speaking," I said. Then I laid out for her the story I knew about Bruce Lutz, Walter McDaniel, and Dick Wolfe.

When I finished, Candice's body posture had changed. Her arms had folded across her chest the moment I mentioned Wolfe, and I thought for sure she was going to refuse my offer. I did my best to make the deal slightly sweeter. "Three months' rent—and I'll throw in an extra mirror for your grandmother."

Candice laughed and seemed to relax a little. "You know, this Wolfe guy is known in my circle as someone you don't want to mess with."

"His reputation has reached all the way to Kalamazoo, huh?"

Candice nodded. " 'Fraid so, Abs. Still, it's obvious to me that you're going to go poking your nose where it doesn't belong whether or not I agree to help you, so in the interest of keeping you out of any new lines of fire, I'm tempted to say yes."

"Four months, Candice, and that's my final offer."

I was rewarded with another laugh and Candice's arms uncrossed. "Again, it's very tempting," she said, tapping her finger against her lips. "But I'm a little reluctant to commit to this, because I know you could use the money."

"I'm fine," I said with a wave of my hand. "I've still got some insurance money and we just got an offer on that investment property I own."

Candice nodded, but her look was still pensive. "I

think what I'm getting at is a more formal agreement," she said.

"What kind of formal agreement?"

"Well, you've certainly helped me out in the past, and I've loved having you on my team. What would you say to forming a real partnership?"

The corners of my mouth turned up. I could see where she was going with this. "You want to go into business with each other?"

"The way I see it, you've let go of most of your clientele, right?"

I squirmed in my chair. This was smacking of the recent lectures I'd received from my boyfriend, and I was never really good at dealing with other people's opinions. "I'm easing back into the idea of starting up again."

"But in the meantime, you've got all this free time. What better way to keep your radar sharp than to work on my cases with me? We can hammer out some sort of hourly trade. It would really help me get established here, Abs. I could cut down on the number of hours I'd need to resolve a lot of my cases and take on more in less time. It's win-win for me."

"And you'd be willing to help me by getting to the bottom of Walter McDaniel's murder?"

It was Candice's turn to squirm. "Yes," she finally said. "But there are a few conditions that I'd need you to agree to."

"Like what?"

"Like, you'd need to put me in charge of the overall investigation. I'm serious about this Wolfe guy. I know for a fact that the FBI's been trying to nail him for years but hasn't been able to get him yet. He's slippery and smart and has one hell of a nasty reputation. Plus, I personally knew someone who got caught up in

Wolfe's business and hasn't shown up to work in two years."

My eyes widened. "What happened?"

"One of the other PIs at my old firm took on an ex-girlfriend of Wolfe's in a paternity suit. The PI— Darren Cox is his name— was a rookie investigator. I thought he was an idiot, but my boss saw some potential in him. Two weeks after he took on the Wolfe case, my boss gets a call from Darren. He tells him that he's taking a vacation. He's just won a ticket to the Caribbean and the deal was that he needed to leave immediately. We never saw or heard from Darren again. Then, an hour after Darren calls us, his client telephones. She wants to pay her bill and close the case, says it was all just a big fat misunderstanding."

"My ass it was," I said, feeling my radar buzz its agreement.

"Those were our sentiments exactly," Candice said.

"Do you think Darren was paid off? Or just scared into leaving town?"

"Probably a little of both, so it's important that we be discreet, Abby. Wolfe isn't someone I want on my ass, especially given your impressions that he had a direct hand in offing McDaniel."

"Got it," I said, making a check sign in the air. "Be discreet."

"There's also your boyfriend to consider here," she added. "Does he know you think that Bruce Lutz was just a stool pigeon?"

"Uh . . . not exactly," I said, looking at my shoes.

"By 'not exactly' you mean not at all, right?"

"That would be a fair assumption," I said with a shrug. "He and Milo are all gung ho on making sure Lutz does as much time as possible. I don't think he'd take kindly to the thought that Lutz wasn't the trig-german."

"And how do you think he's going to feel about finding out that his girlfriend is sticking her nose into the middle of all this?"

"Oh, he'll probably be totally pissy about it, which is why I vote for not telling him."

"I see," Candice said with a grin. "That's fine, but you have to remember that he's FBI, and they *know* stuff, you know? So if this gets back to him, you're going to have to deal with it and make sure I'm left out of the blame game, 'kay?"

"Got it," I said, making another check mark. "Leave Candice out of it. Anything else?"

"Yeah, I need to know how you're doing physically. And don't sugarcoat it. If I help you with this, I'll need you along for the ride, and I'm concerned that it may wear you out so soon after your injury."

"I'm okay," I said with another shrug. Candice dropped her chin and gave me a "yeah, right" look. "Seriously," I insisted. "Yes, I do get tired more easily, but as long as we're not running any marathons I should be good to go."

"Can you run at all?" she asked me. "There have been lots of moments I've needed to get the hell out of a situation fast, and throwing you over my shoulder would just slow me down."

I smiled as that visual came to mind. "If I were being chased, you mean? Yes, I could probably run a short sprint, but I'd need a milk shake or some French fries or a combo like that really soon afterward, you know . . . to get my strength back."

Candice smiled broadly. "French fries and milk shakes—the other Gatorade," she said.

"Is it in you?" I giggled.

"You're making me hungry. Still, I think it would be good if you trained with me in the mornings."

"*Trained* with you?"

"Yeah. If we're going to do this partnership right, you'll need to get your butt in shape. I work out every morning at six a.m. sharp. In fact, before I came over here, I joined that gym right down the street from Nan's. We'll need to get you a membership too."

"Whoa, hold on there, gal pal," I said, holding up my hands. "I don't think my physical therapist is going to go for that so soon after my injury."

"Baloney," Candice said. "I used to be a certified personal trainer, and I had plenty of accident recovery clients training under me. I figure your injury's got to be similar to a car accident, and I know exactly what regimen to put you on."

"Regimen? You want to put me on a *regimen*?" I asked. My heart rate picked up, and I felt my palms go sweaty. I'll admit it: I'd gone soft in my thirties. I hadn't done more than take a few yoga classes, along with the two flights up to my office.

"Yeah, low on the cardio at first. You're looking a little scrawny anyway, and we don't want you to lose weight. We'll build up some muscle first, then ease you into some endurance work."

"Who sent you?" I asked, leaning way back in my chair like she was contagious. "Did my sister put you up to this?"

Candice laughed and reached out to put a calming hand on my knee. "Abby, relax. This will be good for you. It'll give you confidence and you won't be as tired all the time. Trust me. I know what I'm doing."

"How about this?" I suggested. "How about I just come to your gym and root you on? Wouldn't that be fun? Your own personal cheerleader!"

"Tomorrow morning," she said to me, and her eyes meant business. "Six a.m." I gulped and she continued, "Now, about that rent payment . . ."

For the next twenty minutes, we firmed up the financial part of our new partnership. Afterward, I showed Candice her office area and told her that I'd make room for her in the third room, where I kept my computer, fax machine, filing cabinets, and assorted other business equipment. "That's okay," she said at my offer. "Theresa's old room is bigger than your reading room, and I don't need any extra space. I can fit everything in there."

"Great. Here's the extra key, and you'll need to see Yvonne on the third floor in the management's office about getting a parking space assigned to you in the structure across the street. It's a little pricey, but it beats feeding the meter every two hours."

"Got it," she said, taking the key. "I'm having my new office furniture delivered here tomorrow at nine a.m. Is that going to disturb your appointment schedule?"

I smiled. "No. I haven't had an appointment in a long time now."

"No clients are calling, huh?" she asked as she went around my desk to my phone, which had a little red light on it blinking furiously.

I sighed. "Would you look at that," I said as she held up the phone and pointed to the light. "Better return that call, huh?"

"Time to get back on the horse, Abs."

"Yee-ha," I said woodenly.

"It'll be good for you," she insisted as she nosily hit the caller ID button and clicked through the calls. "Holy cow! There are like six new calls here since yesterday."

"Really?"

Candice extended the phone toward me and I took a look. "Five-one-seven area code, hmmm. That's the same as for Kalamazoo, isn't it?"

"Coincidence," she said with a smirk. "I *may* have told a few friends of mine I was moving in with this really amazing psychic and they *might* be interested in a reading with you."

"I'll call them later," I said and set the phone down.

"Abby," Candice said with a sigh.

"I will," I said as I turned around. "Really. But right now I gotta get going. I promised Dutch I'd go grocery shopping if he cooked."

"Okay," she said, but she didn't look convinced.

I left Candice in the office to make a few phone calls and get acquainted with her new surroundings. As I hurried to my car, my cell phone beeped. "Hey there, Cat!" I said happily. "I was just about to call you."

"So you got my message?"

"Dutch said you called while I was taking a nap, and I'm so glad you did, because we got an offer on Fern!" I said excitedly. I was really hoping that I could convince her through my enthusiasm that no matter what the offer, we needed to close on that house before Dave went crazy.

"How much?" I told her and there was a slight pause on her end. Then I heard the sound of fingers clicking on a calculator. "That's not bad," she said when she came up with our profit. "We should counter for ten grand more."

I stifled a groan. "Huh," I said instead.

"What's, 'huh'?"

"Oh, nothing. Just . . . my radar is buzzing like crazy!"

"Really?" she asked, and I could imagine her leaning in over her desk and giving me her full attention. "What's the crew saying?"

"Well, the moment you said counteroffer, I really felt my left side go heavy. . . ."

"Your sign for no," she said.

"Yep. And then when you said to counter by ten thousand, I saw the back of this couple walking away."

"I see," she said, and again I could just see her deep in thought, nodding her head. "So your radar says that if we counter we'll lose the deal?"

"That's about the gist of it."

"Then I think we should accept. After all, the longer we wait for a better offer, the more we lose to interest and mortgage payments."

"You sure?" I asked.

"Yes. But do you think David will agree?"

I smiled as I opened my car door and hopped inside. "Gosh, Cat, I don't know. I'll call him and see if I can't convince him. I mean, he's the one that's really been working to make the house salable."

"Should I call him?" she asked.

"No!" I barked, then followed quickly with, "I mean, let me give it a shot first, and if he balks at the idea I'll have him call you and you can convince him, 'kay?"

"Fabulous," she said and I breathed a sigh of relief. "How are you feeling?"

"Fine. How are you feeling?" I asked, pulling out of the parking garage.

"I'm serious, Abby. Have you been following through on your physical therapy?"

Ever since I'd been shot, my incredibly overprotective sister had been mothering me to within an inch of my life. She'd gone so far as to check up with my doctors (who told her nothing), my pharmacist (who told her nothing), and my physical therapist (who seemed to be telling her *everything*). Of course, I could hardly blame her. Cat had been showering Lori, my therapist, with "tokens of appreciation" since I started therapy. "I've got an appointment tomorrow," I said as I gritted my teeth.

"It's very important that you continue to go until you're back to one hundred percent full range of motion," Cat advised.

I paused at a stoplight and rolled my eyes. "Thanks. I'll keep that in mind. And speaking of which, did you put Candice Fusco up to getting me into the gym?"

"How is Candice?" Cat asked, completely ignoring my question.

"You did, didn't you?"

"That girl is so fabulous, Abby. You should really hang out with her now that she's moving to Royal Oak."

"How did you find *that* out?"

"Dutch told me. Sometimes that man can't find a way off the phone, and the only way I'll let him go is if he gives me a juicy nugget."

"This is an invasion of privacy," I snapped. "Seriously, Cat, you're driving me crazy."

"What did you expect, Abby? You've been so tight-lipped ever since you got back from Denver, and you won't fill me in on *anything* that's going on with you."

"That's because there is nothing going on with me," I said with a sigh. "Listen, I've gotta go. I'm at the grocery store and I'm doing the shopping for dinner."

"Dutch said he can't wait to see what you bring home this time," she chuckled. "He says that the last time he let you go shopping for steaks for the grill, you brought home a rump roast!"

"Bye, Cat," I said and hung up the phone. Sometimes my sister drove me batty. I headed into the grocery store and made my way over to the meat aisle. Pacing back and forth, anxious about selecting a cut of meat that wasn't going to make me the butt end of a joke, I suddenly felt a hand on my shoulder and heard a voice say, "It can't be that bad, can it, Abs?"

I looked up and smiled. "Hey, Milo," I said. "Dutch sent me for meat."

Milo nodded and looked at where I was standing. "Is he into chitlins these days?"

"It all looks the same to me," I said.

"What did he tell you to get?"

"Something good for the grill."

"I see. Well, if I know my old partner, which, lucky for you, I do, I'd say he's more of a rib eye steak–eater."

"Right." I nodded firmly. "Rib eye . . ." I moved away from the gross-looking innards and toward something that looked like steak.

"That's the pork section, kiddo," Milo said.

"I knew that," I said, quickly changing direction and heading back toward the other end of the aisle.

"Yoo-hoo," Milo called, still farther down from me. "Over here." I saw he was holding up a package that looked exactly right.

"This is a rib eye?" I asked, looking at the package he held out to me.

"Extra rare," he said and wheezed his funny laugh. "Now, you'll want three of these," he said, loading up my basket.

"Three? You think Dutch'll eat two?"

"No," Milo said with a wink. "I think he'll put two on the grill and then hear the doorbell ring, and it will be me just dropping by, and what a coincidence, you all just happen to have an extra steak to grill."

"This is the price I pay for your silence about what I almost brought home, huh?"

"Why?" Milo asked me with a twinkle in his eye. "Did you almost bring home something else?"

"I see how we're going to play this," I said. "And what can you do for me in the corn section? Last time I brought home a can of creamed corn and Dutch about split his sides."

"Over here," Milo said and tugged me to the produce section. "Honestly, Abby, one of these days you're going to have to learn your way around the grocery store."

Milo helped me pick out corn and potatoes and a brownie mix for dessert, which I knew from experience was his personal favorite. "Not planning on eating with the family tonight?" I asked as we headed to the checkout counter.

"Nah. Noel's mother is over, and those two will be doing nothing but looking at wallpaper samples and paint samples and tile samples. . . ."

"Not your cup of tea, huh?"

"I just provide the money. Noel's job is to find ways to spend it."

"Well, you're welcome anytime, Milo."

He smiled broadly at me and gave my shoulders a squeeze. "How you doin', by the way?" he asked me as we edged closer to the cashier.

"Good," I said and looked at my shoes. "You know, just about there."

"Your strength coming back?"

"Yeah. It's getting there."

"How's your head?"

I looked at him quizzically, then dodged the question. "Doesn't hurt a bit."

Milo wheezed again. "You know what I mean. How you doin' up here?" he said as he tapped his temple.

Without warning, tears formed in my eyes and embarrassingly, I began to openly weep. As it happened, it was our turn to put the groceries on the conveyor belt, and Milo took the basket from me, set it on the belt, then pulled me close and gave me a squeeze. "Hey there, honey," he said into my hair.

"Sir," I heard the cashier say, "I'll need you to take your items out of the basket."

I could feel Milo stiffen, and I tried to pull myself together, but the more I tried to suck it up, the more the tears flooded down my cheeks and I continued to sob into his shirt. I could see the cashier out of one eye. She looked tired and in no mood for my theatrics.

Milo squeezed me again, then tucked me under one arm and overturned the basket with the other hand. "There," he said at the pile on the belt. "They're out of the basket."

The cashier scowled at him but didn't say another word as Milo pulled out his debit card to pay. "I . . . have . . . mon . . . eeeeey," I blubbered, trying to pull back from him to dig into my purse.

"I got it, Abs," he said and wouldn't let go of me. "Hang in there—we're almost out of here, okay?"

I nodded against his shirt, and in a few moments Milo had our dinner and we walked quickly out of the grocery store together. Milo scooted me over to his big, black, beautiful BMW and held the door open while I got in. He then came around to the other side and settled into the driver's seat. "Here," he said, reaching into the glove box to fish out some tissues.

"Thanks." I sniffled and wiped my eyes. Milo and

I sat there for a few minutes, his hand stroking my shoulder while I dribbled into a tissue. "I don't know what's wrong with me," I managed to say when I felt like I was getting a grip again.

"It's all part of the process," he said to me.

"What process?"

"Post-traumatic stress disorder," he said. "I've seen it a couple times in cops who get shot. You start to feel good again physically, but mentally you feel like you've lost your edge. You begin to doubt yourself and your abilities. Coping with the smallest decision can be a major deal. And just about the time you think you *should* be getting back to work is about the time you're terrified to go."

My eyes got large as he talked. That was exactly what I was feeling. "Whoa," I said to him. "Talk about hitting the nail on the head."

Milo nodded soberly. "Have you considered seeing someone to help you deal with this?"

"Like a therapist?"

"Yeah. I know of a good one if you're interested."

I played with the Kleenex in my hand. "It just seems like I should be able to get over this myself, Milo. Like, what's the big deal? I got shot, I survived, I have a great boyfriend who takes care of me, terrific friends, a pain-in-the-ass sister, a dog I adore . . ."

"Logic has nothing to do with it," Milo said as he wiped a tear off my cheek. "You had a terrible thing happen to you, Abby. And my guess is that right about now you think you should have seen it coming, 'cuz after all, you're psychic, right?"

My mouth opened a fraction. "Jesus, Milo," I said to him, "I'm beginning to think you may be tele-pathic."

Milo smiled. "Naw," he said. "I just know how you

think. You're one of these types that gets all guilty when you miss something, like when Allison was killed. I remember how that mess ate you up."

I nodded. "Yeah, that was bad. But, Milo, this was right in front of my face. I mean, if *anyone* should have seen this coming, it should have been me!"

Milo looked at me for a long, long time before he said, "Abby, you're not God. Underneath that superhero spandex you're still human, and it's human to believe the best about people. And sometimes, my friend, that's counterintuitive. It wasn't your fault. You didn't drop the ball—you just weren't looking for it to come out of left field. You're still the best psychic in town, and you *can* go back to work without worrying about messing it all up."

The waterworks started again, and it was a long time before I could speak. Finally I said in a ragged voice, "Thanks, Milo. That means a lot."

Milo leaned in and gave me a kiss on the cheek. "Now, come on," he said as he started the car. "I'll drive you home, and Dutch can come back for your car after he cooks me a big juicy steak."

Chapter Three

We made it back to Dutch's, and the moment he saw my tearstained face, he came over to protectively hug me and shoot an accusation at Milo. "You just couldn't leave her alone, could you?" he snapped.

"Hey, partner," Milo said mildly. "Good to see you too."

"I told you not to push her," Dutch growled. "Jesus, Milo, she'll talk about it when she's ready."

"And meanwhile she's internalizing all her fear and withdrawing from the world. You said yourself that you were concerned about her," Milo argued.

"Hello," I said, pushing away from Dutch's chest. "I'm standing right here, ya know."

"Are you okay?" Dutch asked me, looking intently into my eyes. "Did you want to go lie down for a while?"

Suddenly, I realized that Dutch and I had fallen into a pattern the past few months. I'd felt wounded, both internally and externally, and Dutch had protectively been wrapping me in the soft cocoon of his house and his care. He'd been enabling me to hide from the world, but now I knew deep down it was time to stop hiding. "Actually," I said, forcing a smile onto my face, "I'm really okay, Dutch. I think I'd like to help you with dinner. And Milo was kind enough to buy us some really good steaks, so how about we all just go into the kitchen and get the hell on with our lives?"

Dutch looked somewhat taken aback as I grabbed the grocery bag from Milo and marched into the kitchen. The fellas followed behind, and I couldn't help but overhear Milo say to Dutch, "Told you so."

While Dutch prepared dinner, Milo and I hung out on the back patio drinking wine and keeping him company. The conversation was noticeably light. Both men seemed to be aware of my rather fragile grip on things, and I couldn't really decide if I was grateful or irritated about that.

Finally, after enough idle chitchat about the weather and the price of a gallon of gas, I said, "Did you get anywhere on Max Goodyear?"

"Who's Max Goodyear?" Milo wanted to know.

"One of the cases I'm working that Abby's been helping me with," Dutch explained. "Yes, I took another look through his finances, Abs. Still can't find a blip, though."

My radar hummed. "What about kids? Did you look into that angle? You know, like maybe he's got a son or a daughter who's the funnel for the money."

"Literal dead end there, I'm afraid," Dutch said as he flipped the steaks. "Goodyear and his wife had a son back in the early seventies, but the baby died of crib death before he was two. There are no other children."

I scowled. The crummy thing about being intuitive is that it can be frustrating as hell when the facts don't match what your radar is suggesting. I sighed and gave him a shrug. "Ah, well, maybe I'm not as sharp as I used to be."

"That's 'cuz you need to work that thing out," Milo said and tipped his wineglass at me. "There's no better way to get it back in working order than to start up your business again."

"Milo," I heard Dutch growl, "lay off, would ya?"

"No," I said to Dutch and laid a protective hand on Milo's arm. "He's right. I do need to get back in the game. In fact, there are some voice mails that I should return. Call me when the steaks are done, 'kay?" I said, getting up from the patio table.

As I left the boys, I had to laugh when I heard Milo say, "Hey, partner, what's up with your hair?"

When I picked up the kitchen phone, my eye caught the red light blinking on the answering machine. I called my office voice mail first, took down all six messages there, and clicked off. My eye kept wandering back to the red light, and before calling back the first prospective client I hit the PLAY button. The message was for Milo. "Hi, Dutch. It's Noel. Listen, if my lunatic husband is there, could you please have him call me immediately? Also, tell him to answer his damn cell phone while you're at it. I've been trying to get a hold of him for an hour."

"Yikes," I said and hurried outside with the phone. "Milo, Noel called and she wants you to call home right away. She says she's been calling your cell for an hour."

I watched Milo pat his pockets, frantically checking for his cell, and then he whapped his forehead. "I must have left it on the charger at work." I gave him the phone, and he trotted inside to call his wife and try to crawl out of the doghouse.

"Dinner's ready," Dutch said. He handed me a plate with steak and tinfoil-wrapped potato and corn.

"Should we wait for Milo?" I asked as he and I took our seats.

"He'll be out in a minute. Dig in," Dutch said, cutting into his steak.

I felt a little guilty, but it smelled so good and I was so hungry that I couldn't help but cut off a piece, favoring my right side a little since the sawing motion of cutting was still very uncomfortable. Noticing the grimace on my face, Dutch asked, "You going to therapy tomorrow?"

I nodded. "And Candice wants to see me in the gym at six a.m. sharp."

Dutch chuckled. "I knew that was going to work out well," he said. "I'm glad she's moved to town."

"Want to come with me?" I asked, thinking that misery would sure love some company.

"Can't, babycakes. I've got an early meeting. Maybe the day after tomorrow."

"You think she'll want me to work out two days *in a row*?"

Dutch laughed. "If I know Candice, she'll be thinking more like five."

I gave Dutch a horrified look as Milo reappeared, his face grim. "Noel got a call from Craig Stanton. He's been looking for me."

"Who's that?" I asked.

"The head of the parole board," Dutch said to me. He turned to Milo. "What's up?"

"Lutz was knifed this afternoon. He's in the hospital being prepped for surgery. They're not sure yet how serious it is."

There was a long silence between Milo and Dutch as the two of them seemed to be working through that. "He'll live," I said into the silence when my radar kicked in. Goose bumps formed along my arms, and in my head I saw that black dog, drooling and snarling. I knew that Dick Wolfe was behind the attack on Lutz.

"That's what you're picking up?" Milo asked me.

"Yeah. Give it a week. He'll be better."

"Did Craig say who knifed Lutz?"

"Conveniently," Milo said sarcastically, "there were no witnesses. A guard found Lutz in a pool of blood and couldn't say who stabbed him. They think it was most likely gang-related."

My left side felt thick and heavy, which meant there was no way the stabbing was gang-related. I held back from commenting, though. "So the parole hearing's been postponed," Dutch said with a sigh.

"Yep. Craig said he'd keep us posted—but maybe this will give us a little more time to prepare anyway."

Dutch nodded. "Sounds good. You still staying for dinner or does Noel want you to get your butt home?"

"Oh, I'm staying," Milo said, taking his seat. "I'll just need to stop off and get her some flowers on the way home."

Later that evening, after returning all the requests for appointments, I came upstairs and found Dutch lounging on the bed in a pair of black boxer briefs with big red hearts. "Interesting underwear," I said to him as I unfastened my watch and set it on the nightstand.

"The interesting part's *under* the underwear, babycakes," Dutch said, giving his eyebrows a wiggle.

I laughed and shimmied out of my jeans, stepping over my two suitcases to toss them in a nearby pile of dirty clothes. "You know I have to get up at the crack of dawn tomorrow, cowboy."

Dutch clicked the TV off and rolled over on his side to rest his handsome head on his hand and make goo-goo eyes at me. "What if I do all the work?" he suggested, his voice deep and throaty.

I sighed as I looked at him. I was starting to waffle. "You know," I said, "I'm not sure I'm ready to jump into this morning routine, but Candice is right. I really do need to start working out."

"Well, how about you come over here and let me give you a workout?"

"I don't know," I said as I took off my shirt and tossed it in the pile. "I may not be in the mood."

I watched as Dutch's mouth set and he stared down at the comforter. Then he said, "Okay," and rolled onto his back, clicking the TV back on.

I stood there dumbfounded for a beat or two. "That's it?" I said sharply. "You're just going to give up and go back to watching the game?"

Dutch gave me a puzzled expression. "Did you want to talk or something?" he asked me, and shut the TV off again.

I looked at the set and back to him, my anger beginning to mount. "What the hell's happened to you anyway?" I demanded. "Seriously, Dutch. I know I got shot, and I'm dealing with this stupid post-traumatic crap, but what the hell happened to you?"

Dutch blinked at me and sat up. "Abby," he said in a very calm voice. "I'm going to need you to give me a hint here, 'cuz I really don't know why you're upset."

I scowled at him and turned to the suitcase where I kept the tank top and shorts I slept in. I paused and folded my arms, trying to keep a lid on the hurt and anger bouncing around inside of me. "I miss us," I said finally. "I miss you."

"Edgar," he said softly, "I'm right here, babe. I haven't gone anywhere."

"The hell you haven't," I barked. "What happened to the guy who used to flirt with me until I gave in? The guy who would know that my saying 'I'm not sure I'm in the mood' means '*put* me in the mood already'!" Dutch was silent behind me and I waited a beat before continuing. "I got injured, Dutch—I haven't died. I'm beginning to think that the reason I keep retreating from the world is because I'm afraid of it. And I think you're making it easy for me to feel that way."

"I see," he said, and I could tell I'd struck a nerve.

"No, you don't," I sighed, opening my suitcase to fish out my jammies. "You think that I'm blaming you, but I'm not. I just want you to be *you* again. I don't want you to tread carefully around me. I don't want you to treat me like I might break, and shelter me from the world. I want you to push me—hard. Every time I back off something that's a step in the right direction, like going back to work, or helping Milo, or working out with Candice, I want you to be there to call me on my shit."

"Fine," he said as I turned around and met those fabulous midnight blues. "I promise I'll push, but I guarantee you're not gonna like it."

"Of course I'm not gonna like it," I said, smiling at him. "But I'll love you for being in my corner, cowboy."

"Get over here," he said, his own mouth curling into a seductive grin. "I have something interesting to show you, and a mood to get you in."

The crack of dawn came friggin' early the next morning, and I so wanted to do nothing more than roll over and go back to sleep. Dutch, however, was taking his new responsibility of pushing me back into the swing of things with relish. He leaped up at the sound of the alarm and came around to my side of the bed. "Morning, sunshine!" he sang, his voice so loud it echoed off the walls. "Rise and shine!"

"Five minutes," I mumbled and pulled the covers up.

"Not even five seconds," he said and yanked the covers right off the bed.

I curled around my pillow and pulled my knees to my chest. I can be a stubborn git when I want to be. "Five minutes!"

Dutch pushed his arms under me and picked me right up out of bed. "You don't want to be late," he said and carried me to the bathroom, where he plopped me down on the side of the tub. "A little cold water should do the trick," he said as I worked to open my eyelids.

A second later the faucet went on and I felt the shock of cold water on my face. "Hey!" I yelled and swatted at him. "Stop!"

"Just pushing you along, Abs." He laughed. "Here," he said, and put my toothbrush in my hand. "Don't want to send you off to the gym with morning breath."

Fifteen minutes later Dutch had dropped me at my car, which had been left at the lot of the grocery store, and was headed back home to take a long hot shower and wake up properly. The clock on my dashboard read five forty-five a.m. and I groaned at it as I swung out of the parking lot and headed to the gym, which was only a few blocks away.

I made it there in time to see Candice's car coming down the street from the opposite direction. She parked next to me and hopped out. "Morning, Abs!" she said happily. "Glad to see you actually made it."

"Is *everyone* cheerful in the morning?" I groused. "It's still officially nighttime until the sun comes up, you know."

Candice yanked on my ponytail while she held the door of the gym open for me. We made our way to the counter, where she signed in and presented the clerk with a coupon for a free guest pass. "We'll get you a membership after we work out," she said and led the way to the locker rooms.

The gym was surprisingly crowded for so early in the morning. "Where did all these people come from?" I asked as I put my keys and sweatshirt in a locker.

"Some people would rather work out before work than after," she said. "Come on, let's find a treadmill before they're all taken."

"I thought we were going to skip the cardio," I complained, slightly panicked that Candice would find it amusing to see how long I could run before collapsing. Little did she know it'd be about ten minutes.

"I'm going to have you walk at a brisk pace for twenty minutes to warm you up. I also want you to increase your protein intake for the next several days. You'll be craving the carbs, but just try and resist and stick with the protein as much as you can."

"Right. I'll order the meat lovers pizza," I said, stepping doubtfully on the treadmill. Candice punched several buttons and I started walking. The pace was fine, and within a few minutes, I could feel the blood flow waking me up.

"You okay?" Candice panted from the treadmill next to me. She was running at a really good clip and I felt like an idiot just walking next to her.

I held up my thumb and hit one of the buttons, which picked up my own pace a little. Candice smiled and gave me a thumbs-up back. "That's the spirit," she said and we finished our time in silence.

Next we headed over to a row of benches. I sat down and looked up at her expectantly. She took off her light sweatshirt and my mouth dropped at the lean muscles running up her arms and shoulders. "Damn, girl!" I said to her. "You look like that chick from *Terminator II*!"

Candice smiled and flexed her bicep. "We'll get you here in six weeks," she said. "You wait, Abs. I'm going to turn you into the bionic woman. Now, we're going to do butterfly exercises first," she said as she selected two dumbbells from a rack in front of us, then made her way over to the bench next to me and lay back on it. "The motion looks like this," she said as she raised the dumbbells directly above her, then moved each out to the side and down, then back up in one fluid motion.

"Looks easy enough," I said, and lay back on the bench while Candice selected two dumbbells for me and came over to place them in my upraised hands. "Go slow, Abs, and let me know if they're too much weight."

I tested the dumbbell in my left hand a little. It felt just right. "No sweat, Candice. This is fine." My hands separated as my arms brought the weights out, but just when my right hand had reached about a quarter of the way down, a sharp pain tore across my chest. I dropped the dumbbell from my left hand, which tilted me off balance, and I rolled right off the bench onto the floor. *"Shit!"* I said when I hit the floor.

"Ohmigod!" Candice said as she bent down next to me. "Abby! What happened?"

Every breath I took sent ripples of pain through

my chest. "I think I tore something," I said through gritted teeth.

"Can you stand?" she asked me.

"Give me a sec," I said, holding up a finger. "Just give me a sec."

"Is she okay?" I heard a male voice say above us. Squinting up, I saw some sort of Greek god hovering over us, wearing a skintight T-shirt with STAFF in big white letters on the front.

"I don't know," Candice said. "She was shot in the chest a few months ago, and I think I may have re-opened her wound!"

"I'm fine," I said as I moved to a sitting position. "Really, I'm okay," I added when the two of them didn't look convinced.

"Maybe we should call an ambulance," Candice said, her eyes pinched with worry.

"No!" I barked. There was no way I wanted to ride in another damn ambulance—not for a long, long time. "I'm fine, really," I added, realizing that the seizing pain in my chest had subsided substantially. "I think it's just the scar tissue. My physical therapist warned me it would be tight."

"She was really shot?" Staff Guy wanted to know.

"Yes. In the heart," Candice said dramatically as she swept her hair demurely behind her ear.

"Is she a cop or something?"

"No, but I'm a PI."

"Get out of here! My brother's a PI."

"Really? Here in town?"

I glanced up at Romeo and Juliet, who had completely forgotten about their friend Mercutio, lying on the floor, holding her chest. "I'll be over at the water fountain," I said, as I got to my feet.

Candice turned back to me, "Oh, God, Abs, I'm sorry. Do you want some help?"

"No, no," I said, wagging my finger at her. "I'm fine. You two continue your conversation. I'm going to rest over there."

A little while later, Candice came trotting over, a piece of paper in her hand. "How you feeling?" she asked me.

"I'm fine," I said and meant it. "I have a session with Lori, my physical therapist, later today. She can take a look at it, but I really think it's just the scar tissue."

"I never should have started you out on butterflies," she said. "I'm really sorry."

"Maybe something in the bicep or triceps area would be better until I can stretch this out."

"No problem. Let's wait until tomorrow after your therapist okays it, though."

"Deal. So did you get his number?"

"I did," she said with a big grin. "His name is Simon."

"When are you two going out?"

"Tomorrow night. You and Dutch want to double with us?"

"Can't," I said, smiling. "I've got appointments."

Candice clapped her hands. "You called my friends!" she exclaimed.

I nodded, feeling a teensy bit of pride. "Yep. Working my way back into my old life."

"Good for you," Candice said. Then she stood up. "Come on, Abs. Let's treat you to some breakfast, and after that I'm going to head to the office and see what I can start digging up on Walter McDaniel's murder."

"Oh!" I said, slapping my forehead. "I totally forgot

to tell you. There's been an update that you should know about."

While we retrieved our things from the locker room, I filled her in on Lutz's stabbing, including the bit about my radar hinting that Wolfe was behind it. "Why would Wolfe want Lutz dead now?" she asked me. "I mean, if he was going to blab, wouldn't he have done it by now?"

"I'm not sure," I said as we made our way to the front and Candice grabbed a membership application for me. "But if we're going to dig into this, we might want to try and find out."

Dutch's car was gone when I got home about an hour later. In its place was a beat-up blue Chevy pickup with a familiar face behind the wheel. "Hey there," I called to Dave as I parked and got out.

"Heard you went to the gym," he said, getting out of his own vehicle.

"I did," I said and clicked my heels together smartly.

"How'd it go?"

" 'Bout like you'd expect a field trip with me to the gym would go," I said and headed up the walkway to the house.

"I'm picturing dropped dumbbells and lots of swearing." Dave chuckled.

"Now who's clairvoyant?" I said, opening the door.

Dave followed me inside and greeted Eggy, who was much more glad to see him than me. "Want coffee?" I asked as I headed into the kitchen.

"Love some. Say, have you had a chance to talk to your sister yet?"

I smacked my head. "Crap!" I said and wheeled around to face him. "Dave, I'm so sorry. I called Cat and she's totally good with the offer. Call the agent and accept. We can close as soon as they're ready."

Dave looked up at the ceiling and mouthed, "Thank you," then glanced back at me. "I hope they want to close soon."

I cocked my head at him. "You hurtin' for money?" I asked.

"Kind of," he said and avoided my eyes.

It was then that my radar buzzed and in my mind's eye I saw a red heart with a split down the middle. "Oh, my God, Dave," I said breathlessly. "She left you."

Dave looked sharply at me. "Turn that thing off," he said, pointing to my head.

"When?" I asked, coming over to him and grabbing his hand to lead him to a chair.

Once he'd gotten seated, he began to make little circles on the table with his forefinger. "Last week," he mumbled. I opened up my intuition and tried to get the skinny. Dave looked up at me again and scowled. "Stop with the mind reading, Abby," he said, and his tone meant business.

I turned away and fiddled with the coffeemaker. I didn't know what to say. Dave had been in a common-law marriage forever. I had no idea what his wife's true name was, since he always referred to her as "my old lady," which sounded demeaning unless you knew, like I did, that Dave absolutely worshiped the ground she walked on.

Dave was silent until I returned to the table with two steaming cups in hand. I sat down across from him and sipped at my brew, waiting him out. "I can't talk about it," he said gruffly.

I nodded, but just couldn't keep myself from saying, "There's no other guy, you know."

Dave's eyes met mine and there was a hint of relief there. "That what your team says?"

I nodded. "Yep. She's gone because of a broken promise."

Dave sucked in a breath. "Shit, Abs. You should be on television or something."

I smiled over the rim of my cup. "It's a gift. Sure you don't want to share?"

Dave sighed and picked up the sugar bowl from the center of the table. After spooning in four teaspoons, he began softly: "I came home last Tuesday, you know, after my usual poker game, and she was gone. All her stuff was gone too and there was no note or nothin'. She wouldn't answer my calls and I just about called the police, I was so worried about her. And then I passed by the fridge and I saw that the calendar had been taped to the door. She'd circled the day before in big red marker. That was my only clue about why she'd gone."

"Something to do with the promise," I said, feeling a connection. "And a celebration missed," I added.

I got another gasp of surprise from Dave, along with a small, mirthless laugh. "I may kidnap you for my next poker game. We could make a killing."

"What was the date?" I asked, wanting to put the pieces together.

"It was our twentieth anniversary."

"And you forgot it?" I said, cocking my head. That fit in my head, but it didn't feel like that was all of it.

"Not only did I forget, even after being reminded about it for months beforehand, but I failed to deliver on the promise I made to her ten years ago."

"Which was?"

"Well, we'd been together a long time then, and she was pestering me for a ring. The law already recognized us as common-law husband and wife, but my old lady really wanted the diamond. As you know, I've never been a big fan of the whole ceremony, so to put her off I made her a solemn vow. I told her that if she and I hung in there for another ten years, I would buy her the biggest diamond I could afford, and make it official."

It was my turn to suck in a breath. "Oh, Dave," I said as I set down my coffee. "How *could* you forget? Don't you men realize that women take stuff like that *seriously*?"

Dave's eyebrows lowered. "Of course I didn't!" he snapped. "If I did, I would have planned better!"

"Well, have you been in touch with her? I mean, have you tried to find out where she is?"

"She's at her sister's house in Gaylord," he said more calmly. "Her brother-in-law called me a few days later and said that he'd been sworn to secrecy but he thought a brother should know."

"So she won't talk to you," I said.

"Nope."

"You need to buy a ring, Dave!" I said to him excitedly. "You need to buy a gigantic honker of a diamond, run up there to Gaylord, get down on bended knee, and tell that woman you love her once and for all!"

"Sure, Abby. Let me just go down to the bank and withdraw the thousand dollars I've got stashed away in my bank account and buy a diamond just larger than a grain of sand."

"A thousand dollars?" I said to him, my eyes large. "*Why* would you have only a thousand dollars, Dave? You've been working steadily since fixing Fern."

Dave squirmed in his chair and fiddled with his spoon. "I bought a flat-screen TV the weekend before she left," he said very softly.

"You *what*?" I shouted at him. "Are you *kidding* me?"

"It was a great deal!" he argued. "I couldn't pass it up."

"How much could a flat screen possibly cost?" I asked him, completely exasperated.

"Seven grand after the rebate." I shook my head back and forth wondering how men could be so incredibly stupid. "And the rest of the money is tied up in all the building supplies that went into Fern. Plus, I might have needed a new tile saw for Milo and Noel's place."

"Call the Realtor, Dave, and after you tell her that we accept the offer you and I are going to make a trip into town."

"I gotta get over to Milo's," Dave said.

"No, what you've got to do before that is come up with a plan to make up for being an idiot. I'm going to introduce you to a friend of mine, Bobby Miller. He's a client, and he owns a wholesale jewelry business. We're going to have him start work on a ring that's got enough bling to be seen from outer space."

Two hours and several arguments later, I was back home, waving to Dave as he peeled out of the driveway and headed down the street at a good clip. He'd failed to thank me for spending ten thousand of his hard-earned dollars from Fern, once it closed. I was in too good a mood to hold it against him, though. Someday, he would see that getting his girl back meant making sure she knew she was worth more than a flat-screen TV.

I headed inside just as my cell phone rang. I figured it was Dave thinking better of peeling out. "Abby Cooper," I said into the phone.

"Hey, there," Candice said. "I need you to come

to the office. I've found something interesting about that case you wanted me to look into."

"I've got physical therapy in an hour," I said, looking at my watch. "Can it wait until after that or would you like me to come down now?"

"Now."

My eyebrows lifted. "Okay, be there in a flash." I clicked off and hurried to my car. Candice's *now* had been filled with urgency, and I'd known her long enough to understand that she didn't toss that tone around lightly.

I arrived at the office just a few minutes later and rushed up to the suite. Candice was finishing up a phone call and pointed to a chair in front of her when I walked in. I sat and took a look around the office that had sat empty for the past year.

Since her arrival this morning, she'd already moved in most of her office furniture. Her taste matched well with mine, but had a little more chrome and art deco in the mix. Her desk had a glass surface with chrome legs and a black metal hutch. A white Macintosh laptop was in front of her and she typed on it while she was on the phone.

The matching chair to the one I was sitting in was smoke-colored crushed velvet, with a short, circular back and spiked wooden legs. Two paintings were propped against the wall, both swirls of earth-toned colors that complemented each other and the room. A framed PI certificate of license already hung on the wall over Candice's desk.

Candice said good-bye to the caller and focused her attention on me. "You'll never guess who that was," she said.

"I'm a pretty good guesser," I said. "How many chances do I get?"

Candice smiled. "Don't bother. That was Darren Cox."

My brow furrowed. The name sounded familiar, but where had I heard it? "That would not have been one of my guesses," I admitted.

"You remember," she said, realizing I was trying to place the name. "The PI who worked on that case where Wolfe was involved—the one who cleared out of town without notice?"

"Ah," I said, nodding vigorously. "I remember. So that was him?"

"Yes. And you will never believe where he works," she said excitedly.

My radar buzzed. "He works with houses, but he's not a real estate agent," I said, following the thought. "It's more like accounting . . . oh! He's in the mortgage business!"

Candice shook her head back and forth. "You never cease to amaze me," she said. "Yes, he's a loan officer at a mortgage company. You'll never guess who he works for."

An ugly black beast appeared in my mind's eye. "He's working for Wolfe," I said with a scowl.

"Remind me never to throw you a surprise party," she said, sitting back in her chair and crossing her arms.

"Sorry. When someone says, 'You'll never guess,' I take it as a personal challenge. So tell me how Cox ended up working for the very guy who ran him out of town."

"Not sure yet," she said. "But I have a plan."

My left side felt a little thick, and I knew I wasn't going to like Candice's plan. "Uh-oh," I said.

"What's uh-oh?" she asked. "You haven't even heard it yet."

"Fair enough. What's the plan?"

"You have a date with him tonight, and on said date you can ask him. Indirectly, of course."

"I'm sorry, what?" I asked, cocking my head and cupping my ear. "I don't think I heard you correctly."

"You can ask him on the date."

I threw my head back and laughed. Granted, it was a rather forced laugh, but I wanted Candice to appreciate how *hilarious* I found her. "That's a good one, girlfriend! Man, you had me going for a minute there."

"I'm serious, Abby. We need to pump him for information, and I certainly can't go out with him."

"Why not?" I demanded.

"Because I may have slept with him. Once. A long time ago. When I was very, *very* drunk."

"Again, you're hilarious," I said to her. "Truly, you need to take this act on the road."

"Plus I'm seeing Simon now," Candice added.

"Really? Gee, I thought you'd just met. Didn't realize the wedding invitations were going out already."

Candice rolled her eyes at me. "I'm a one-man girl, Abby. When I say yes to a date with someone, I don't like to complicate things by having other distractions."

"You don't say? Gee, have I introduced you to *my* other distraction? Special Agent Dutch Rivers? That tall drink of water I've been seeing for a year—you remember, the guy with the *gun*?"

Candice waved her hand airily at me. "It's just a pretend date," she said. "And if it will make you feel any better, I'll call Simon and see if we can switch our drink to tonight and we'll double with you. That way I can keep an eye on you."

"Yeah, 'cuz I'm *totally* worried about Darren lighting my world on fire and me losing control," I deadpanned. "This is ridiculous. Candice, call him back and tell him the date's off."

"Fine," she said and picked up the receiver. Her finger hovered over the number pad. "But just remember, I was doing this for you."

I stared at her without blinking.

"This was your big case," she added. My expression didn't change. "And this was our only good lead into finding out about Wolfe."

"You're not going to call it off, are you?" I said to her.

"No," she said and put the phone down. "Abby, I've known you long enough to know that when you get a hunch about someone, it's right on. And if this Lutz guy didn't kill Walter, then I think we owe it to Walter's family—and Milo—to uncover the truth of it."

Aw, crap. She had to play the sympathy card. "How the hell am I going to explain to Dutch that I'm going on a pretend date tonight?" I said, starting to give in.

"The same way you explained to him that you're looking into Walter's murder—you don't."

I sighed heavily. "Fine. But the ground rules are that we have one drink while I pump him for info before I remember I have to be somewhere, and I am outta there. Then, you can tell him later that I thought he was cute, but I'm still not over my old boyfriend, 'kay?"

Candice held up two fingers. "Scout's honor," she said.

You'd think I'd know better than to take that two-finger salute seriously, but Mama always did peg me for a slow learner.

Chapter Four

Later that afternoon I stopped off at my place, a cozy little ranch-style house that Dave had fixed up before he'd started on the Fern project. I'd barely been here since returning from being shot in Denver three months earlier. Feeling eerily like a stranger in my own home, I walked through my front door, then paused in the living room and looked around.

The place felt smaller. My new furniture had arrived just after Christmas, and it was nice enough, but truthfully, this house really hadn't grown on me like I'd expected it to. Granted, I'd spent very little time here since moving in. Usually I was over at Dutch's, and I genuinely liked his place, even though we were really cramped for personal space. But since I was now on this whole "taking my life back" crusade, perhaps the next logical step was to move back home and settle in.

I resolved to talk to Dutch about my living situation later. Right now I had a half hour to change and get back downtown to go on my pretend date. I boogied into the bedroom and headed for my walk-in closet.

As I was looking at my choices my cell phone rang. "Abby Cooper," I said, after flipping it open.

"Abby? This is Lori. Are you on your way?"

"Ach!" I sputtered. "Oh, crap, *crap*! Lori, I completely forgot about calling you to cancel our session today!" I said, slapping my forehead.

"I was wondering," she replied. "You're usually right on time."

I leaned my head on the wall of the closet. "You must hate me," I said, silently cursing myself. There was nothing worse than having someone skip out on an appointment—trust me, as a psychic who used to live her life around her appointment book, I put clients who skipped out on their appointments without even bothering to call right up there on my list of super-loathsome people.

"No," she laughed. "It's fine. When would you like to reschedule?"

"Uh . . ." I said, considering the commitments I'd already made. "Tomorrow?"

"Three o'clock?"

"Yeah, that should be good—and I swear to you, I will be there, and on time."

"It's no sweat, Abby. Really. It happens to everyone."

"Thanks for understanding. Lori, while I have you on the phone, can I ask you something?"

"Sure?"

"Is there any reason why I shouldn't be doing weight training at the gym? Like maybe I'll pull something and this might not be such a great idea for at least another year?" Even though I'd only walked at a brisk pace for twenty minutes that morning, my ass was sore as all get out, and I was hoping to weasel out of another training session.

"No reason at all," she said easily. "In fact, I think it's an excellent idea. You need to stretch out that scar tissue, and some resistance training would be great for it."

"Ah," I said with a scowl. "Okay, that's great, 'cuz I really want to get back in the swing of things and all."

"Glad to hear it. I'll see you tomorrow at three."

I clicked the phone off and shoved it into my back pocket. Then I pulled a blouse off a hanger and walked over to my full-length mirror. Holding it up under my chin, I looked at my reflection. "This'll do," I said and ducked back into the closet for a clean pair of jeans.

Forty-five minutes later I had showered, dried my hair, and put on only a hint of makeup. I really didn't want to appear interested in Darren, but I also didn't want to seem like a slob. I locked up the house and a minute later was back in my car and headed toward town.

I was meeting Candice and Darren at Tom's Oyster Bar on Main Street for happy hour. I was kind of nervous about how I was going to get information out of him on Wolfe, but Candice had assured me that she would do most of the talking. Her instructions to me had been to look sexy, but not too sexy. I hoped the blue cotton button-up and jeans were what she'd pictured when she handed out the instructions.

I found a parking space on Fifth Street and pumped the meter full of quarters, then hoofed it down to Tom's. Candice had gotten a table right out front and waved at me when she spotted me. "Hey," I said as I took a seat at the table. "You the first one here?"

"Yep. Simon doesn't get off work 'til six, so it may just be you, me, and Darren for a while."

"Fine by me," I said. "I'm not planning on staying long." Just then, my cell rang and I pulled it out of my pocket and looked at the caller ID. "Ugh," I said, showing her the display. "It's Dutch."

"So answer it," she said as she picked up her martini and took a sip.

"He'll want to know where I am," I said, looking around nervously.

"So tell him you're out with me," she said simply.

"Good call." I flipped the phone open. "Hey, guy!" I sang. "What's movin' and shakin'? What's rockin' and rollin'? What's happening?"

"You're in a good mood," he said.

"You betcha! I am a happy, happy girl!"

Dutch paused, then said, "So, I'm at home."

"That's great! Good for you. Home is good. Home is where the heart is. Home on the range. Home sweet home."

"Where are you?"

"Er . . . I'm out with Candice. You know, hanging out. Just us girls. Nothing special. Just talking. And hanging. Her and me. She and I. Gabbing it up . . ." Did I mention I'm not good on the phone when I have to lie to my boyfriend?

"Edgar, how many drinks have you had?"

"Oh, ha, ha! No, I'm fine," I said. "Really. We're just hanging, and talking. Mostly just gabbing, not a lot of drinking, 'cuz that's not safe, and I'm a safety girl. Which is why we're just talking. About girl stuff. You know . . . like PMS."

I was rewarded with another pause. "Okay, then. Have a good time—and call me if you feel you've had too much and I'll come pick you up, okay?"

"Sure, sure. No worries, cowboy. I'll probably just

hang with her for a bit and be home later. In a little while. After we finish our conversation. About girl stuff."

I noticed Candice making a slashing motion across her throat. I said a quick good-bye and hung up. "Jeez, Abby. Don't ever think about having an affair on him. You are the worst liar I ever met."

"Ohmigod!" I said as I tucked my phone back in my pocket. "*Why* did you make me answer that?!"

"Relax," she said, looking over my shoulder. "Here comes Darren. Try and get it together until we find out how he managed to get a job with Wolfe and then you can bail."

I shook my head a little, trying to clear all the blubbery thoughts racing through my mind. When I get nervous I tend to chatter, and I needed to play it cool for this pumping session with Darren. "Hello, ladies," a strikingly handsome man said as he came to our table. "I'm Darren," he added, offering his hand to me.

"Abby," I said as I shook his hand and discreetly gave him the once-over before he turned toward Candice and gave her a big hug. I guessed that he was a little shorter than Dutch, with curly dark hair and a nice square jaw. His nose was thin and delicate, and he had really nice green eyes.

"Man, it is so good to see you!" he said to Candice as he stepped back and took his seat. "What's it been, like three years?"

"Just about," she said, and motioned to our waiter.

We all ordered drinks, and Darren leveled his gaze at me. "Candice tells me you two work together."

I nodded. "Yeah. We just started. Working together, that is." God, I was awful at this.

"Only officially," Candice said easily. "Abby and I have had an informal working relationship for years."

"So you're a PI too?" Darren asked me.

My eyes darted over to Candice. I didn't know how to do this. Should I lie? Should I tell the truth? Should I pretend my contact had just popped out of my eye and dive under the table? "No. She's a professional psychic," Candice said. "Careful, Darren. She'll be reading your mind in a minute."

Darren's eyes got large and he sat back in his chair. "Really?" he asked me. "Are you really a psychic?"

I nodded and played with the straw in the amaretto sour that our waiter had just put in front of me. "It's true."

"That is so cool!" he said enthusiastically.

"She's fantastic," Candice said. "She can tell you all about your future—right, Abby?" She gave me a look that suggested I roll with her.

"Guilty as charged," I said, taking a big sip of my drink.

"I'll bet you have a fantastic future ahead of you," Candice added, laying it on thicker. "I'll bet she can see big things for you. Go ahead, Abby, tell Darren what big things you see for him."

"Uh," I said, looking at her quizzically. I wasn't really sure where she was going with this.

"Like tell him what you see with regard to his career," Candice encouraged.

"Ah," I said as the lightbulb finally clicked on in my head. "Okay," I said, turning to focus on him and switching the radar on. "I already know you work at a mortgage company, but the first thing I'm picking up is that there is something to do with . . ." I paused. What the hell was this image in my head? I kept seeing a horde of snakes slithering all over each other. "They're showing me snakes."

"Snakes?" he asked thoughtfully. From the look on

his face, I could have sworn he knew what I was referring to but was holding back to see what else I could
give him.

"Yes. Where you work, does one of your coworkers
have some pet snakes or something? This has to do
with the environment you work in. They keep showing
me snakes crawling all over each other."

Darren tilted his head back and laughed. "Whoa!"
he said. "That was awesome!"

"Someone does have snakes at your work?" I
asked.

"No. But at my mortgage company there's this one
large room where all the loan officers sit. It's called
the snake pit."

Candice gave Darren an elbow. "See? I told you
she was really good. Abby, what else are you getting?"
Candice made sure to mouth the word "wolf" to me
while Darren wasn't looking, and I gave her a tiny
nod in return.

"Well," I said, feigning concentration. "Your boss.
They keep showing me this big black dog—or maybe
it's a wolf. Yeah, I think it's a big black wolf."

Darren laughed again. "My boss's last name is
Wolfe," he said, then seemed to catch himself. Turn-
ing to Candice, he said, "You remember that last case
I was working on before I quit the firm?"

Candice's face scrunched up a little and she rubbed
her forehead with her fingers. "Vaguely," she said.

"The guy I was investigating is now my boss. I
ended up meeting with him the night I flew out on
vacation, and we talked and he explained that our
client was his former girlfriend and she had made up
this whole thing about being pregnant with his kid
when she caught him cheating on her."

In the back of my mind I heard *Liar, liar . . . pants*

on fire, my sign that Darren was telling a big fat fib. Candice's eyes flickered to me. She wasn't buying it either. "You don't need to explain it to me, Darren," she said. "Who you work for is your business."

My radar buzzed and I followed the thought. In my mind's eye I kept seeing one of those street scammers who lure tourists into a shell game where they have to find the bean. I wondered about it, but waited to see if Darren would offer up anything else.

"Dick's a great guy," he said, and my radar buzzed again at the lie. "He heard I'd moved to Royal Oak and offered me a job."

"I'm glad you're doing well, Darren," Candice said.

"It's a great business to be in," Darren said, and I noticed how hard he seemed to be trying to convince her. "We specialize in providing mortgages to people who get turned down by local banks. We're helping people own a home for the first time in their lives." I felt his insincerity again and I got such an acrid taste in my mouth that I took a sip of my drink to try and clear it.

"That's great," Candice said. "It's really good to enjoy what you do, isn't it?"

"That it is," Darren said.

"Abby, what else do you see for Darren?"

"That's okay," he said quickly. "She's on a date, after all. I don't want her to think she needs to work while we're just getting to know each other."

I nodded as I played with my drink, feeling someone staring at me over Darren's shoulder. I did a quick double take as I realized that Dutch Rivers was across the patio, saluting me with the beer in his hand.

"Ohmigod!" I yelped.

"What?" Darren and Candice both said together.

I slapped my hand over my right eye and said, "My

contact! I think it's gone under the table!" With that, I dove under the table and began to pat the pavement.

Candice poked her head under too. "What's going on?" she whispered.

"Dutch!" I hissed at her, and just then I heard a familiar baritone above the table.

"Hey there, Candice," Dutch said.

Candice mouthed "Oh, shit!" at me and lifted her head from under the table. "Well, hello, Dutch," I heard her say. "What brings you by?"

"I'm looking for Abby. Seen her?"

"I'm right here," I said as I emerged from under the table and poked convincingly at my eye.

"Did you find your contact?" Darren asked.

"Sure did." I smiled at him. "Mr. Rivers, this is a pleasant surprise. I didn't realize our appointment was for tonight."

"Yes, and you're late," he said to me, thankfully going along with the ruse.

"Aw," Darren said, "does that mean we won't be able to finish our date?"

I jumped up so quickly that I nearly flipped the table. "Oh, so sorry!" I said, putting a steadying hand on the tabletop. "Yes, some other time. You and Candice can catch up for a bit. Mr. Rivers, come on. We'll head up to my office and get started, okay?"

I hurried away from the table, hoping Dutch would be right on my heels. He was, and the moment we were out of earshot he gripped my elbow and said in my ear, "Want to tell me what that was all about?"

I kept walking and said, "*What* are you doing here?"

"You sounded tipsy on the phone. I came to make sure you were okay to drive."

"How the hell did you find me?"

Dutch wiggled his cell phone. I had its twin, and I knew from past experience that the two could be easily linked and my location pinpointed via the GPS chip inside. "Dirty pool," I said as we turned the corner, heading to my car.

"It's dirty pool to make sure my girlfriend isn't impaired?"

"You should know me better than that," I said, keeping my pace brisk.

"Well, I thought I knew you well enough to think we were exclusive," Dutch snapped, and I winced at the jealousy in his voice.

I stopped walking and turned to look at him. "It's not what you think."

"Neither was the wedding invitation to Denver," he said coldly.

I sucked in a breath. "You *know* I thought we'd split up!" I said, referring to the small, not even worth mentioning, *teensy* affair I'd had with a very old friend just before I'd been shot.

Dutch sighed heavily and ran a hand through his short blond hair. "Yeah, well, I was willing to let that one go, babycakes, but now three months later, here I find you testing those waters again."

I stared at my boyfriend for a full minute. Half of me wanted to walk off in a huff and not speak to him for a while. The other half realized that if the situation were reversed, I certainly wouldn't have been so understanding about his sleeping with another woman. Luckily, my reasonable half won out. "I never really told you how sorry I was about that, did I?"

"No," he said, leaning against a tree. "You didn't."

"Well, I am, you know. I'm really, really sorry, Dutch."

"Okay," he mumbled, not meeting my eyes.

I walked over to him. His arms were crossed and his face was hard as granite. I reached my hands out to his waist and gripped him firmly. "I will never understand how you put up with me," I said after a moment.

A tiny smile cracked the granite surface. "I get paid extra," he said. "Cat sends me a big fat check every month."

I laughed, then leaned in to wrap my arms around him. "I love you, cowboy," I said. "And I'm sorry about Denver."

"Got it," he said and lowered his chin to my head. "Now what was going on back there?"

"I was helping Candice with a case. She needed someone she could trust to go along with pumping some info out of that guy. She decided to have me play single white female."

"What's the case about?"

"It's confidential."

"I don't think I like you getting so personally involved with this stuff, Edgar," he said.

"I know. But I've got my radar on high, and I'm going to be careful."

"More careful than you've been all those other times your radar was on high?"

I looked up at him and smiled. "Definitely."

"And yet I'm still worried," Dutch said as he stroked my cheek.

"You have no faith," I said, taking his arm and leading him toward my car.

Later that night, as we were curled up in bed, my head resting on Dutch's chest, I brought up the topic of moving back home. "I was thinking," I began.

"Always a time to worry," Dutch quipped as he stroked my hair.

"Maybe it's time for me to head back to my place."

Dutch's hand paused on the top of my head. After a moment he said, "You know you're welcome to stay as long as you want."

"I know, but it's really a tight fit for the two of us. I mean, my stuff is just lying all over the place here," I said, motioning toward the suitcases on the floor. "And besides that," I added, "I think that the longer I stay, the longer I put off getting back into the swing of things."

"Okay," he said. "But make sure you come back to visit."

"I will." I smiled, then switched topics. "Did you have any more luck with Max Goodyear?"

Dutch sighed, his breath tickling the hairs on my head. "No. For the life of me I can't figure out how this guy plays into the waterworks pension fund leak."

In my mind's eye I saw Goodyear, a line leading down from him to a male figure; then a line leading from that male directly across to another male. I raised my head from Dutch's chest and said, "I know that you said his son died, but I get such a strong connection to a son figure. Are you sure he didn't have a kid out of wedlock or something?"

"None that I've been able to track down yet," Dutch said.

I sat up and focused hard on the extra male energy in the scenario. "It's so weird," I said. "Because when I ask the question about where the money's being filtered to, I'm shown Goodyear, then a line down to a son figure, then a line directly across to another male."

"Another male?"

"Yeah. My interpretation is that the money is being funneled through a close friend of Goodyear's son."

Dutch seemed to consider that for a moment. "So you're convinced that he's got a son who's alive?"

My left side felt thick and heavy, which surprised me. "Huh," I said. "That's weird."

"What's weird?"

"No, I don't think he's got a son who's alive."

"You think there was a son, born out of wedlock, who is now dead?" Dutch asked, and I could tell by his expression that he'd have a hard time believing that one.

Again, my left side felt thick and heavy. "Hold on," I said to him as I closed my eyes and tried to sort out exactly what my crew was telling me. Silently I asked how many children Goodyear had. I was shown the number one. Then I asked if the money was being filtered through someone associated with this dead child. My right side felt light and airy. "Dutch," I said, opening my eyes, "I know this is going to sound really out there, but the money is going through someone who had a close connection to Goodyear's son. They might have been playmates when they were babies, and now this man is grown and he's handling the money."

Dutch scratched his head. "So I should be looking at who the playmates were from thirty years ago?"

"Yeah. Sorry," I said. "But there's this connection— I just know it. And there's a good chance that the parents still may be close. I mean, obviously Goodyear and this playmate of his son's are close, so the odds are pretty good that the adults might still hang out together."

Dutch nodded. "Okay, Abs. I'll work on that in the morning. You getting up at the dawn of time again?"

"No. I told Candice that I'd need to check in with Lori first and make sure I didn't pull anything before I headed back to the gym."

Dutch gave me a sideways glance. Clearly he doubted my intentions to get back to breaking a sweat. I decided to change the subject by giving him a big fat smooch.

The next day I took a load of clothes and other belongings over to my place. I wasn't quite ready to leave Dutch's, but I figured I'd at least start the process. Next I headed to the office and found Candice already there, tapping away on her laptop. "Morning!" she said as I came through the door.

"Hey there," I replied, coming into her office and taking a seat.

"Missed you at the gym this morning," she said as she took a sip of coffee.

"I have an appointment with my physical therapist this afternoon. I want to make sure she clears it before I hand my physical well-being over to you again," I said.

Candice set her mug down and hung her head a little. "I'm really sorry about that, Abs. I totally forgot about your wound."

"It's fine," I said with a wave of my hand. "It's just the scar tissue's really tight. I'll have Lori give me the lowdown on what areas to work that won't affect it so much and then we can build a program from there."

"Good," she said. "And how'd it go with Dutch?"

"Fine," I laughed. "Can you believe he was jealous?"

"I can," she said with a wink. "But after you left, things got even more interesting."

"Dish," I said.

"Turns out Wolfe's company is looking for more loan officers."

"Really?"

"Uh-huh. And I might have mentioned to Darren that you have a background in the mortgage biz."

"Excuse me?" I said, squinting at her. "You told him what?"

"Weren't you a loan officer at that bank that went under a few years ago?"

"Yes, but—"

"He's really into the fact that you're psychic and that you know your way around a mortgage. I think you're a shoo-in."

I shook my head a little. I was aware that Candice was speaking, but I wasn't really getting the words that she was stringing together. "A shoo-in for what?"

"For the job, of course," Candice said. "Here, this is an application. Fill it out and I'll fax it to Darren. He said he could cut through a lot of the red tape."

I resorted to blinking rapidly as I stared at the paper in front of me. "You're kidding me with this, right?"

"Abby," Candice said, leaning forward and lacing her fingers together. "If you want to find out about Wolfe, we're going to have to do a little undercover here. I can't go in. My PI license is still current, and Wolfe's going to sniff that out right away. We need a mole, and since there's just the two of us, that mole's gotta be you."

I sputtered for a few seconds, then said, "But why can't we just dig around outside his organization? I mean, what the heck are we going to learn by going in this way?"

Candice sat back in her chair and regarded me for a long minute. Finally she turned to her computer and typed a few keystrokes, then said quietly, "Were you aware that before he died, Walter McDaniel was the owner of six rental properties throughout the metro Detroit area?"

I blinked again. "So?"

"And were you aware that he had a mortgage pending on a seventh house?"

"Again, I'm having a hard time following you here, Candice," I said to her.

"And were you aware, Abby, that prior to McDaniel owning these properties, at least two that I can trace were owned by known drug dealers?"

My mouth opened as my radar hummed loudly in my mind. "What mortgage company did the paper?" I asked.

Candice smiled. "Wolfe's," she said.

"Son of a bitch," I said. "He was dirty?"

"McDaniel?" Candice said. "Not sure yet, but it sure looks suspicious, doesn't it?"

I sat back myself and lifted the application off her desk to look at it again. "What made you look into McDaniel?"

"A hunch," she said. "And I'm still digging, but in the meantime we need to get to the bottom of the link between these two. The more we poke around the outskirts of it, the more we call attention to ourselves. But if we get you inside the organization and have you root around, we might be able to come up with some solid evidence to not only link Wolfe to McDaniel's murder but put him away for good with some other illegal shit that I think's going on down there. Since you've got a background in mortgages, you're the best person to go digging for something incriminating."

"How dangerous is this?" I asked her, knowing the answer.

"Very," she said. "So if you want to stop, we need to do it right now."

So there it was. I could step out onto the curb and know that a bus might come along and flatten me, or I could stay in the safety of the little padded room I'd created for myself. I was shaking inside. There's nothing like a near-death experience to make you want to take the safe route for the rest of your life, but the part of my personality that had always pushed me to do things that I wasn't comfortable with was yelling at me to get in there and start digging. "No," I said. "We move forward. I'll fill this out and get it back to you in a few minutes."

I marched into my office, filled out the application, and made up a quick résumé to attach to it, stating "counselor" as my current occupation. I was done in an hour, and gave both to Candice. She looked them over and said, "Good job, Abs. I'll get this to Darren this afternoon."

I busied myself the rest of the day with errands and readying my office for the three clients I'd scheduled that evening. They would arrive at six, which left me plenty of time to meet with Lori and take a shower before coming back to the office.

I walked into the physical therapy building promptly at five to three and found Lori just finishing up with her previous patient. I smiled and took a seat as I waited, watching her with an elderly woman who was trying to bend a knee that looked like it had just seen some surgery.

Lori stood about an inch taller than me, with chestnut-colored hair that reached her shoulder, brilliant green eyes, and a light, creamy complexion. She was patient, kind, and devoted to everyone who came to her for therapy. When she was done with the elderly woman, she wheeled her out to the lobby, then turned to me.

"How ya feeling?" she asked as she picked up a clipboard and began scribbling on it.

"Good," I said.

"That's great. How's the range of motion coming along?"

I showed her by extending my right arm straight out and moving it sideways, squinting a little when it was fully extended, perpendicular to my side. Lori nodded. "Range looks great, but you've still got some pain at the farthest points, huh?"

"Yeah. Yesterday I tried doing butterfly curls with weights and thought I'd ripped my chest wide open."

This got another nod from Lori. "Best to go really slowly with the weights," she said. "At least until you've stretched that tissue out."

"So I shouldn't be lifting for a while, then?"

Lori smiled. "On the contrary. It's the best thing for you. You just need to use very light weights and go nice and slow when you're making the motions. Here, lie back and I'll show you."

For the next hour Lori and I went through examples of exercises that I could do with Candice at the gym. All of them seemed to sting, but at least I knew the proper way to work out until I was fully healed.

"So when would you like to see me again?" I asked as Lori made a few more notes on her clipboard.

"Actually, Abby, I think you're good to go," she said, looking up at me with a wide smile.

"Really? I'm done with therapy?"

"Yep," she said, getting up to walk me to the front. "You have full range of motion, and the stiffness will eventually go away. I've monitored all your cardiovascular levels since your surgery, and they're all stable and at normal levels. You seem to have healed really well. So the rest you can do on your own."

A mix of emotions washed over me as we hit the lobby. Part of me was relieved I didn't have to drive across town once a week to be put through some pretty difficult paces, but there was also a part of me that felt like a bird hovering on the edge of the nest, while its mother nudged it to take off. "Thanks for all your help, Lori," I said, and gave her a hug.

"My pleasure, Abby. And tell your sister I said thank you for the bath salts. I got those in the mail yesterday."

"You do realize she's been bribing you, don't you?"

Lori laughed. "Of course," she said. "But it's taken her focus off of all the other people involved in your recovery. Talking to me lets your sister feel like someone's looking out for you and filling her in on your progress. And that way she leaves Dutch, your doctors, and your other friends alone. Am I right?"

I grinned. Lori was smarter than I thought. "For the most part," I said.

I left the physical therapy office and went back to Dutch's to take a shower, then returned to my office. As I was unlocking my door I could hear the phone ringing inside the suite. I left the keys in the door as I rushed to answer it before it went to voice mail.

"Abby Cooper," I said.

"Hello, Ms. Cooper," chirped a woman's voice. "This is Andrea LaChance from Universal Mortgage Corporation. I've got your application for employment in front of me, and I was hoping we could get you in for an interview in the next few days or so."

I set my purse down, swung around to the chair behind my desk, and pulled my desk calendar close. "I'm pretty open next week," I said.

"I have a two thirty available Monday afternoon. Would that work for you?"

"Works fine, Andrea," I said and made the notation. "You guys are over on Old Woodward Avenue, in Birmingham, right?"

"Yes, six seventy-five Old Woodward."

"Great. Shall I ask for you?"

"No, you'll be meeting directly with our owner, Mr. Wolfe." I sucked in a surprised breath. I hadn't expected to do the meet and greet with the big nasty guy right off the bat. "Is something wrong?" Andrea asked me.

"No," I said quickly. "I just gave myself a paper cut. I'll see Mr. Wolfe at two thirty Monday, then."

I clicked off with Andrea and immediately called Candice. "Hey, Abs," she said happily into the phone when she answered. I could hear what sounded like restaurant noise in the background. "I'm having drinks with the ladies before they come see you. They're all excited."

"That's swell. Listen, I just got a call from Universal Mortgage. They want me to come in for an interview Monday afternoon."

"Perfect," Candice said.

"No," I snapped. "It's not perfect, Candice! They want me to meet with Wolfe. He's my interviewer."

Candice chuckled into the phone. "Well, who did you think you were going to interview with?" she asked me.

"I don't know," I said as a little wave of panic swirled uncomfortably in my tummy. "Some lackey from HR?"

"Abby, relax," she said. "He's just a guy. You're on an interview. Just go in there, tell him about your experience at the bank, and you'll get the gig."

"Easy for you to say," I groused.

"May I remind you that this is *your* case?"

"Okay, okay," I said, giving in. "I hear ya. I just get nervous around murderers."

She chuckled again. "I will make sure nothing happens to you. Okay?"

I grumbled my good-byes and hung up with Candice. After taking some deep breaths, I headed into my reading room and sat down in my new leather chair. My adrenaline was still pumping, but just being in this room seemed to be helping. I glanced at my watch and realized that Candice would be leading the first of her girlfriends back here in a few minutes. I'd need to prepare. I closed my eyes and got into my zone. By the time I heard the light knock on my door, I was much calmer and ready to go.

The three readings were fantastic. It was like I'd taken a shot of intuitive speed or something. The information I received about the women was strong, detailed, and right on the money. When the last one had left the office, Candice turned to me and beamed. "They were totally blown away by you," she said.

I blushed and gave her a wave of my hand. "It's what I do."

"And you were afraid to jump back in," she continued. "Abby, you're as good as ever. And those were the right women to blow away. They know everyone," she said. "Totally hooked in to the community in Kay-zoo."

"You think many people will make the trip?"

"For you? Definitely," she said.

I headed back to Dutch's feeling really good about myself. I'd stepped up to the plate tonight and hit three right out of the park. The old radar wasn't broken, or even rusty. It had come right back, just as

strong as it ever was. As I started up the walk, the
front door opened and six feet, two inches of gor-
geousness stared out at me. "Hey there, beautiful,"
he said.

"I could say the same to you," I said as I eased
into his arms, giving him a tight squeeze.

"How'd your readings go?"

"Really well," I admitted. "Which was a surprise."

Dutch pulled back to look down at me. "A
surprise?"

"Yeah. After such a long hiatus I figured I'd be
pretty rusty."

He took my hand and pulled me inside, where the
dining room table was decked out with candles and
place settings for two. "What's all this?" I asked.

"A celebration," he said.

"What are we celebrating?"

"Your radar."

"How'd you know the readings would go so well?"
I asked, turning to him.

"I didn't. Or rather, what I had intended to celebrate wasn't so much your readings as your impressions on the Goodyear case."

"You solved it?"

"No," he said, leading me to a chair at the table.
"You did."

"Huh?" I asked as he disappeared into the kitchen.

Reappearing with two plates of my favorite dish,
pork tenderloin over linguini in a delicious lemon
cream sauce, he explained, "Remember you told me
to look into the friend of the son?"

"Yeah," I said as he set down my plate.

"Turns out that Max and his wife joined a grief
counseling group shortly after their son died in
seventy-nine. In the group they met another couple,

and the four of them became close friends. They even moved next door to each other in the late eighties."

"Okay," I said, and twirled some pasta onto my fork. "I'm following you. The couple has a son and Max has taken him under his wing."

"Not exactly," Dutch said, and I noticed the twinkle in his eye. There was a twist here.

"So tell me," I said as I took a bite of pasta. I added a small moan, it was so fabulous.

"The couple, Mark and Patricia Hiller, had a son, Jeffrey, who died of crib death the same week as Max's son. Turns out the boys shared a birthday." I nodded and gave a roll of my hand for Dutch to continue. "Jeffrey Hiller has a bank account at Goodyear's bank. Regular deposits have been made in some pretty significant funds, and are later cleared out with checks to a guy who's a known bookie here in Royal Oak."

I dropped my fork. "No way!" I said. "He stole the little boy's identity?"

"Yep. Back in the seventies and eighties you didn't have to have a Social Security number at birth. You could wait until you were sixteen. Somehow Goodyear got hold of Jeffrey's birth certificate and presented it for a Social Security number in the late eighties. He held on to it for years, then used it to launder the money from the waterworks fund."

"Wow," I said. "Do you think the Hillers know?"

"I'm still looking into their bank records, but my guess is no. Mark Hiller is an architect at a firm in Southfield, and his wife works as a buyer for a department store."

"They're clean," I said, feeling a buzz in my head. "They had nothing to do with this."

Dutch nodded. "I'll do the check anyway, just to

make sure they're not implicated. That only leaves the question of who Goodyear's accomplice at the waterworks is."

I tried to tune in on that thought, but came up empty. "You sure he's not working alone?" I asked.

"It'd be pretty tricky," Dutch said as he curled pasta around his own fork. "He'd have to know a password that he shouldn't have access to. And the password changes on a regular basis. Someone would have to update him every time the password changed."

My crew chimed in with an opinion. "Are there cameras in the office where the people who have the passwords work?" I asked.

"No."

"Can you guys put some in?"

"Yes," he said, looking thoughtfully at me. "You think he's breaking in and stealing them?"

"Something's going on," I said. "The crew says you need to watch his comings and goings in the office."

"Tell the crew I said thanks," Dutch said with a wink.

Later that night while we were watching the news, Dutch said, "I noticed you've already cleaned out some of your stuff."

"Yeah," I said with a sigh. "It may take me a few trips to get it all back home."

"When's the move-out date?"

"Not sure," I said evasively.

"Soon, then, huh?" he pressed.

I took my chin off his chest and looked up at him. "Maybe. Why? You in a hurry to see me outta here?"

Dutch smiled and knuckled the top of my head. "No, Edgar, I'm in a hurry for you to go home, spend the night away from me, miss me like crazy, and hurry back."

That made me smile. "You're convinced I'll miss you, huh?"

"Yep."

I nodded. "You're probably right, but what I won't miss is that cat." As if on cue, Virgil hopped up on the edge of the bed and regarded me with a particularly disdainful look.

"Aw, cut him some slack, Abs. He's just protecting his turf."

"He's evil," I said as Virgil flicked his tail at me.

Dutch laughed and ruffled my hair. "He is not, you goof."

"I swear he's got it in for me. The other day he almost killed me when I was coming down the stairs. He purposely tripped me!"

"You sure he wasn't just going up the stairs and you tripped over him?"

I scowled at my boyfriend. "I'm telling you, he's got it in for me, and this house ain't big enough for the four of us."

"I see," Dutch said, the playful grin never leaving his face. "Fine. Go home. Miss me—not my cat—then come over and visit anyway, okay?"

I sighed dramatically. "Oh, if I *must*!" Dutch's grin deepened, and that was when he nudged Virgil off the bed with his foot and rolled over on top of me.

The next morning at five thirty sharp, the alarm sounded and I bolted upright. "Huh? Wha? Huh?" I said as my heart raced and my mind worked hard to shake off its sleepy contentment.

"Time to go to the gym," Dutch said with a yawn. "Better get a move on, Abs. You don't want to be late for Candice."

I groaned and looked longingly at the pillow.

"Don't you think last night counted as a good work-out?" I asked.

The corner of Dutch's mouth curled up, and his hand reached out to stroke my arm. "Yep. And if you'd like to get in another workout with me, I'd be willing to make that sacrifice for you."

I seriously considered it for a few seconds, but just then I saw Dutch's eyelids close and noticed that his breathing slowed to a steady, heavy rhythm. Man, I envied his ability to drop off to sleep in seconds. Quietly I eased out of the bed and grabbed my workout clothes, heading for the bathroom. A few minutes later I was out the door and driving to the gym.

I arrived right on time and found Candice already inside, stretching out on the floor. "Morning!" she said happily.

"Mmmph," I replied. Mornings have never been my strong suit.

"I'm assuming that your therapist gave you the all clear?"

I nodded. "She said the only thing to proceed slowly with is my upper chest. The scar tissue needs to be stretched out over time, not all at once."

"Great. We'll go easy on the chest exercises," said Candice. "Come on, let's get you stretched out for your cardio workout first, and then we can focus on shoulders and triceps."

Candice and I worked out for a good hour and a half, and by the end of it I didn't think I liked her anymore. "Did you ever do a stint in the army?" I asked. " 'Cuz you could teach a drill sergeant a thing or two."

Candice laughed. "You'll thank me in about six weeks when you've got the body of a twenty-year-old."

"I look better now than I did when I was twenty," I said, remembering all the extra weight I carried from dorm food and keg parties back then.

"You'll still thank me," she said. "But I'll go easy on you and give you this weekend off." As we made our way into the locker room Candice asked, "When is your interview with Wolfe again?"

"Monday at two thirty."

Candice nodded as she retrieved her Windbreaker from her locker. "Word to the wise—Wolfe is apparently a big fan of low-cut blouses and short skirts."

I scowled. "Shocker."

Candice gave me a knowing look. "You were hoping to go in with pants and a turtleneck, weren't you?"

"No," I said, avoiding her eyes. "I was thinking a nun's habit would be more appropriate."

Candice laughed. "You're just playing a role, Abby. There's no need to be nervous."

"Fine," I said. "I'll look in my closet and see what I've got in the slutty-office-girl category."

"Good," she said with a pat on the back as we walked out of the gym. "Call me Monday when it's over and let me know how it went."

I headed back to Dutch's and noticed that his car was gone. He'd left for the office early, probably wanting to get a jump on installing those cameras in Goodyear's office before the staff came in. I went straight to the kitchen and did a little "hoo-ya!" when I saw that he'd nicely set out a mug for me and had left a pot of coffee brewing. There was also a note clipped to a file, reading, *Hey, sunshine. Sorry about missing the workout this morning. Let's reschedule for tonight. And if you get a chance, any impressions you can give me on this case would be great.* I poured the mug of coffee and felt a nudge on my leg. Looking down, I saw a pair of big brown eyes giving me the "Good morning, I'll have my breakfast now" once-over.

"Hey, buddy," I said, and stooped to pick up Eggy. My arms fiercely protested as I held him up and he gave me a wet, slobbery kiss. "Okay, okay," I said, setting him down again. "One egg over easy coming up."

Eggy was just polishing off his egg and I was putting the finishing touches on a fantastic ham-and-cheese omelet when there was a knock on the door. I groaned as I looked at the fluffy perfection in the frying pan. "Come on in, Dave," I called. I put the omelet on a plate and reached for the door of the fridge to get out more eggs.

"Morning," Dave said as he entered through the back door. "That eggs I smell?"

"Here," I said as I set the plate down on the table. "Chow down on this. I'll just make myself another one."

Dave eagerly sat down while I brought him over a cup of coffee. "Man, that looks good," he said, picking up a fork. "You definitely know your way around an omelet."

"Too bad it's the only thing I can cook," I said. "I get ribbed a lot around here for not having mastered any category other than eggs."

"I got a buddy who could hook you up," Dave said, readying a forkful of omelet. "His name's Adam. He works over at the Kroger grocery store on Maple and Lahser."

"How exactly is he going to hook me up?" I asked.

"He's a great cook, and the store manager has set him up with a little kitchen near the meat aisle. He prints up these recipes that are really easy to follow, pushes the higher-end sauces and marinades, and gets a commission on the total he sells every month."

"Really?" I said as I poured more eggs into the frying pan. "He could teach me?"

"Sure," Dave said. "Just tell him Dave sent you. He'll turn you into Rachael Ray in no time."

"Okay," I said, locking that idea away. Secretly, I would love to cook a meal that Dutch could actually eat without eyeing the phone number for poison control. When my omelet was done I took a seat next to Dave and asked, "So what brings you by?"

"Dutch said he needs a little work done."

I blew on my forkful of egg to cool it. "Really? He didn't mention anything to me. What's he having done?"

"I don't know," Dave said as he scratched his head. "He told me to take some measurements upstairs and he'd catch up with me later to discuss it. It's probably shelving or something."

I nodded. "His closets are ridiculously small," I said. "Most of my stuff here is in the spare bedroom closet, which reminds me, I have to take another load back to my house today."

"You moving home?"

"Yep. I think it's time for me to get back in the groove. It's too easy here, too comfortable."

Dave cocked his head thoughtfully. "In other words, I'm not the only one with a commitment problem."

My eyes widened. "I don't have a commitment problem!" I sputtered.

"Really?" Dave said. "Seems to me that you two have never gotten along so well as the past three months, and just when things are humming along, off you go back to your bachelorette pad."

"That's ridiculous," I scoffed. "I just think it's a good thing for me not to rely so much on someone else."

"Uh-huh," Dave said.

"I'm used to my independence," I insisted.

"Sure, sure," he agreed.

"I like my stuff and my space and my things in their rightful place, and as you can tell by the upstairs, it is *cramped* here!"

"Right."

I gave him another scowl. "Speaking of commitment issues, how's your wife?"

Dave seemed to brighten. "She actually talked to me last night."

"Yay!" I said, giving him a pat on the arm. "That's great, Dave! What did she say?"

" 'Stop calling me.' "

I blinked at him a few times. "Well," I said, trying to think of a positive spin. "At least it's a start."

"Exactly," he said, pointing his finger at me. "Which is why we need to hurry up and close on Fern. The Realtor said the title search should be complete by the end of the day today. You available to close next Friday?"

"Sure," I said. "The sooner the better, 'cuz my bank account's starting to look pretty scary."

"You should get your practice back up and running," Dave encouraged. "You were doing pretty well there before you got shot."

"I know," I said as I stood up and took our plates. "One step at a time."

While Dave took his measurements I quickly showered and dressed, then began loading the car with stuff going back to my place. I had to wait for Dave to finish in the spare bedroom before I could get at most of my clothing, and when I pulled open the doors I let out a horrified gasp. Several shirts hung in shreds on their hangers. I reached for one of them, pulling it from the closet as I looked at it in horror. "Ohmigod!" I squealed.

"You okay?" Dave said as he came back into the room. I held up the garment for him to see. "Yikes," he said. "Looks like Virgil has struck again."

"*That . . . I'm going to . . . Just wait until I . . .*" I sputtered, the ruined blouse on the hanger preventing me from forming coherent sentences.

"What'd you do to that cat, anyway?" Dave asked. "Seriously, Abby, you should try being nice to him."

I whirled to face him. "*Nice?* You want me to be *nice*? Have you *seen* this closet?!" I shrieked as I took out one hanger of tattered clothing after another.

"Maybe he just likes your scent," Dave said, backing away from my wild-looking eyes.

"*What?*"

"You know," he said meekly, "maybe he likes the smell of you and he climbed on your shirts 'cuz he likes the smell."

I threw the shirts on the floor. "That. Is. It!" I yelled, reaching back into the closet and grabbing an armload of clothes. "I will not wait around here one more minute for that little mutant to destroy one more thing! Come on, Dave. Give me a hand. I'm moving home, *today*!"

Reluctantly, Dave helped me load not only my SUV but his truck. We packed up every single item that I could lay claim to and drove it over to my house. As we were unpacking, Dave said calmly, "You know, Dutch is going to think you're blaming him by moving out like this."

"It's his cat," I snapped. "I've told him a hundred

times that Virgil is an evil spawn of Satan, but does he believe me? Nooooo! He thinks it's *funny*!"

"Maybe he just thinks you're overreacting a little."

I glared at Dave. "It's come down to me or the cat," I said. "I can't live in that house without wanting to kill that overstuffed furball, so it's probably safer this way anyway."

"You're right," Dave said as he grabbed an armload of clothes. "I'm sure it has nothing to do with your fear of commitment."

Once Dave and I had finished unloading, he took off for Milo's to finish up the bathroom while I got busy putting my things away. Around noon Dutch called my cell. "Hey there," he said. "How's your day going?"

"I hate your cat," I snapped. (Sometimes I'm *just* a ray of sunshine.)

"You're kidding," he said with a chuckle. "You do? I've never noticed."

"I'm not joking, cowboy," I growled. "He shredded four of my favorite shirts and there are claw marks in my suede coat!"

"Sounds bad," Dutch said seriously. "Can I offer to replace them?"

"No."

"Okay. Can I cook you dinner?"

"No."

"Back massage?"

"Uh-uh."

"Hot bath with a foot rub?"

"I've moved out," I said flatly.

Dutch was silent for a long minute. Then, very softly, he said, "I'm going to miss having you around, Edgar."

I sighed into the phone. I was still really, really mad,

but I didn't want to give Dutch the impression that I was being unreasonable. "I took your file home with me. I'll focus on it this weekend and drop my notes off early next week, okay?"

"Cool," he said. "Call me before you go to sleep tonight, okay?"

I hung up feeling really shitty. I hated that Dutch was being so understanding about this whole thing. Inwardly I wanted him to fight me a little more. I wanted to be angry at him, and that made me wonder. "Goddamn it, Dave," I muttered as I went back to putting my things away. "I hate it when you're right."

Chapter Five

I spent most of my weekend unpacking and avoiding Dutch while getting resettled into my own space. I'd also devoted much of that time to sweating Monday's interview with Dick Wolfe.

Candice had called a few times to offer a pep talk or two. She'd also grilled me about what to say—and more importantly, what *not* to say—during our early morning workout at the gym on Monday. And while I appreciated her coaching, I found that what I really needed was to get the damn thing over with already.

Promptly at two twenty-five Monday afternoon, I stepped out of the elevator and into the lobby of Universal Mortgage Co., Inc. Taking in the marble floors, plush furniture, and art deco reception desk, I walked up to one of the three receptionists, the one wearing an earpiece connected to a telephone lit up like a Christmas tree, and made my introduction.

The woman I spoke to, a pretty redhead with inch-long nails and a low-cut sweater, told me to have a seat and that Mr. Wolfe would be with me shortly. I sat down in one of the gorgeous leather chairs and tightly crossed my legs. The skirt I was wearing was three inches higher than I was comfortable with, and I was nervous about giving someone a lookey-loo at my cha-cha.

I glanced at my watch as the minutes ticked by, and watched the hustle and bustle of people streaming through the lobby. Most of the people I saw had their heads down and serious looks on their faces, intent on moving fast and not being distracted.

I waited patiently for more than half an hour, but then I started to get pissy. It irked me that this Wolfe man would have so little regard for my time. I already knew he was a rat bastard, but leaving me to hang out in the lobby for such a long time was downright rude.

Finally, forty minutes past my appointment time, a woman came out of some double doors at the end of the lobby and eyed me with purpose. "Hello," she said as she drew close. "I'm Andrea LaChance. You must be Abigail."

"Nice to meet you," I said, standing up to shake her hand. "I'm not sure I got the appointment time correct," I added. "I thought we said two thirty."

Andrea gave a wave of her hand, as if it were nothing that I'd been kept waiting so long. "Mr. Wolfe is a very busy man," she said. "He squeezes these things in where he can. Now come with me and I'll get you started on the paperwork."

If I'd actually been applying for a real job here, I would have walked out right then. It's been my experience that the heads of companies with this type of attitude usually regard their employees as one notch above indentured servants, and expect fealty no matter how badly they treat the people who work for them. Still, I set my jaw and followed Andrea.

We rounded the corner into a medium-sized conference room, and I was told to take a seat and fill out the information on a clipboard Andrea handed to me. "I'll be back to check on you in a few," she said and left me alone.

I completed the application and attached my résumé to the clipboard as instructed. Then I waited. And waited. And waited. At four o'clock the door opened and Andrea walked in. "Are you finished?" she had the nerve to ask me.

"For a while now," I said, plastering a tight smile on my face.

"Mr. Wolfe has one more phone call to make and then he'll be right with you," she said, taking my application and walking out the door. I gave her behind a snarl and sat back in my chair. My radar buzzed and I knew I was in for another long wait.

At five fifteen the double doors opened and in walked Dick Wolfe. The hair stood up on the back of my neck the moment he came into the room. He was a very tall man, with wire-rimmed glasses and curly brown hair, broad-shouldered and impeccably dressed in Armani.

He moved with a precision that revealed his calculating nature, and as he drew near I physically braced myself. "Dick Wolfe," he said, extending his hand.

"Abigail Cooper," I said, standing to shake his hand.

He flashed me a toothy grin and copped a look down my blouse. "Nice to meet you," he said.

"Likewise," I lied, taking my seat.

"I hear you know Darren," he said, sitting down across from me.

"Yes, a friend of mine introduced us the other day. He seems very nice."

Wolfe nodded as he looked through my application and paperwork. "You worked for Fidelity Bank, I see?"

"Yes, for about four years. I was a senior loan officer there."

"Terrific. We're always looking for experience," he said, looking up to stare at my chest again. "Let's start you tomorrow. You can mentor with Darren for a few weeks, learn the ropes, then we'll give you a few leads and see how you do."

"Uh . . ." I said, taken by surprise that this was moving so quickly. "That's . . . uh . . . terrific," I said. "May I inquire about the pay?"

"You'll be paid a small commission on the loans that you work with Darren, and then when you close your own deals you'll be paid a ten percent commission on the points you charge in the closing fees."

"I see," I said with a nod, while inwardly fuming. A ten percent commission rate was robbery in this business, and I knew it. "That's terrific. What time tomorrow, then?"

"Be here at eight," he said. He stood up, already turning away from me.

"Thank you," I said as he held the door open for me and I passed into the hallway.

"Nice meeting you, Angela," he said, extending his hand again.

"You as well," I answered, shaking his hand while vowing to wash mine the first chance I got.

When I reached my car, I immediately called Candice. "My God!" she said into the phone. "A three-hour interview? What the hell could he have asked you?"

"Anything," I said moodily. "He could have asked me anything. Instead, he kept me waiting for two hours and fifty minutes, then sat down with me for less than ten minutes and basically told my chest to show up tomorrow. Or at least I think he told me. He called me Angela, so I'm not really sure he knew who he was speaking to."

"Huh," said Candice. "Well, at least you got in, Abs. I mean, if he's going to be so nonchalant about who he hires into his organization, you should be able to do some pretty good snooping around."

I started my engine and pulled out of the parking space. My head hurt, my stomach was growling, and I was in a foul mood. "What exactly am I looking for again?" I asked.

"Henchmen," Candice replied.

"I'm sorry?"

"Cronies. Homies. Brothers. Wolfe has to keep the guys who do his dirty work close, and my thinking is that you may be able to get some good dirt from one or two of them."

"So I'm not supposed to spy on Wolfe per se?" I said.

"No!" Candice said quickly. "That guy you've got to steer clear of. He's dangerous, Abby. Someone who's managed to skirt the law as long as he has must have his own finely honed sixth sense. If you go for him directly, he'll smell you coming and play dirty. You just keep it relaxed for a while, see what some of those loan officers are up to and what kind of business Universal Mortgage does. They have a really awful reputation for driving people into big debt, so it would be great if we could get the scoop on what happened to Walter and bring down Wolfe's big business at the same time."

"Okay," I said, wondering what the hell I'd gotten myself into. "What should I do if someone gets wise to my being nosy?"

"First and foremost, you don't let them catch on, and second, you get the hell outta there the minute things get dicey. You feel me?"

I scrunched up my face. "What are you, some sistah from the hood these days?" I asked with a laugh.

"I mean it, Abby. Someone there notices that you might know a little more than you should, you better have a back door and a flight plan."

"I feel ya," I said to her.

"Cool. Now go home and hug that tall blond drink of water."

I didn't have the energy to fill her in on the latest spat between Dutch and me, so I said my good-byes and clicked the phone off. On the way home I stopped at Just Noodles and picked up a big, steamy portion of comfort food. When I got home, the light on my phone was blinking. I had messages.

While I slurped up some carbs I listened to the three messages. The first was from Cat, who was wondering if I was still alive, since I hadn't spoken to her in over forty-eight hours. Her voice sounded slightly panicked, and I knew I'd have to call her before going to bed, lest she contact her good friends in the merchant marines to drop in and check up on me.

Dave had also called, to say we had a closing date on Fern for Friday. I was to be at the title office at noon. The last message was from Dutch. "Hi, sweetie," he said. My eyebrow arched. He only used "sweetie" when he was really in the doghouse. "I'm cooking mahimahi on the grill tonight. If you'd like some, come on over, okay?"

I looked down at the container of noodles and scowled. Mahimahi was one of my favorites and sure would have been good. "Damn," I said as I put my feet up on the ottoman and leaned back against the couch cushion. "Cowboy, you don't play fair."

After supper I called Cat. "Hey," I said when she answered.

"*Where* have you been?" she demanded.

"Working the streets, hanging out with the wrong crowd, and getting into all sorts of trouble. You know—the usual."

Cat sighed. "You drive me crazy," she said flatly.

"Back atcha, my sistah," I said with a laugh, then changed the subject. "We close Fern on Friday."

"This is good news," she said, perking up. "I'll have my attorney review the closing statement and give you the clear to close before you go."

"Great. The closing's at noon."

"I'll mark it down. Say," she said, and I could hear her voice take on a breezy tone. This, of course, put me on high alert. "I called over to Dutch's place, and he said that you moved out."

"Uh-huh," I said. I had no intention of sharing the intimate details of our cat-versus-dog fight.

"He sounded really sad," she went on.

"He's probably just tired."

"Well, he said he was sad, so I think he really *was* sad," she insisted.

I rubbed my temple with my fingertip. I didn't want to talk about this right now. "I'm sure he's fine. Hey, I'm back in the gym this week," I said. Sometimes you could divert Cat with another tidbit of information that she was likely to pounce on.

"The gym? You mean you're working out?" she said. (Yahoo! It worked.)

"Yep. Lori gave me the all clear last week, and Candice has agreed to be my personal trainer."

"Just be careful about your injury," Cat said, the worry in her voice making it a bit shrill. "You could do more harm than good if you're not careful!"

"I'm fine, Cat," I said. "Really. I'm not pushing it. I just want to get my stamina back."

"I'm asking Sven about what regimen would be best for you," Cat said, referring to her personal trainer.

I rolled my eyes. "Don't ask Sven. It's fine. I'm fine. I'm healed, and getting fit, and everything's good, okay?"

"Maybe I should fly him out to you," she said, completely ignoring me. "He can show Candice how to properly train you."

"Oops!" I said, my patience at an end. "That's my call-waiting, Cat. Gotta go!" And with that I hung up the phone, then promptly headed to the kitchen for an aspirin. While I was gulping down two with a glass of water, my eyes wandered to the FBI file from Dutch, still resting on my kitchen counter. My shoulders sagged when I saw it. I'd promised him that I'd give him my impressions and drop it off for him soon.

"Well, there's not much on television tonight anyway," I said as I took a seat at the table and grabbed a notepad and pen. I sat there with my eyes closed for a while, allowing my mind to clear and my radar to kick in. I placed my hand over the file and waited for a few impressions to hit, then jotted some notes.

The first impression I had was of a flag and a rat in a maze. I smiled. Together these two symbols were my sign for a government position. I opened my eyes and wrote down, *Someone who works in government.* Next I saw a postcard I'd had on the bulletin board in my room as a kid. It was from this place up in the northern part of Michigan called Sea Shell City. I wasn't quite sure what to make of it, but just then the phrase "postcards from the edge" floated through my mind.

I shrugged my shoulders, opened my eyes, and wrote that down. Next I glimpsed a map of the United States. Michigan stood out on the map, but so did Ohio, Illinois, and Indiana. "Weird," I muttered and recorded all that as well. The last symbol sent a shudder through me: I saw a dagger dripping with blood— my symbol for murder. After I'd scribbled that onto the paper, I opened the file and read about a Michigan state senator's daughter who disappeared from her dorm one night in early December and hadn't been seen since.

The case had been turned over to the FBI because an Ohio state congresswoman's son had also disappeared from his dorm four weeks prior to the other incident. The cases sounded similar, since both abductions had occurred on the first Monday night of the month.

There were photos of the students, and I frowned as I stared back at their flat and plastic images. Both of the images looked dead, and the notes in the file indicated that the FBI firmly believed the students were dead as well. They were great kids with bright futures, doing well in school, with no reason to run away from their friends and families.

An intensive search had been conducted on both campuses, but not a single clue had shown up to lead the police or the FBI in a specific direction.

I closed my eyes again and focused hard, but the same clues came back to me, and that phrase, "postcards from the edge," just swirled around and around in my mind. Finally I opened my eyes and looked back at my notes. I underlined *Indiana* and *Illinois*. What did these two states have to do with the murders? And further, what the hell was this constant reference to postcards? Did the kids send a postcard before they died? There was nothing about it in the file, and my radar said that the clue didn't fit that way. I sighed and continued to try and puzzle it out for another hour before I gave up, closed the file, and called Dutch.

"Hey there," he said when he answered the phone. "I was wondering when I'd hear from you."

"I've been working on your case file," I said, feeling a bit guilty about avoiding him recently.

"Yeah?"

"I'd love to tell you I cracked the code, but right now I'm really stumped."

"Did you get anything at all?" he asked.

"Yeah," I said wearily. "One thing, but it's weird."

"What was it?"

" 'Postcards from the edge.' "

There was a pause. "I don't understand," he finally said.

"Makes two of us," I replied.

"You think there's a postcard from one of the kids?"

"No."

"Is one of them going to send a postcard?"

"Big no," I said sadly. "They're both dead, Dutch."

"We were afraid of that."

"Can I keep this file for a little while and try again in a day or so?" I asked.

"Keep it as long as you like, babe. We've been working both cases hard for five weeks now and haven't made an inch of progress."

"I do think there's a connection," I said.

"We were afraid there would be, but until something points us to either a body or the killer, we're stuck."

I rubbed my temple and changed the subject. "So how was the mahimahi?"

"Missing something," he said, with a hint of mirth in his voice. "Like maybe a little spice that usually sits next to me at the dinner table."

"I had noodles," I said. "Yours sounds better."

There was a low chuckle in my ear. "Next time just get your butt over here, Edgar, and join me for dinner, okay?"

" 'Kay. Good night, cowboy."

I went to bed that night exhausted but was unable to sleep well. It's amazing how quickly you miss that warm body sleeping next to you.

The next morning I was already awake when my alarm went off at five thirty. I joined Candice in the gym, and during our workout we went over the game plan again for my first day at Universal Mortgage. "Stick close to Darren for a while," she advised. "Pick his brain about the politics of the place, see if any of the other employees have been around for a long time."

"Won't he get suspicious?"

"Not if you phrase it right. Just tell him you're getting the impression there's a lot of competition among the other loan officers and ask him who you should steer clear of, et cetera. He should buy that."

"Got it."

"Also, try to focus on using their software. I want you up to speed as quickly as possible. That way you can start searching their internal database and see if any familiar names pop up."

"Uh-huh," I said, already feeling nervous. "I swear, I don't know how you do this on a regular basis, Candice. This shit scares the crap outta me."

Candice set a pair of dumbbells on a nearby rack.

"You'll be okay," she said, flashing me a grin. "Remember that you can leave anytime. If things get sketchy, head out to lunch and don't go back."

I nodded, feeling a little better now that I had a quick "out." "How long am I supposed to nose around before I can quit?"

"Well," she said, "till the moment you get something concrete, I would imagine. I also want to do a little nosing around on Bruce Lutz. I'll start with his family, see if anyone close to him is willing to talk, and then you and I should take a trip up to Jackson and see if he's accepting visitors."

"Won't that get back to Wolfe? I mean, what if he and Lutz are tight?"

"It won't get back to Wolfe if he's the one trying to get rid of Lutz, which seems highly likely."

I sat down on a nearby bench and worked through a set of arm curls. Then I asked, "Should we look into Walter's past too?"

"Absolutely," said Candice. "But I want to save that for last. Cops get upset when you start sniffing around one of their own, and I don't want to alert the media until I have to."

I drove home from the gym feeling high on endorphins but nervous about my first day at the fake job. I arrived at Universal Mortgage ten minutes early and was given a quick tour around the massive office by one of the receptionists. The mortgage company was divided by department. Underwriters were at one end of the building and loan officers at the extreme opposite end. Between them were the processing and closing departments, and two small additional suites housed an appraisal firm and a title company.

The walls of every corridor were painted with the

slogan, WE CLOSE LOANS *FAST!* and I had no doubt that was true.

After getting a cup of coffee I was shown to Darren Cox's cubicle and told to wait until he arrived. At eight thirty the first of the loan officers trickled in. One or two of them gave me a cursory nod, but no one came over to introduce themselves. "Friendly," I mumbled under my breath as one heavyset man came in, looked me up and down wordlessly, then sat down to enjoy his jelly doughnut and coffee.

Finally, at quarter to nine, Darren showed up. "Good morning," he said as he fumbled with his tie.

"Morning, Darren," I said. "Ready to show me the ropes?"

"Sure," he said, taking his seat and flipping on his computer. "You used to write mortgage paper a few years ago, right?"

"Yeah," I said. "I worked for a bank and closed quite a few in my day."

"What was the most you ever wrote in one month?" he asked.

I thought back. "Probably half a million," I said proudly.

Darren chuckled. "Half a million here will get you fired," he said. "We're given a quota of nothing below seven hundred fifty thousand a month."

My eyes bulged. "You're kidding!" I said. I knew that was an incredibly aggressive figure. "How do you do it?"

Darren smiled confidently at me and leaned forward to whisper, "I've got a system."

"What kind of system?"

"The kind that allows me to close four million a month," he said quietly.

"Get out of here!" I whispered. "That's amazing!"

"My last paycheck was for ten thousand dollars, Abby," he said cockily.

Again my eyes bulged. If he made ten thousand, that meant Wolfe made ninety off Darren alone. "Wow," I said, trying to play to his ego. "You must really have a fantastic system!" My radar buzzed, and intuitively I had a feeling that Darren's "system" wasn't exactly aboveboard.

"And if you play your cards right," he said, putting a hand on my knee, "I could give you a piece of that sweet apple pie."

I stifled the urge to slap the snot out of Darren and opted to politely laugh as I moved his hand over to his own knee. "I'm excited about making money," I said. "You don't make a lot of money as a psychic."

"Really?" he asked. "Well, then, you've come to the right place. I figure with your psychic abilities, you can probably let me know which prospects to pursue and which ones to back off on."

I smiled. That was my in. "Of course," I said.

The rest of the morning I sat next to Darren and watched him call all the applicants in his pipeline, confirming figures, status, and gathering additional information. We broke for lunch and agreed to meet back at his cubicle in an hour.

I called Candice the moment I hit the street and gave her an update. "Have you seen his system yet?" she asked me.

"No," I admitted. "Mostly I'm sitting there watching him make phone calls. Everything seems legit at this point."

"Have you had a chance to hop on their computer?"

"Nope. I offered to enter data for him, and Darren said he'd think about it after lunch."

"Okay. Well, stick with it, Abs. So far, so good."

"Have you been able to get anything on Lutz?"

"Not yet. No family nearby that I can identify, so we may be at a dead end until we head up to Jackson."

I was back at Darren's cubicle at quarter to one. The place was fairly empty save for one man who was having a heated conversation with a customer on the phone, who had apparently changed his mind about going through with the loan. The longer I listened to the conversation, the angrier I became, because it was clear that the man was using fear and lies to get the customer to the closing table.

Finally Darren returned, and as he took his seat I asked, "Who's that guy over there?"

Darren looked in the direction of the man who was yelling into the phone. "Sheldon Jacob. He's been here since Dick first opened."

"He doesn't take no for an answer, does he?" I said.

"Nope. And of anybody in here, he's the guy you want to steer clear of."

"Really?" I asked. "Why?"

Darren lowered his voice to barely a whisper. "He's Dick's stepbrother, and he has one hell of a bad reputation. I've seen him beat the snot out of an appraiser who came back with a value that was too low for Sheldon's deal to go through."

"He *beat* him?"

Darren smiled, but there was no mirth in his eyes. "It can get pretty rough around here. Just stick to your own business and stay out of everyone else's and you should be okay."

I gulped. "Why would you work someplace that is so volatile?" I asked quietly.

"Four words," he said seriously. "Ten-thousand-dollar paycheck."

"Ah." I nodded. "Okay, for that amount of money I suppose I'd be willing to put up with a lot too. Now, about this system you were talking about. Show me." I was being bold, I knew, but the longer I was in this atmosphere the more I just wanted to get the hell out.

Darren looked over both shoulders and discreetly reached into his briefcase. He pulled out a CD and carefully loaded it onto his computer. "This is the same software we used at the PI firm," he said. "Now, watch this." The screen filled with a GPS map of a section of Bloomfield Hills, one of the priciest neighborhoods in all of metropolitan Detroit.

Next, Darren positioned the cursor over one of the addresses on the screen. A window popped up and revealed a name and a plus sign next to a dollar figure. Darren moved the cursor to the next residence and the same type of information appeared. He did this six more times until finally, instead of a plus sign next to a dollar figure there was a red negative. "Gotcha," he said.

"Got what?" I asked, squinting at the screen.

"See that?" he asked, pointing to the dollar figure. "Mr. Ron Weis hasn't paid his property taxes in over a year."

I blinked a few times. "Okay," I said. "Why is this important?"

"Hang on," Darren said, copying Ron Weis's name and address. Then he minimized the program, opened up a new window, called CreditSearch, and typed in the copied information. In seconds we were looking at Ron Weis's full credit history.

"You pulled his credit?" I whispered.

"Yep," Darren said as he scanned the information.

"Isn't it illegal to do that without his permission?" Darren looked at me, and I knew I should have kept my damn mouth shut. "Technically, yes," he said. "But I'm about to save this guy's ass, so I don't think he'll mind."

"Good point," I said, turning my attention back to the screen. "He's two months behind on his credit cards, and his mortgage payment is thirty days past due," I said.

"He's sinking fast," Darren said. "And I'm about to bring him to the Promised Land."

I sat quietly while Darren printed out the credit report and made some notes in the margins. Next he went to the end of the report and highlighted a phone number. "See that?" he said, pointing to a notation. "That's his home number."

I was amazed at the amount of information that Darren was able to retrieve. A moment later he was back to fishing around in his briefcase. He took out a small black box and plugged one end of the gadget into his phone and the other into his computer. Another small window appeared and he asked me, "Abby, what's your cell phone number?"

I gave him a puzzled look. "My cell number? Why do you need that?"

Darren winked at me. "Watch and see. Now, come on, give me the number." I did and he typed it in, then opened another window and told me to look away. I did and waited for him to tell me when I could look again.

Just then, my cell phone rang. "Go ahead," Darren said. "Look at the display first, then answer it."

I pulled my cell out of my purse and looked at the display. It read, "County Clerk's." I answered the phone with a tentative "Hello?"

Darren picked up his receiver and said, "Hey there," in my ear.

My mouth dropped. I knew what he was doing and it was so far beyond the boundaries of fair play that I wanted to bolt for the exit right there. Instead, I played along. "Wow! That is so cool!" I said. "I'm assuming the next phone call will be to Mr. Weis, regarding his overdue property taxes?"

Darren winked at me as he clicked the phone off and began to type on the computer. He had his phone on speaker so that I could listen, and I heard a woman's recorded voice announce that Ron and Barbara were unable to come to the phone and to please leave a message after the tone. I listened as Darren's voice lowered an octave or two and he gave a garbled introduction of a name I couldn't catch followed by a rather scary message about the overdue property tax bill and the risk of foreclosure. He then left a number and an extension and urged the Weises to call soon to discuss the matter.

"I'm assuming you left your own number and extension?" I said.

Darren smiled broadly. "When Wolfe set up the phones, he purposely got a number that was one digit off the Oakland county clerk's office."

"So they're going to assume they misdialed or wrote the number down wrong," I said.

"Yep. And when they call, I'm going to take care of all their overdue bills."

"What's it going to cost them?" I asked.

"Couple of percentage points at the closing table," Darren said. "That house has gotta be worth close to a million, and their mortgage is only for six hundred fifty thousand. It's the perfect loan."

"It's the Weises' lucky day," I said, working hard to hide my disgust.

"And the beauty is that I got a guy down at the

county clerk's office who's willing to field the calls
should they bypass calling here."

"That's quite a system," I said. "No wonder you're
doing well."

"Everyone here has something," he said. He must
have noticed my doubtful expression because then he
added, "Don't worry. We'll get you hooked in, Abby."

"That's great," I said, trying to force some enthusiasm into my voice. "Just great."

It was six p.m. before I was able to escape for the
day. I had watched Darren click through neighborhoods and nose his way into countless people's personal and private information, leaving the same
message on every voice mail. The more he "worked,"
the happier he became, and the more my skin crawled.

I stopped off at home and took care of Eggy, who'd
been home alone all day, poor thing. I then changed
and went to my office. Something was really eating at
me and I intended to deal with it, pronto.

When I arrived I found Candice in her office, tapping away on her computer. "You're here late," I said
in greeting.

"Hey, Abs," she said, taking her eyes off the screen.
"My grandmother's driving me a little batty, so I came
here for a little peace and quiet and a lot less pink."

I laughed. Candice's grandmother was a character,
and her living room looked as if it had been sprayed
with a gigantic bottle of Pepto-Bismol. "At least it's
free," I offered.

Candice sighed. "I know, I know, I'm sounding un-
grateful. But I've always found that with Nana, less
is more."

My radar kicked in and I offered, "The good news
is that I'm seeing a move in your very near future."

"Really?" she said hopefully.

I nodded. "And it's somewhere tranquil and fabulous and you're going to *love* it. I also get the feeling the price is right and the terms are fair. They keep saying it's a perfect solution."

Candice cocked her head at me. "Wow, that would be fantastic. But I really don't want to get myself into a lease situation. I'd rather wait until the old business is rockin' and I can afford to buy a place. So I can't imagine how that would happen."

"The crew's insisting that there is a compromise you can definitely live with," I said. "Something will turn up."

"Okay, I trust you. And I did get a case today, so maybe lots more will follow real soon."

"Need any help with it?"

"Naw. It's your typical cheating husband. I'll have it wrapped up in a few days."

"Cool," I said as I took a seat across from her and gave her a tired smile. "I had forgotten how much I hate corporate America."

Candice grinned at me. "Not ready to head back to a nine-to-fiver, huh?"

"Definitely not," I said with a yawn.

"How'd the rest of the day go?"

I stretched in the chair and said, "For starters, your boy Darren is breaking about six laws that I can think of, and I'm sure investigators would be more than happy to nail him on a few others."

Candice shook her head and frowned. "I had a feeling he'd gone over to the dark side. What's he doing?"

"Pulling unauthorized credit reports, committing fraud, impersonating a county official—it goes on and on."

"How about the rest of the office?" she asked. "Anyone else up to no good?"

I nodded. "No one there is innocent, Candice.

There's one guy in particular who strikes me as being a person of interest. His name is Sheldon Jacob, and Darren says he's Dick's stepbrother and he's been there for years. My guess is he's a henchman."

Candice jotted down the name. "Awesome. Anyone else?"

I sighed. "No. Unfortunately Darren kept me close today, so I didn't have a chance to snoop around."

"There's always tomorrow," she said brightly. "By the way, I've got some time on Thursday to head up to Jackson prison. Tell Darren you've got a doctor's appointment and won't be around in the afternoon."

"Sounds good," I said, pushing to my feet.

"Hey," she said to me, "what are you doing here so late, by the way?"

I gave her a grin. "Making sure the only office I ever *have* to go to is my own," I said. When she gave me a quizzical look I explained, "I'm sending out postcards to all my clients, thanking them for their patronage and letting them know I'm officially back at work."

"Good for you," Candice said brightly. "Way to hop back on that horse, Abs."

I left Candice to work her case and went into my office to pull out files and get organized. While I was working on my mailing list, my cell phone buzzed. "Hey, cowboy," I said when I answered it.

"Where are you?"

"The office."

"It's ten p.m.," he said.

"Thank you, Father Time," I said. "Want to give me the weather report now?"

"Rain," he said. "Nothing but rain."

I glanced out my window. "Looks pretty clear to me."

"Then bring that sunshine over and spend the night," he said. "I miss you."

"You miss getting some," I teased.

"Yeah, but I promise to cuddle afterward if you'll come over."

I rolled my eyes. "How about I come visit this weekend?" I suggested.

Dutch sighed. "You really don't want to see me tonight?"

I looked at the stack of client information and release forms on my desk and the nice little spreadsheet I'd just created. "Dutch," I said seriously, "I'm in the middle of something important, and I was hoping to make some headway tonight. I'll call you Thursday and maybe we can go away for the weekend or something."

Dutch didn't say anything for a long moment. Then he said quietly, "Okay, Abby. I'll talk to you Thursday" and clicked off.

I scowled as I closed the phone. It wasn't that I didn't want to see him. I just felt like a little space might be good for us. Besides, he'd flip out if he found out I was working at Wolfe's company, and I wasn't in the mood to explain that one to him. It was better if I just kept a little distance between us for a while so he could assume I was keeping my nose clean and out of trouble.

Candice popped her head in around eleven. "I'm headed home," she said. "You going to be at the gym tomorrow?"

I groaned. "I forgot about the gym. Yeah, I'll be there," I said, hitting the SAVE icon on my computer and standing up. "Wait up. I'll head out with you."

Candice and I left the office and walked to our cars. As I drove home, I thought about the next day and how I hated the fact that I had to go back to the mortgage company. The place had horrible energy. I gave an involuntary shiver as I thought about it.

I was hoping that I could find out something incriminating about Wolfe and deliver that to Dutch so that he and the FBI could open a new investigation. I didn't know if I'd be able to find anything out that would connect Wolfe to Walter's murder, but something told me that if this mortgage company was around when Walter died, there might be something there.

The other intriguing tidbit was that Walter had used Universal Mortgage Company to finance his rental properties. I wondered what that was about, and I was determined to dig into the database to find out.

Chapter Six

The next morning I met Candice at the gym, and she put me through my paces. "Are you sure we should be working this hard?" I asked, panting between squats.

"This is your warm-up," she said. "The hard stuff comes later."

"Nazi," I grunted as I dipped low.

"Pansy," she replied. "Come on, five more and we can move on to something else."

"Great," I said through gritted teeth. "I'm totally motivated."

I arrived at Universal Mortgage promptly at eight again. I knew that Darren wouldn't be in for a while, but just in case anyone was taking notice I wanted to give the appearance of being an eager beaver. To my surprise, Sheldon was already in his cubicle, and he was talking to a heavyset man with thinning hair and a severe underbite. "This is the best list so far," the man was saying.

Sheldon took the list and scanned it. He gave a scowl that gave me the willies. "Fuck, Benzie. What the hell is this shit?'' and he threw the paper at the other man.

"Those are good!" insisted the man. "I swear, Sheldon! I drove by 'em myself and none of 'em are burnouts or crack houses."

"You think I don't know my own shit?" Sheldon said. "You think I'm just sitting here for you to fuck with me?"

I was sitting in my cubicle trying to avert my eyes, but the mounting tension in the room was making me incredibly uncomfortable. "I swear this is a good list!" said Benzie. "And if you don't want it, then maybe one of these other guys will!" With that he turned and stared directly at me. Like a deer caught in the headlights, I couldn't look away. "You!" he said to me.

I gulped. "Yes?" I asked.

"You work here?"

"Uh . . ." I said.

"Here!" he said, striding forward to shove the list at me. "You take this list and see what you can get for it!"

"Benzie," said Sheldon with a low growl, "cut that shit out."

Benzie turned back to Sheldon and said defiantly, "You think I don't know what goes on here?" he demanded. "I know what you guys do!"

The list was in my hands and I quickly scanned it, looking for anything incriminating, but it was simply a list of names with addresses. There didn't seem to be anything unusual about it. At that moment the paper was snatched away and Sheldon Jacob bent down to put his face inches from mine. "This ain't none of your fucking business, bitch," he said to me.

I gasped. It wasn't just the way he had spoken to

me; it was the venom coming from his eyes. "Okay!" I said as I backed my chair away from him. "I was just sitting here and that guy gave it to me."

Sheldon narrowed his eyes. "You see a lot of other bitches around here in the pit?" he asked me.

"Right now I don't see much of anyone around here," I said, looking pointedly around.

"You're a smart-ass," he said to me. "I don't like smart-asses."

"Noted," I said, standing up. I refused to let this foulmouthed jerk get to me. "I'm going to get coffee. Would you like some coffee?" I asked Benzie, who had been closely watching Sheldon and me.

"That'd be great," he said.

"Black?"

"Cream and sugar," he said.

I strolled past Sheldon as if he didn't exist, heading in the direction of the kitchen. When I got there I gripped the counter and took a few deep breaths. When my heart rate had calmed, I poured two cups of coffee, added cream and sugar, and walked them back to the pit. When I got there Sheldon wasn't at his desk, but Benzie was.

"Here you go," I said.

"Thanks, doll," he said. "Sorry about before, but I wanted Sheldon to stop dicking me around, and sometimes you gotta call his bluff, you know?"

"He doesn't seem the type that enjoys having his bluff called," I said, taking my seat.

"Aw, he's okay. We've been doing business together for years and years. I was the one who did his bond way back when."

My brows furrowed. I had no idea what he was talking about, but decided I should play along a little. "Really?" I said. "So you've known him a while?"

"Yeah, goin' on twenty years now. I'm Ben Zimmerman, by the way," he said, extending his hand. "Most folks call me Benzie."

I shook it and gave him a big fat smile. "Abby Cooper. I'm new here."

Benzie nodded. "I got that. Not many of the women stick it out," he said. "Most of 'em get a taste of Sheldon or Ron and don't come back."

I cocked my head. "Who's Ron?"

Benzie laughed. "You ain't met Ron yet? That's right. He's on vacation this week. He's Sheldon's twin brother, and if you can believe it, he's the more hot-headed of the two."

My eyes widened. "You're kidding."

"Nope. See that?" he said, pointing to a pile of broken plastic and wires sitting on top of a desk.

"Yeah?"

"That was a fax machine. Last time I was in here one of Ron's deals went bust, and he smashed that to pieces. You never saw a room clear out so fast." He chuckled. "It took the big guy to chill him out."

"Mr. Wolfe?"

"Yeah. I've known him for years too," he said, puffing his chest out.

"Wow," I said, playing into it. "Maybe you should work here."

Benzie laughed. "Naw. I do okay with the system I've got with these guys," he said. "I do all the work on the front end, and they close the deals."

"That's great," I said just as Sheldon came back into the room.

"Where's my coffee?" he snapped at me.

"In the kitchen," I snapped back, meeting his eyes and folding my arms. I'd dealt with scarier dudes than him before.

Sheldon's upper lip curled slightly. I truly hoped it was a smile. "Benzie!" he said and shifted his attention. "Stop fuckin' around and get over here. I just talked to Adam and a couple of these I might be able to do something with."

Benzie headed back over to Sheldon and I discreetly pulled my cell phone out of my purse. As quickly as I could, I texted Candice the names Ben Zimmerman and Ron Jacob, then figured I could also pass along the names I'd remembered from the list Benzie had given Sheldon, so I typed out *Carmen Perez, Livingston St.* and *Chandra Brown, Grossebeck Ave.,* followed by *I'll xpln later,* and hit the SEND button.

As I flipped the phone closed Darren walked in. "Morning," he said as he pulled out his chair. "You're in early."

I tucked my phone into my purse. "Just eager to get to work," I said.

"Great. I have a closing this morning, and since you're already familiar with how those work, I thought I'd partner you up with my loan processor. She can show you our software and get you familiar with our desktop underwriting system."

"Perfect," I said with a broad grin. This spying gig was turning out to be easier than I thought.

Fifteen minutes later I was seated with a perky blonde named Bree. "This is your second day?" she asked me as I pulled my chair closer to her computer.

"Yeah. You guys do things a little differently than we did them at the bank I worked at," I said.

Bree gave me a wry smile. "I'm sure we do," she said. "I've been here for almost a year now. Before that I worked as a paralegal for a real estate law firm that tanked."

"There are a lot of businesses doing that these days," I said, thinking of my own practice.

"It's this crappy economy," Bree grumbled. "My husband was an engineer for Chrysler, making great money. He was downsized last year and hasn't been able to find work since."

"That's tough," I said, automatically turning my intuition on. "Must make it difficult for the two of you to get along, huh?" I was sensing some major tension in Bree's marriage.

"You said it. It's been all on me since he got laid off. I've had to take on extra work here, and thank God I've also got Darren. He's been slipping me a little on the side and I swear it's the only way we can pay our bills."

I frowned. There was nothing good happening in Bree's energy. I sensed that she was pushing the ethical envelope and that she was in way over her head. I also sensed that she and her husband were separating—soon. "I'll keep my fingers crossed for you," I said. "Now, how about you let me enter a loan or two so I can get used to your software?"

Several hours later we broke for lunch, and I was damn happy to get away from the monotony of data entry. Bree offered to have lunch with me, but I begged off, saying I had an errand to run. Hurrying to my car, I called Candice the moment I locked the door. "What's happening?" she asked me.

"Did you get my text?"

"Yep. Want to explain who they are?"

I told her about the morning confrontation with Benzie and Sheldon, and where I'd gotten the other names. When I'd finished she said, "Okay, Abs, I'll run these and see what I can come up with."

"Cool. I'll check in with you later." I did the drive-thru at Burger King, happy that I could finally order a Whopper and fries without feeling guilty, thanks to all my gym workouts. I ate in my car on the way back to the mortgage company, dreading another long afternoon.

I beat Bree back to her desk, and smiled as I glanced at my watch. It was twenty to one, so I figured I probably had a good buffer before she made her way back to work. I sat down at her desk and pulled the paperwork on one of the loans we had already entered close to me, thinking that if someone walked up it would look like I was entering the data. And if Bree came back early, I could always say that I was just going over the application one more time.

Clicking on the keyboard, I headed to the main menu, found the search field I needed and entered *Lutz, Bruce.* There was no match, but several other Lutzes came up, all with different first names.

Next I tried Walter McDaniel, and the message *Check Version Three* flashed in front of me. "What Version Three?" I asked the screen quietly. It didn't reply, so I clicked out of that.

Thinking for a minute, I decided to try Ben Zimmerman's name. That was a bust. "No such record," the computer said.

"Okay," I whispered, "how about this?" I typed *Wolfe, Dick* and a new screen came up. It asked me for a password. "Interesting," I muttered and quickly clicked off the name. I also tried *Jacob, Sheldon,* and I got the same request for a password. Finally I went with *Bree Mills,* and a loan application came up right away. "So not all of the employee loans are password-protected," I muttered.

Just then my radar buzzed a warning, and I glanced at the little clock in the corner of the computer. It was five to one. Quickly, I logged out and closed the loan file I'd had in front of me. No sooner had I put it in the rack next to Bree's desk than I saw her enter the room. "Hey," she said as she approached with an armload of folders. "Sheldon just gave me this stack. Feel like entering them?"

I took the armload from Bree and we got to work. When I got to the second to last loan, I was surprised to see the name Carmen Perez on the application. "Huh," I said as I typed in the name.

"What?" Bree asked.

"Sheldon works fast," I said. "Ben Zimmerman just gave him this woman's name."

Bree lowered her voice to a whisper. "You really shouldn't talk about where Sheldon gets his leads," she said.

"Why?"

Bree looked around nervously. "You just shouldn't," she said.

"Okay," I conceded. But in the back of my mind I continued to wonder what the big deal was. I looked closely at the address as I was typing and memorized it, then noted the approximate value of the house and made a mental note of that as well. When I was done entering the loan data I told Bree that I had to go to the little girls' room, and while I was there I sent a text message to Candice with the address and the value, again telling her I'd explain later.

Finally, at five thirty, Bree called it quits. "I've got to go pick up my son from day care. Have a good night. I'll see you tomorrow."

"Do you think I'll be sitting with you again?" I asked.

Bree nodded. "You caught on really fast, but most of the loan officers train with a processor for a couple of days, then with a closer, then an underwriter. Finally, they go back to their mentor—Darren, in your case."

"Ah," I said with an inward groan. With my background, I already knew the ins and outs of processing, underwriting, and closing. This was going to be one long week. "I have a doctor's appointment tomorrow afternoon. Do you think it'll be okay to only spend a half day with you?"

"Should be fine. We can send Darren an e-mail in the morning, but he's really cool, so you should be good to go."

I said good-bye to Bree in the parking garage and pointed my car toward home. Eggy had been all alone again today, and I felt bad for the little guy, since I usually made time in my day to stop off and let him out around lunchtime. That is, I did when I used to set my own schedule.

After taking care of his needs, I changed and went to my office. Candice wasn't in when I got there. "Bummer," I said when I read the note from her that said she had a dinner meeting with a prospective client and that she'd call me later.

I ordered up some pasta from the Italian restaurant downstairs and ate at my desk while I sifted through my spreadsheet and typed in names and addresses for my big mailing campaign. At ten o'clock I heard a key in the front door and saw Candice come in. "Hey," I said, blinking my tired eyes a few times.

"You look like crap," she said to me. "You been in front of that computer all night?"

I rubbed my eyes and said, "All day and all night. But I'm almost done with the list. I figure I can start sending out the postcards by this weekend."

"How many are you sending?"

I turned to my spreadsheet. "I've got nearly a thousand so far and a good three hundred or so left to enter."

"That should be good for business."

"I hope you're right, Candice, 'cuz I can't continue this daily grind. I swear I'm bored outta my gourd."

Candice came into my office and took a seat. "I know what you mean. I love being my own boss. No more sitting at my desk trying to look busy."

"I thought you were the busiest investigator at your old firm," I said.

"I was. But the owner flooded his own market with investigators. He made a percentage on every single case that came in, so the more investigators, the merrier his take. We were climbing all over each other and there were too few cases to go around. Out here, the market is ripe for the picking."

"So your meeting went well tonight?"

"Very. A guy who's got a booming software business wants to expand, and he wants me to do his background checks."

My radar hummed. "What's his connection to Texas?"

Candice smiled. "The company's home base is in San Antonio."

"You'll get the deal," I said confidently. "He liked you."

"I'm really digging this partnership," Candice said. "I get all these little free tidbits. Dutch must love dating you."

I sighed. "Not lately," I admitted. "I'd be willing to wager that right about now he's feeling like I've ditched him."

"Have you?"

"No," I said. "I just need to reclaim my independence." Quickly switching topics, I asked, "Did you manage to dig up anything on those names that I sent you?"

"As a matter of fact, I did," said Candice, pulling a folder out of her shoulder bag. "I'm not sure if any of them mean anything, but this is what I've got. Ben Zimmerman owns Benzie's Bond Agency down on Eight Mile and Gratiot. He lives about three blocks from there, and according to all the data I've looked at, the guy is squeaky. No criminal record, owns his own home—and it's paid for. He's got clean credit too. The only bump in the road I could find was a pretty nasty divorce back in ninety-eight. He owes a few bucks in back child support and alimony, but as far as I can tell he's clean."

"That's interesting," I said, thinking back as I made the connection to what he'd told me earlier about Sheldon's bond. "He told me that he posted the bond for Sheldon Jacob, so if he did that, Sheldon must have a record."

Candice nodded. "And how," she said as she flipped forward a few pages. "Sheldon Jacob is one *bad* dude, Abby. He's got a record that goes back to the late seventies, everything from extortion to armed robbery to assault to drug dealing. Word is he used to supply a lot of the old Motown groups with their drugs."

"You're kidding," I said. "He strikes me as a wormy sort of guy, not someone I would expect to see associating with the in crowd."

"Maybe his ten years in prison had something to do with making him a little more wormy, a little less popular."

"He spent ten years in prison?"

"Yep, for possession with intent to deliver. And get this—he got out right before Walter was murdered."

"What about his brother?"

"Ron? Same rap sheet, but he beat a lot of the charges. Zimmerman's also posted bond on him."

"Interesting," I said. "Zimmerman gets around."

"He does a healthy business, from what I can gather."

"What about the other names I gave you—the two women? Anything on them?"

Candice turned a page in her file. "There's no criminal history for them, but I did find an interesting connection to Zimmerman."

"What's that?"

"Both have sons who've had run-ins with the law, and guess who secured bond for them before trial?"

"I'll take Ben Zimmerman for two hundred, Alex," I said.

"You would be two hundred dollars richer," Candice answered with a wink.

"I'm assuming the houses were the collateral for the bond?"

Candice nodded. "Yep. That must be how Zimmerman is getting these lists to Sheldon. The women come in, want to bail out their boys, and he jots down their info to pass to Jacob once the trial's over."

"Wonder what's in it for Zimmerman," I said.

Candice closed the file. "Gotta be some kind of a kickback," she said. "He's certainly not the type to do it for the goodwill."

"I saw the loan application for one of the women, Carmen Perez. She's taking a ton of money out of her equity."

"She paying off debt?"

"Nope. She's only got one credit card, and that has a small balance on it."

"Maybe she's investing it."

My left side got thick and heavy. "I don't think so," I said. "She's got no savings to speak of and no retirement account."

"Doesn't mean she can't start now with the cash-out of the equity in her house," Candice said reasonably.

I nodded and tried to stifle a yawn. "I'll keep my fingers crossed that that's what it is."

"I think you need to go home and get some rest," Candice said, eyeing me critically. "Why don't we skip the gym tomorrow morning and hit it after we get back from Jackson?"

"Sounds good," I said, clicking my computer off. "Are we meeting here?"

"Yeah. Meet me in the parking garage at noon and we'll take my car."

"Sounds good," I said again, wearily. Candice and I parted at my Mazda and I drove home, dog-tired. Eggy greeted me with a rousing round of running in circles followed by a few good yaps. The poor guy had to be getting lonely with all the time I was spending away from home.

At eleven o'clock I crawled into bed and was about to turn out the light when my phone rang. "Hey, cowboy," I said sleepily.

"Did I wake you?" he asked.

"Nope, but I am getting ready to turn in."

"I hadn't heard from you all day," he said. "I even stopped by your office around noon, but you weren't around."

"I was running errands," I said easily. "Next time give me a heads-up on the cell and I'll meet you for lunch."

"I wanted to let you know that we nailed Max Goodyear today."

"The guy from the waterworks?"

"Yep. And I have you to thank," he said with a chuckle. "We put those surveillance cameras up in his office, and sure enough, we caught him this morning coming into one of the comptroller's offices, picking up her keyboard, and jotting something down from a piece of paper she had there. Later we learned that the woman who sits there writes down the new password every week and hides it under her keyboard."

"He's been stealing it all this time," I said.

"Uh-huh. We tapped his computer too, so the moment he logged in and used the password to get to the account and siphon off a few grand we had him."

"Did you arrest him?"

"Yep. One of the most gratifying busts I've ever made," Dutch said. "And I'm taking you to dinner to celebrate."

I gave a loud yawn into the receiver. "Sounds good, Dutch. Let's plan on Friday night after my closing on Fern, okay?"

"It's a date," he said and then there was a pause before he added, "I miss you, Edgar."

I smiled. "You'd better," I purred. "See you Friday, cowboy." I disconnected. I rolled over onto my side with a sigh of contentment. I loved that Dutch and I were in such a good place, and just as I had that thought, I heard a faint buzz from my intuition that bothered me. I had a feeling that there was trouble ahead for the two of us, and for the life of sleepy old me, I couldn't figure out why.

Chapter Seven

I slept in until the last possible moment before bolting out of bed, taking a quick shower, and dashing out the door to Universal Mortgage. I made it there by eight thirty and still beat Darren by ten minutes.

"Morning," he said happily when he saw me.

"Morning," I replied. "Should I go sit with Bree again?"

"Actually," he said, "I have to shoot out to Bloomfield Hills to take a loan application. Want to ride shotgun?"

"That would be great," I said with relief. I was going to die of boredom if I had to enter one more loan into the system. "But I have to be back by lunchtime. I have a doctor's appointment this afternoon."

"Nothing serious, I hope?"

"No. Just my allergist. I have awful allergies." Man, I was good at making stuff up on the fly—as long as it wasn't to my boyfriend.

"No problem," Darren said. "Come on, let's go make some money."

I followed Darren out to his car and paused before getting in. "Nice," I said as he clicked the locks for the gray Mercedes.

"Work here for a while and you could be driving one of these babies too, Abby."

"Good to know," I said, forcing a smile. I got in and Darren pulled out of the space, cruising down the ramp and into traffic.

We'd gone about three blocks when my crew sent an intuitive alert to me. I had the feeling that I needed to be very aware of my surroundings. I sat up straight and looked around. To my right, I saw a familiar face in the car next to us. "Oh, shit!" I said as my boyfriend locked eyes with me.

"What's the matter?" Darren asked. Without thinking, I dove out of sight, my head landing in Darren's lap. "Abby, what the—"

"Drive!" I yelled at him. "Just drive away!" I felt his leg muscles tense and the car accelerated. Just then my cell phone rang. Reaching into my back pocket, I pulled it free and worked it up to my ear. "Hello?" I said, craning my neck to speak into the phone.

"You okay?" asked Dutch.

"Fine," I said lightly. "Why?"

"Because your head is in the lap of a guy driving a Mercedes-Benz, Edgar, and that's rather strange behavior—even for you."

"Huh?" I said, keeping my voice casual. "Don't know what you're talking about, Dutch. I'm at the office."

"Really?" he said, and I could hear the tension in his voice. "That's odd, because your cell phone is currently in the possession of someone bearing a striking resemblance to you and heading east on Long Lake Road."

"Oh, crap," I muttered. I had forgotten again that he had that stupid GPS locator on his cell that allowed him to track my every movement. "Hello?!" I suddenly yelled into the phone. "Dutch? Can you hear me?"

"I'm here," he said.

"Hello?!" I said again.

"Abby, I'm here."

"Darn," I said, pulling the phone slightly away from my ear. "I always drop calls in this area." I quickly turned the cell off, then twisted in my seat and eyed Darren. "Can you move this thing any faster?"

"You want to tell me what's going on?" he asked.

"Sure," I said. "Just tell me when we're clear of the black Range Rover tailing us."

About three minutes later Darren said, "We're clear. I dropped him at the red light behind us."

I sat up in my seat and straightened my hair and clothing. "I am in trouble," I said.

"Will you tell me what's going on?"

"That was my boyfriend back there," I admitted.

Darren's eyebrow arched. "I thought you were single."

I frowned. "I suppose that at this very moment that is a true statement."

"Are you afraid of this guy?" Darren asked me, his features lined with concern.

"No," I said, looking behind us. "It's just that he's a little on the jealous side, and I don't think he'd like it if he knew I was driving around with another guy."

"I see," said Darren. "Do you think he saw you?"

"Most definitely," I said with a heavy sigh. "And I have no idea how I'm going to explain this to him."

"Just tell him that your new job requires you to travel with an experienced loan officer. It's just business."

I nodded absently while my thoughts whirled. There was no way I could tell Dutch that I was working for Universal Mortgage. He'd be furious that I was within a hundred feet of Dick Wolfe. "I am so dead," I muttered.

A few minutes later, Darren and I arrived at the house of Tim and Tina Schalube. They were a nice couple who were struggling to assist with the housing and medical expenses of Tina's ailing parents. They'd gotten behind in their property tax payments, along with a few of their credit cards. I listened as Darren smooth-talked them into overextending themselves with a three-year interest-only balloon mortgage that allowed them to take a good chunk of their equity out and increase their loan to property value. He told them that given the neighborhood and the size of their five-thousand-square-foot home, the value of their property was likely to increase ten to twenty percent over the next three years, which meant that they'd still have plenty of equity if and when they wanted to refinance.

As I listened to him, I had a hard time holding in my anger. I knew both intuitively and from a practical sense that with Michigan's struggling economy and the current downsizing of all the local automotive firms, there was no way this house was going to appreciate so much in such a short period. The Schalubes stood a really good chance to lose money, not make it. What's more, by being locked into a balloon mortgage, they would be forced to refinance in three years—which meant they might have a much higher interest rate too. Still, in order to keep my cover, I had to play along, smiling and nodding at all the right times as the couple nervously scanned the application paperwork and signed the forms.

We left their home only an hour after we'd arrived, and Darren was riding high. "Did you see that?" he said to me as we pulled out of the driveway. "They didn't even flinch when I tacked on the origination fee!"

"I saw," I said, keeping my voice even.

"Easiest six grand I ever made," Darren continued, exuberant about sticking it to the Schalubes. "There's a sucker born every day!"

That was it. I'd had enough. "Doesn't that bother you even a little?" I snapped.

"Doesn't what bother me?" he asked, looking puzzled.

"These people are really struggling financially and you're most likely putting them in a much worse situation, not to mention taking a good chunk of their equity in closing costs with it."

"Did you see me holding a gun to their head?" Darren said defensively.

I scowled at him and turned my head away to look out the window. "Whatever," I said, wishing I'd kept my mouth shut.

"They got themselves into their own mess, Abby. Not me. And if the universe wants to teach them a lesson by having them hand over their money to me and suffer for it down the road, then I'm actually helping them, aren't I?"

I felt my face grow hot as my temper reached the boiling point. Turning back to Darren I said, "Did you ever consider, Darren, that the universe isn't trying to teach the Schalubes the lesson? Maybe the powers that be are trying instead to teach *you* a lesson about doing the right thing."

Darren gave me a huge roll of his eyes and turned back to watching the road. "You know, you're never going to make it in this business with that kind of an attitude."

Damn skippy, I thought, *and thank God for that.*

A short time later Darren dropped me at my car and I wasted no time getting to my office so I could meet Candice. I wanted to be as far away from the cutthroat environment of Universal Mortgage as I could get.

When I pulled into the parking garage, I could see Candice's car already parked in the space next to mine. I rolled into my slot and pulled a little coin purse out of my shoulder bag that held my ID and credit cards, shoving it into the pocket of my blazer. Next, I pulled out my cell phone and clicked it on, then tucked that back into the bag and shoved it under the front seat. I then joined Candice in her SUV. "Tough day at work?" she asked, looking at me critically.

"Darren Cox is an asshole," I snapped.

"Tell me something I don't know," Candice said. "Want to fill me in?"

I sighed heavily. "It's not even worth getting into," I said. After we drove for a minute or two, I had an idea and asked to borrow her cell phone.

"Where's yours?" she asked as she handed it to me.

"Under the seat of my car. I figure if Dutch has any ideas about tracking my whereabouts via his cellular GPS system, he'll see I'm at the office."

"You left your purse behind too?"

"Yeah, but I brought my ID. One less thing the guards at the prison have to sort through," I said as I punched a phone number into her phone. The call was to an old friend of mine, Tracy Gibson, who still worked at the bank where I used to work. She was the woman who had handled all of my own loan applications. I gave her all the details about the Schalubes, including the phone number I'd discreetly managed to jot down from their loan application. I told her to give them a call and offer them a competitive rate and program. "They're being raked over the coals, Tracy," I said. "I know you can do better on rate and terms, and I also know your fees will be a fraction of what they're currently being charged."

"How exactly do you know that they've got an application in at Universal Mortgage?"

"If I told you I'd have to kill you," I joked. "Seriously, though, you can't mention that you got this from me."

"And how exactly am I going to broach the topic?" she asked me.

"Pretend you're a telemarketer," I said.

"Which is against FCC regulations if they're on the National Do Not Call list, Abby. I'd rather not get fined five thousand dollars."

I scowled. This was harder than I'd thought. "Oh, crap, I'd forgotten about that. Well, can't you be creative?"

Tracy giggled. "I miss working with you, girlfriend."

"Does that mean you'll do it?"

"I'll see if I can't come up with something. Keep me posted if you hear anything on your end, though."

"Absolutely. And thanks, Tracy. You're a lifesaver."

I hung up feeling much better and flashed Candice

a winning smile. "I love beating an asshole at his own game," I said.

Candice smiled and pulled off the highway. "You hungry?"

"Famished," I said, noting that she was heading toward a Denny's restaurant.

"We can talk strategy over lunch," Candice said as we pulled into the lot.

After we'd placed our order, Candice pulled out a legal pad and began to make notes. "I made a call up to Jackson this morning to see if Lutz was accepting visitors, and apparently he's recovered enough from his stab wound to meet with the public. When we get in we'll need to go through security and then I'll give my name and see if Lutz is curious enough to let us see him. Most of these guys are so bored that they're willing to see complete strangers if it means breaking up the monotony."

"I gather you'd be the one doing all the talking?" I asked.

Candice nodded. "You just sit there and let that radar hum. Along with asking him about Walter, I want to know who stabbed him, and why. Not that he'll tell me, but maybe your radar can give us an insight or two. It'll also let us know if he's full of shit or not," she added with a smile.

"Inboard lie detectors do come in handy." I grinned back.

"I think we should also try and get a word with the warden. He's not obligated to talk to us, but he might open up about who's been visiting Lutz and if there's any inside scoop about the stabbing."

I nodded. "Sounds like a plan."

We finished our meal quickly and hurried out the door, anxious to be on our way since the drive was long. We made it to Jackson about two hours later, and I was struck by the starkness of the place. The prison was out in the middle of nowhere, far removed from anything even remotely civilized. A huge facility complete with watchtowers and razor wire strung along the top of mammoth brick walls, it stood imposingly surreal against the emptiness of the open terrain.

There was nothing warm or inviting about it, and I felt the hairs on my arms and the back of my neck stand on end as we entered the first set of gates leading into the main prison. We were stopped by a guard and asked to show our IDs and state our business. Candice did most of the talking and I simply nodded as she explained that we were here to visit with one of the prisoners.

We were let through the first set of gates and came to a second and a third before we were finally allowed onto the main grounds. We had to pay to park, but we found a good slot near the main entrance and hurried inside, both of us eager to complete our errand and get the hell out of there.

Once we were inside, though, the process was anything but swift. We were taken through security, which involved lots of unloading of pockets and Candice's purse, pulling off shoes, being swept by a handheld metal detector and peppered with questions about who we were there to see and why. Once we'd passed the gauntlet of security and were allowed into a small waiting area, I turned to Candice and said, "We'd better make this visit count, because I sure as hell don't want to come back through all of this again."

"You find this at the maximum-security level," Candice said. "I mean, this is where the worst of the worst get sent, so they have to be thorough."

I shivered as I looked around at the bleak waiting

room and the even bleaker faces of relatives and friends of inmates, all waiting to spend a few minutes with them. "Makes you really want to keep your nose clean," I said with another shiver.

A few minutes later, our names were called and we were led through a set of iron prison gates into a corridor lined with barred windows. Our footsteps echoed along the corridor as we followed the guard, and I found myself trying to quiet them. We turned a corner and were led through two more sets of gates and corridors until we were finally admitted to a narrow room set up with little cubicles. Plexiglas divided those of us in the free world from the prisoners on the other side.

We were shown to the last cubicle near the wall and told to wait while Lutz was brought down from the infirmary. I took a seat beside Candice and we waited in silence for a minute until Candice looked down at her cell phone and said, "Crap, I gotta take this. Abby, if Lutz shows up, tell him I'll be right back." Off she went to a corner of the room to take her call.

I was sitting, anxiously wondering how long it would be before Lutz came down, when snippets of the conversation in the next cubicle caught my attention. "The man came to the house yesterday," said a portly Hispanic woman next to me. "He gave me the papers to sign and drop off to him tomorrow. This way we won't have to sell the house to get the money."

Out of the corner of my eye I glanced at her. She was talking earnestly into the phone that connected her with the convict on the other side of the Plexiglas, and I noticed that her swollen belly showed signs of late pregnancy. "He said it would take about two weeks before I could get the check." There was a pause as the woman listened to what the prisoner said before she snapped, "There's nothing I can do! I already asked him to hurry, Nero! I can't make this go any faster!"

It was then that I noticed my intuition buzzing like crazy in my head and I swiveled in my chair to get a full look at the woman and focus on her energy. She wasn't just pregnant; she was scared out of her mind. Her energy was frantic. She held one arm protectively over her stomach while she gripped the phone with the other hand. Something was terribly wrong, and the fact that she was incredibly nervous and talking about taking two weeks to get some money had me on high alert.

Just then the woman turned her head slightly in my direction, and the look she gave me was harsh. "You want something?" she snapped.

"Sorry," I said, holding up my hand in apology. "You remind me of someone I know."

"Yeah, right," she scoffed as she looked me up and down. "I know plenty of white folks like you. I clean their houses and pick up their shit and get paid dirt for it."

I nodded soberly. "I'm truly sorry," I said. "It was rude of me." I scooted my chair a little farther from her, hoping that she'd drop it.

She gave me a loud "Hmph" and turned back to the inmate, saying, "Nothing, just some white bitch thinkin' she's all better than me. Listen, I gotta go. I'll be back next week, okay?"

Thankfully, at that moment Candice came back and took her seat. "Did Lutz come down yet?"

"No, not yet," I said.

"You okay?" she asked me as she noticed the way I was trying to blend into the wall.

"Fine," I said quickly. "I'm just anxious to talk to Lutz and get the hell outta here."

We didn't have long to wait. Bruce Lutz appeared in a wheelchair on the other side of the Plexiglas a few moments later, and although his face didn't register anything other than a deep scowl, his eyes held a hint of curiosity. "What?" he asked as Candice picked up the phone and held it between the two of us.

"Good afternoon, Mr. Lutz. My name is Candice Fusco and I'm a private investigator. I'd like to ask you a few questions, if I may."

"What's in it for me?" he asked as his eyes roved over her chest.

"Parole," Candice said simply.

The corner of Lutz's lip turned up slightly. "That so?" he asked.

Candice nodded. "I'm looking into the murder of Walter McDaniel, and I have reason to believe you were not the triggerman."

Lutz actually laughed. "That's funny," he said. " 'Cuz I seem to recall confessing to the crime, Miss PI."

"Lots of people confess to crimes they didn't commit," Candice said easily. "The question is why."

Lutz waved his hand impatiently. "Well, I hate to disappoint you, sweetheart, but I shot that cop, and you can let the parole board know that I'm really sorry about it."

My lie detector went haywire. I tapped Candice's foot with my own, a sign that she and I had agreed upon at the restaurant would indicate when Lutz was lying. "I'll be sure and let them know, Mr. Lutz," she said. "But are you sure your memory is serving you correctly? Are you sure that someone else didn't shoot Detective McDaniel and get away with it?"

Lutz scoffed as he looked at her. "You're a pretty dumb broad even if you are a looker," he said. "I told yous, I shot that cop. Okay?"

Again my lie detector sounded and I gave Candice's foot another tap. "Fine," said Candice. "Have it your way, Mr. Lutz. I was hoping I could help you, but that's obviously not something of interest to you. So sorry for wasting your time."

"That's all I been doin' for nine years, honey, wastin' time. Say, who hired you anyway?"

"One of the family members," Candice said easily, then quickly changed topics before Lutz had a chance to ask which one of Walter's relatives had hired us. "Just one more thing before we go, Mr. Lutz. Mind sharing with us who stabbed you?"

Lutz's face seemed to flush slightly. "Yeah, I mind," he snapped and promptly hung up his end of the phone. Flipping Candice the bird with one hand, he pulled on his wheelchair with the other and spun away from the counter. A moment later he was out the iron gate and heading away from the visitors' room.

"Charmer," I said as he pushed himself along the hallway on the other side of the Plexiglas.

"He had me at hello," Candice scoffed. "Come on, let's see if we can get a word with the warden."

We made our way out of the visitors' room and followed the guard back to the prisoner information desk where we'd first given our names and reason for visiting. Candice pulled out her wallet and flipped it open to her PI license so the guard could inspect it. "We'd really appreciate any time the warden could spare," she said to the woman behind the desk, who looked completely disinterested in how appreciative we were. "Wait over there," she said as she picked up the receiver on her desk phone and punched in an extension.

Candice and I headed over to a row of rather bleak-looking chairs and sat down. While we were waiting I glanced out the window and saw the pregnant Hispanic woman I'd been caught eavesdropping on earlier. My radar kicked in and I knew I needed to talk with her.

"I'll be back in a minute," I said to Candice and headed outside. As I approached the woman, I waved my arms to catch her attention. "Yoo-hoo!" I called brightly. "Can I talk to you for a minute?"

The woman stopped and scowled at me. "What are you, some kind of psycho stalker?" she asked as I walked up to her.

I smiled, allowing the insult to roll off me. "I just want a quick word with you," I said.

"Make it quick," she said impatiently. "I gotta get back to my kid."

I nodded. "The thing of it is," I began, going for honesty, "I'm a professional psychic."

"Shut up," she said, pulling her head back and eyeing me out of the corner of her eye.

I held up my hand as if I were taking a vow. "Honest," I said. "And I know you thought I was being rude back there, but it's just that you have some really interesting energy and I couldn't help tuning in on you."

The woman turned her whole body to face me. She might not have believed me, but at least I had piqued her interest. "What did you see?"

"For starters, you're having a little girl. Correct?"

"Lucky guess," she said, crossing her arms. She wasn't going to be so easy to convince.

"You're right. But at least now you'll have one boy and one girl. And your little boy's around four, right?"

The woman's mouth dropped open ever so slightly. "He turns five in August."

"And there's an older woman living in the house with you—a mother figure who helps watch out for your son while you're at work, right?"

The woman nodded, and her large, unblinking eyes told me that I had her full attention. "What else you gettin'?"

I smiled. "So much," I said as I turned the radar to full throttle. "I'm getting that the man you were talking to is connected to you, but not in a romantic way."

"He's my older brother," she said.

"And you're really worried about him," I said. Okay, this was technically cheating because I'd seen the lines of worry on her face when she was talking to him, but I'd done all the other stuff on my own.

The woman nodded. "I am," she said, and her eyes welled up slightly.

My radar hummed, and I had to admit I didn't like the energy surrounding her brother at all. "I feel you have reason to be," I said. "He's in trouble, and it's got nothing to do with what he's doing time for."

The woman placed a hand to her heart as one tear slid slowly down her cheek. "I'm doing everything I can to help him," she said. "I just need some time."

I nodded. My crew suggested there was some legal paperwork being drafted that would require her signature. "You've gone to the authorities," I said.

Her face scrunched up in shock. *"Hell, no,"* she said.

I cocked my head, wondering how I'd misinterpreted. "Really?" I said. "Because I've got this con-

nection to some legal paperwork and a hope that it
will help your brother out—but I want to warn you,
there's something not good about signing these docu-
ments. I'm getting the feeling this will chain you in
some way."

It was her turn to give me a puzzled expression.
"Chain me?"

"Yes," I said, nodding to her. "Like, bind you or
trap you in a way you hadn't anticipated. I want you
to be very careful about signing any legal paperwork."

She stared at me for a long moment, her face showing conflicting emotions that ranged from despair to
anger to hopelessness. "There's nothing else I can
do," she said and began to turn away.

At that moment I clearly saw the face of my boyfriend. "I know someone who can help you," I said,
trying to hold her attention. She looked questioningly
over her shoulder at me. "Here," I said hurriedly as
I fished around in my pocket for the coin purse I'd
tucked there. After thumbing through my ID and
credit cards, I came up with Dutch's business card and
handed it to her. "I know him. He can help. Think
about calling him, okay?"

Reluctantly she took the card and pocketed it. Then
she turned away and waddled to her car. I watched
her until she got in, then turned back to the prison—
thinking that I didn't even know her name.

"What was that about?" asked Candice when I re-
joined her.

"I'm not sure," I said, glancing outside as the woman's car pulled away.

"Well, the warden is willing to see us at four thirty,"
she said. "Gives us half an hour to twiddle our
thumbs."

I leaned my head back against the wall and closed my eyes, weary beyond belief. "Wake me when he's ready," I said and drifted off to sleep.

Sometime later I felt a little nudge on my arm. "Abby," Candice said softly. "Come on, honey, time to go."

I opened my eyes and stretched. "Man, I needed that little catnap," I said. "Is the warden ready to see us?"

"Uh-huh. Come on. We don't want to keep him waiting." We followed a guard through another maze of bar-lined corridors and up a flight of stairs, after which we were escorted through a locked steel door and into a completely different environment.

"Nice digs," I said, looking around at the attractively decorated lobby where a woman with black glasses and a hairdo that would have been all the rage about fifty years ago glanced up at us as we approached.

The guard in front of us halted at the corner of her desk and said, "Candice Fusco and Abigail Cooper to meet with the warden, Evelyn."

"Thank you, Jeb. I'll call you when they're finished." After Jeb left she turned to us and said, "Please take a seat. Warden Sinclair will be right with you."

We sat down in two of the overstuffed and incredibly comfortable lobby chairs—a far cry from the flimsy plastic chair I'd just taken a nap in. After we'd gotten settled, Candice leaned over and said, "Let me do the talking in here, too, Abs."

I nodded and tried to keep my sleepy eyes open. It was hard, given how comfortable I was. After about ten minutes Evelyn's phone bleeped and she picked up the receiver. Saying something we couldn't catch, she replaced the phone and stood. "Warden Sinclair

will see you now," she said, coming out from around
her desk.

We followed her down a short corridor and waited
while she opened a door and gave us a nod. "In there,
if you please," she said.

Candice and I filed in and I worked hard to contain
my surprise at the size of the place. It was gigantic as
far as offices were concerned. The mammoth room
had a heavy oak desk at the far end, and behind the
desk a row of huge windows overlooked the prison
grounds. Several formal-looking portraits of previous
wardens hung on the walls. I was surprised to see
that one of the men in the portraits bore a striking
resemblance to the rather short man with a receding
hairline and thin mustache behind the desk who had
stood to greet us. The nameplate on the desk read,
WARDEN A. SINCLAIR.

"Good afternoon," he said as we hurried across the
room to greet him. "I'm Warden Sinclair."

Candice stepped forward as he came around the
side of his desk and extended his hand to her. "Good
afternoon, Warden. I'm Candice Fusco. Thank you for
seeing us on such short notice."

The warden pulled his rather thick lips back in what
was probably a smile, but it looked to me like more
of a grimace. "You're lucky that my calendar is fairly
clear today," he said as he turned to shake my hand.

"Hello," I said. He gave my hand one quick pump
and turned back to Candice.

"I understand you're a private investigator here to
see prisoner Bruce Lutz?" he said as he took his seat
and waved at us to sit down too.

"Yes," Candice said. "I used to work for the PI
firm of Phitzburger and Weinstein, but I've recently
gone out on my own."

The warden's eyebrows gave a bounce. "I know Phitzburger personally," he said. "How is David?"

"He's doing well," Candice said. I could tell she was waiting for Sinclair to ask her why she'd requested the meeting. "We keep in touch through e-mail, and I'd be happy to send along your regards if you like."

The warden nodded. "What can I do for you today, Ms. Fusco?"

Candice smiled warmly. "We're actually here to help Mr. Lutz," she said. "We believe we're on to something that could help him at his parole hearing."

"Oh?" said the warden. "He's hired you?"

"No," said Candice. "We were retained by another party."

"Who?"

Another bright smile from Candice. "I'm afraid that's confidential," she said. "But I was wondering if you could shed some light on this recent stabbing incident. Do your guards have any leads about who might have stabbed Mr. Lutz?"

The warden gave a snorting sound, as if Candice had said something funny. "That suspect list gets longer by the minute," he said.

"Lutz has a lot of enemies?" Candice asked.

"I'd say he's got far more of those these days than he has friends."

Candice hesitated for a moment, then asked, "How has Lutz's prison record been?"

"Up until a few weeks ago he was the model prisoner," said the warden. "In fact, I'd been prepared to testify to his good behavior before the parole board until he began acting inappropriately."

Candice leaned forward slightly in her chair. "Inappropriately?"

"The change was quite drastic, in fact," said the

warden. "He began picking fights and getting into skirmishes. In fact, at one point we had to put him in solitary confinement."

"Why do you think he began acting up so close to his parole hearing?" Candice asked.

The warden shook his head. "Who knows why these men do the things they do, Ms. Fusco? After all, they're criminals."

I'd been following the conversation quietly in my chair, but just as Sinclair finished speaking, my lie detector went haywire. I discreetly nudged Candice's foot with my own. She gave my foot a quick glance, then stood up. "We don't want to keep you, Warden," she said to him. "Thank you for your time."

We waited in the lobby area for Jeb to come get us, said our farewells to Evelyn, and made our way out of Jackson Penitentiary. I was never more relieved to get out of a building in my life, and that included the once very haunted house I was about to sell. "Thank God I keep my nose clean," I said to her as we pulled out of the parking lot.

"Not your taste in living quarters, huh?"

I shivered a little as I watched the building become a little smaller in the side mirror. "I'd go bonkers in there."

"Might be the reason Lutz has been acting up," Candice said. "Maybe he went a little crazy."

"Who knows, Ms. Fusco? After all, he is a criminal," I said, mimicking the warden.

"And how creepy was that guy?" Candice said. "That was one toady-looking dude."

"And a liar," I said with a scowl. "He knows why Lutz was acting up."

"He strikes me as the type who likes playing mind games," Candice said, then looked up through the windshield at the darkening sky. "Looks like we've got a nasty storm brewing."

I glanced up too. "Yikes," I said as a flash of lightning in the distance broke against a deep gray cloud. "And it looks like we're headed right into it."

"You buckled up?" Candice asked me as she flipped on the SUV's lights and gripped the steering wheel with both hands.

"Always," I said, noting that she looked a little nervous. "You okay?"

"Yeah, I just hate driving in stormy weather. I was in a bad accident when I was a little kid. My sister was driving and we got into some weather she couldn't handle."

"Ah," I said, suddenly remembering that Candice had once mentioned that her sister had been killed in a car accident. I figured this was the same one she was referring to, but I didn't want to have her elaborate when she was trying to concentrate. "I'm sure we'll be fine," I said, but just then my left side went all thick and heavy. *Ah, shit,* I thought as I sat up straight in the seat and tightly gripped the bar above my door.

We were fine for the first hour, even though rain and wind racked the car and lightning crashed all around us. We drove in silence and I nervously watched Candice as she strained to see out the windshield. I kept hoping that the weather would break, but about an hour from home it only got worse, and Candice gave me a quick, rather frightened glance. "We need to pull over," she said.

"Good idea," I agreed.

We got off at the next exit, not wanting to stop on the shoulder in the severe weather. We were in a remote area, and Candice looked right and left at the stop sign at the top of the ramp, trying to decide which to choose. I was about to tell her to go left, which was what my radar suggested, but she turned right and I didn't feel like second-guessing her—she was stressed out enough.

The road we were on was long and straight and there weren't any buildings or driveways for us to pull into. "Damn," she said as we were about to drive onto a long bridge. "I think we should go back and try the other direction," she said.

I was about to agree when we felt a tremendous bump from behind. "What the . . . ?" I said as I squirmed in my seat and saw the windshield of an enormous Hummer coming toward us.

"That son of a bitch!" Candice yelled. "He's been on my tail ever since we got off the highway! He should freaking know better than to get so close in this weather."

Candice put on her turn signal. "Let's get off this bridge and pull over to get his insurance information," she said. But just then there was a roar of an engine and the Hummer cruised up next to our backseat.

"What the hell is he doing?" I asked, panicking as I saw how close he was cutting to us.

Candice was staring wide-eyed into her side mirror and she barely had time to say, "Abby, hold on!" before we were rammed again, from the side. My neck snapped to the right and my head hit the passenger side window. *"Ow!"* I yelled.

"Shit, shit, *shit*!" Candice said as she tried to work the steering wheel. "I think he's done something to the axle! I can't get this thing to turn!"

Again there was a roar of an engine and we were hit for a third time. The blow from the Hummer slammed us into the guardrail on the side of the bridge. "Jesus!" I hissed as I looked out the window at the twenty-foot drop into a ravine below. "Candice! We've got to get outta here!"

Candice depressed the accelerator and we screeched forward a few feet, but the Hummer came at us again and knocked us up onto the curb of the bridge. We were now lodged against the rail. "Goddamn him!" Candice yelled as she shook her fist at the Hummer. The truck answered her by ramming us again.

"Ow!" Candice and I both yelled. The SUV wasn't the only thing taking a severe beating. "Abby!" Candice yelled as she worked at the buckle on her seat belt. "We've got to get out of this car! Can you get out on your side?"

I unfastened my own seat belt and grabbed the door handle. It clicked and the door opened a centimeter. "It's jammed against the guardrail!"

A second later we heard yet another roar and the screeching of metal as we were knocked against the guardrail and all the way up onto the curb, which caused a section of the guardrail to fall off the bridge. A second later we heard it crash at the bottom of the ravine. Again the Hummer came at us and we both screamed as Candice's SUV gave a tremendous jolt. The back wheel hitched over the side of the bridge and pitched the front up in the air.

The Hummer backed up, and Candice and I looked behind us at the drop through the back windshield. "He's going to push us over the side!" Candice yelled.

"Do something!" I screamed, my knuckles white as they gripped the dashboard.

Candice bent forward and I saw her reaching under the seat. The SUV teetered like a seesaw, and through the window I could see the Hummer sitting there, revving its engine as it mocked us. "My gun is under here," Candice said anxiously. "I know it's here some-where!"

"Hurry, Candice! Hurry!" I cried. "He's getting ready to ram us again!"

There was a roar from the Hummer just as Candice pulled her arm free from underneath and came up with a silver Glock Nine. She pulled back on the safety and swiveled in her seat in the second or two before the Hummer reached us.

"Shoot him!" I screamed, and three explosions rocked through the car. In the next instant, the Hummer reached us and Candice came flying into me as the crash into the side panel sent everything in motion.

The SUV swiveled sideways and there was a terrible noise of metal scraping on metal and pavement. The back of our car fishtailed and the second tire went over the edge. I felt the cab pitch straight up into the air, and if I hadn't been holding on to the little handle above my head I would have toppled to the back of the SUV. I held on to it and Candice for dear life.

I thought for sure the next thing I would feel would be the pain of impact as we tumbled over the side of the bridge into the gorge below, but time seemed to stand still as we dangled there in space, teetering back and forth.

I was breathing hard, my eyes wide with panic as I waited for the fall, but the seconds ticked by and we continued to hang there. "What's happening?" I finally said.

"I think we're hung up on the guardrail," whispered Candice.

"Where's the Hummer?"

"Gone."

Neither of us spoke for several seconds. Then, in a soft voice I said, "How do we get out of here?"

"Very slowly and very carefully," said Candice. "My driver's side window is probably our best bet."

I looked over her shoulder and noticed that the Glock had done a nice job of clearing out most of the glass. The rain was still coming down hard and heavy outside, but right then I'd have given anything to be drenched and cold outside. "Can't we just sit here real quietlike, until someone comes by?"

"You want that someone to be the Hummer again?"

"Good point," I said, trying hard to calm my rapid heartbeat. "You first."

Candice gave my arm a pat and very carefully pushed herself away from me. "You follow right after me," she instructed.

"Don't you worry about it," I said, holding my breath and watching as she reached up to grab the armrest of the driver's-side door. "You're doing great," I said encouragingly. "Keep going."

Candice paused for a second and used her gun to knock the rest of the glass out of the frame. "Watch yourself on the glass, Abby," she said as she tucked her gun into her waistband, then moved up level with the window.

"That's it," I coaxed. "You can do this, Candice!"

As she eased one leg out of the SUV, there came a groaning sound and Candice stopped moving. We both held our breath again and listened. "Abby!" she squealed as she pulled her head up to look over the dashboard.

"Yeah?"

"The guardrail is giving way!"

I closed my eyes and swallowed hard. Crap. I'd survived a friggin' bullet to the chest and *this* was how my life was going to end? Just then my crew came into my head loud and clear with an urgent message. Snapping my eyes open, I said sternly, "Candice, the guardrail will hold, but we have to move. *Now!*"

Without a backward glance, Candice shimmied as carefully as she could out of the window. I saw her drop out of sight and heard her call, "Come on, Abby!"

I didn't need the added encouragement, as I was already up and pushing myself toward the window. There was more groaning outside, but I ignored it and grabbed the door handle with one hand and the window frame with the other. There was a slicing pain in my hand, but I didn't pause as I pulled hard and got my head and torso free. I felt Candice's arms reach around my chest, and I let go of the car as she pulled me through the window and free of the SUV. Not even a split second later the guardrail squealed and snapped and Candice's car dropped out of sight. Time seemed to stop as I blinked, once, twice, three times, and we heard an awful crashing noise from the ravine below.

We both stood there panting hard in the rain, looking at the spot where there had just been a car. "Christ," I said with chattering teeth as I realized I was shivering from head to toe.

"He might have had something to do with getting us clear in time," Candice said as she placed an arm across my shoulders. "I was definitely sending him a thought or two there before we got out."

"Now what?" I asked, turning to her.

Candice reached for the cell phone clipped at her waistband. "We get the hell outta here."

Chapter Eight

A county sheriff's deputy showed up within about ten minutes of our 911 call. After viewing Candice's crumpled SUV at the bottom of the ravine he quickly called for backup, then offered us blankets and the back of his patrol car to warm up in. I continued to shiver long after we'd warmed up. I couldn't believe how close we'd come to looking like compacted trash.

After backup arrived, the deputy took us to a highway station and got our statements. It was while we told our story that Candice and I realized we knew very little about our assailant. The only relevant information we were able to give was that we'd been rammed several times by a black or dark blue Hummer and neither of us knew why. At least, that's what we told the deputy.

After we gave our statements, Candice called her grandmother for a lift, then her insurance company. "They are so going to drop me," she muttered after she'd hung up the phone.

My right side felt light. "Yep," I agreed. "Time to start looking for another carrier."

We sat in stunned silence for a while, each of us lost in our own thoughts. It would be at least an hour and a half before Madame Brijitte Dubois—Candice's rather eccentric grandmother—could get to us, so we had time to ponder things.

Finally, after almost an hour, Candice said, "I think we were tailed from the prison."

"My thoughts exactly," I said. "Did you notice the Hummer at any point on the drive?"

Candice sighed heavily. "Nope. I blew it. I was concentrating so hard on seeing the road in front of us that I wasn't even looking in the rearview mirror."

"Kinda tough to see anything in that rain," I offered.

Candice nodded and was silent for a few beats before she said, "The real question is, who did we piss off?"

I scoffed and rubbed my neck, which was starting to stiffen. "Someone who owns a Hummer."

"How's that hand?" she asked, looking down at my crudely wrapped right hand.

"I think there's still some glass in it. I'll need to go home and soak the heck out of it."

"Might want to see a doctor," she offered helpfully.

"No thanks," I said. "I've seen enough of them for a while."

We waited in the lobby of the sheriff's station, listening to the rain outside, for nearly two hours. Finally the doors opened and a beautiful elderly woman toting a bright pink umbrella entered. "Bonjour!" she said as she spotted us, her voice thick with an authentic French accent.

"Bonjour, Nana!" Candice said, getting to her feet and looking at the clock on the wall. "I was beginning to worry about you."

Madame Dubois gave her a wink. "Ze traffic! *C'est horrible!*"

"May I drive us back?" Candice asked, reaching for the keys.

"Mais oui," Madame Dubois answered, giving them up easily. " 'Ow is your car, Candice?"

Candice glanced at me and gave me a guarded look. "Fine, Nana. Just a little fender bender, but enough that I didn't want to risk driving it any farther in this stuff. Thanks so much for coming to get us."

"Oui, oui," Madame Dubois said. "Shall we bee off, zen?"

We exited the station and I followed numbly behind Candice and Madame Dubois. I was tired, still a little damp, and becoming stiff and sore all over. All I wanted to do was get the hell home and climb into a tub of hot water. We got to Madame's car and piled into her powder pink Volvo—Madame is *big* on the color pink—and headed for home.

I fell asleep before we'd gone ten miles, and the next thing I knew I was being gently shaken. "Abs," Candice said. "Come on, girl, time to get in your own car and go home to bed."

I opened my eyes and blinked a few times. "We're here?" I mumbled.

"Yep. That's your car right over there," she said, pointing out her window. I nodded and said my good-byes to her and Madame as I got out of the car. Shuffling painfully over to my Mazda, I hopped in and started the engine. Candice waited for my car to start before she gave a wave herself and exited the parking garage.

I drove home in a stupor. My eyelids felt like lead and my body ached so much that I tried to move as little as possible. I arrived not ten minutes later to see a black Range Rover in my driveway. "Great," I muttered. "Ricky's home and Lucy's got some 'splainin' to do."

I parked next to the SUV and headed inside. Dutch was sitting in my living room cuddled up with Eggy, and it dawned on me as I entered that I'd forgotten all about the little guy; but then, I had rather expected that I would have been home long before now.

"Hey," Dutch said, watching me closely as I dropped my purse on a side table and walked stiffly over to the couch.

"Hey, yourself," I said. "Been here long?"

"A while," he said. "Good thing too, 'cuz your little guy was hurtin' for some supper and a chance to water the lawn."

I smiled as I reached over to pet Eggy. "Thanks for taking care of him."

"No sweat. Mind telling me what happened to you?"

I leaned forward and rested my head on Dutch's shoulder. "Candice and I are working a case."

"I figured as much."

"And we had to go visit one of the witnesses today, but on the way home it started to rain really hard and Candice was trying to pull over when . . ." My voice trailed off as I thought about a way to explain what'd happened that wouldn't get him too worked up.

"When what?" he asked, cocking his head to look me in the eye.

"When she lost control of her car and we had a little accident."

"You okay?"

I sighed. "I'm sore and a little bruised, but I'm okay."

"Is Candice all right?"

"She's the same."

Dutch set Eggy to the side and pulled my bandaged hand forward to inspect it. "What happened here?"

"Cut my hand on some glass. I think there's still a little glass in it."

"Come on," he said. He got up and eased me to my feet. "You need a bath."

A little while later I was soaking in soothing bathwater while Dutch worked on my hand by the side of the tub. He had a pair of tweezers, a magnifying glass, and some peroxide. As I watched him work I noticed that his long hair looked pouffy. Apparently he'd taken my suggestion about the hair mousse seriously.

He glanced up as he caught me looking at him. "What's up?" he asked.

I grinned. "Just remembered that John Oates called for you. He wants to know when the Hall and Oates reunion's going to take place."

Dutch rolled his eyes. "I haven't had time to get to the barber, okay?"

"I can tell," I said. "Pretty soon you'll be trying out for Flock of Seagulls."

Dutch gave a patient sigh. "Now that I know about the car accident, you mind telling me about the guy you were with this afternoon?"

I gave him a narrowed look. "Methinks you could tell me more about him than I could tell you."

The corner of Dutch's mouth curled up slightly. "Darren Cox, the guy whose lap you were inspecting today and the guy you played single white female with the other night, is thirty-three, resides on Glengary

Road in Bloomfield Village. Has a PI license that's up for renewal in January."

I shook my head. "Heaven forbid I should ever step out of line with you around," I said.

"Oh, you step out of line all the time, Abby. I just let you get away with most of it."

I rolled my own eyes. "Darren is an old coworker of Candice's. He's helping us with this case."

"This case, this case," Dutch mimicked. "Who and what is this all about, Edgar?"

I squirmed uncomfortably as he dug around in my palm for the shard of glass I could still feel there. "It's confidential," I said with a wince.

"Maybe I could help," he said. "I do have some pretty good resources at my disposal, you know."

I reached up with my other hand and ran my fingers along his sideburn. "I know," I said softly. "But until Candice gives the okay, I can't divulge anything." I hated that I was putting Candice in the middle of this, and I really hoped that Dutch didn't get a chance to approach her directly with his offer for help—she'd have to give him a solid reason why she couldn't accept.

"Okay," Dutch said as he pulled up with the tweezers and smiled triumphantly. "Got it."

He showed me the shard and I made a face. "That little bugger was driving me nuts. Thanks for working it out."

"No sweat," he said, dousing the wound with peroxide.

"Yikes!" I said as my hand burned.

"That's for the Flock of Seagulls comment," he said with a smile. "Now stay there while I go heat you up something to eat."

"There's no food here," I admitted.

"None?"

"I ran out of eggs this morning."

"How do you live?" Dutch asked me seriously.

"I take it day by day, cowboy."

Thirty minutes later, I was just rubbing myself dry with a towel when I heard the doorbell ring. I dropped the towel, got into my robe, and gave a contented sigh when I smelled the delicious scent of fresh pizza. "Have I told you lately that I love you?" I said to Dutch as he set out a plate and napkin for me on the coffee table.

"Not really. I suggest that you say it more often and follow it up with a lot more sex."

I giggled as I sat down and took a huge bite. "Mmff . . . it'sh good!"

"Little hungry, are we?"

I nodded, then noticed that the file I'd been working on for Dutch was open on the coffee table next to the pizza. "I'm still working on that," I mumbled, motioning to it.

"I can tell," he said. "Have you figured out what 'postcards from the edge' means?"

I shook my head. "No, but I know it's important. All of the contexts that I want to put it into feel wrong to me. The only thing I can think of is that it's a clue that hasn't surfaced yet—but when it does, we'll know."

"So for now we just have to wait, huh?" he said.

" 'Fraid so, cowboy."

"Well, I brought you the other one, too, just in case you felt like switching to a new case."

"Sure," I said. I set down the pizza and picked up the folder. Flipping through it, I remarked, "This thing's almost older than I am."

"I know," said Dutch. "Each agent gets one cold case to work on with their regular caseload. This one's a real dud. I've been over it and over it half a dozen times and nothing's jumping out at me."

I scowled as I read out loud, "Cynthia Frost, age forty-one. Divorced and living with her six-year-old daughter on the seventeen-hundred block of Fourteen Mile Road. Found dead from a broken neck in her home on September Twenty-second, nineteen seventy-eight." I read on silently for a bit, then turned back to Dutch and asked, "What makes this a federal case?"

"Cynthia was CIA."

"Get outta here!" I said as I glanced back to the photo of Cynthia, which was likely taken from her driver's license. "But she looks so matronly."

Dutch nodded. "Which was why she was so good. She was an operative during the Cold War, and from what I've been able to ascertain, she was one of the best in the biz."

"You think she was killed by another spy?"

"That was the prevailing theory for a while, but no leads ever developed. This was with the CIA until about ten years ago, and that's when we got it."

"Why'd it flip agencies?"

"Frost's boss switched houses. He got out of the spy business and into more domestic interests. He's now the SAC for all of Michigan."

"SAC?" I asked.

"Special agent in charge," Dutch explained. "Anyway, he gave it to my boss, the ASAC."

"Let me guess," I said, interrupting him. "That would stand for assistant special agent in charge?"

"Bingo," Dutch said with a wink. "So the ASAC has been giving it to every new agent for the last couple of years, thinking that a new set of eyes might help spot something someone else missed. The rookie who investigated it before me worked it hard, trying to impress the brass, but he got bubkes."

"Ex-husband?" I asked going back to the word "divorced."

"Was giving a speech at a convention in Hawaii. Had two hundred eyewitnesses to place him eight thousand miles away."

"Ex-boyfriend?"

"Nope—looked into it and nothing."

"Angry neighbor?"

"Double nope."

"Did the daughter see anything?" I asked, noting that the report mentioned that the six-year-old daughter was at the house when the crime took place.

"Asleep upstairs, and was grilled repeatedly by both the police and the federal agencies investigating. Doesn't remember anything beyond coming downstairs in the morning and finding her mom dead in the kitchen."

"Have you talked to her recently?"

"No. The last time an agent interviewed her was three years ago, and the interview was pretty thorough. The record shows she works for some attorney in Birmingham. I suppose I could track her down and do one more follow-up, but I really don't think she's got any more to give us, and I don't see the point of having that girl relive the worst day of her life over and over."

"Wow, this really is a stinker," I said as I closed the file. "They either hate you down there, or they love you and think you can work miracles."

Dutch shrugged. "Maybe all I need is one good lead from my favorite little miracle worker." And with that he reached forward and pulled me into his arms.

I allowed myself to be enveloped. God, I loved the feel of him. "You know," I said softly, "if I weren't so tired, I'd mount you right here and now."

Dutch wiggled his eyebrows and flashed me his gorgeous smile. "Giddyup," he said and kissed me.

The next morning he was off early to shower and change at his place. I moved around slow and easy, since my entire body felt like it'd gone a few rounds with Evander Holyfield. Candice called while I waited for the coffee to drip in the coffeemaker. "How you feeling?" she asked.

"Sore as hell."

"I hear you. I think I'm going to see my chiropractor today. My neck is killing me."

"At least you get to stay in bed if you want to. I've got to go to the mortgage company this morning."

"You gonna make it?"

"I made the coffee extra strong. I'm hoping caffeine also works on pain."

"Take it easy, kiddo. You've had a rough year of it."

"Really?" I said. "What's a few pints of blood between friends?"

"What we need is something solid," said Candice, ignoring my sarcasm. "We need a lead to tie some of this stuff together."

"Maybe we should start with the guy who rammed our car yesterday?" I said.

"Great idea, Nancy Drew. I'm already working on that. But without a license plate and a good description of the driver, we'll have to rely on forensics to find anything."

"Which means it could take months."

"Right," she said. "I still say there's something going on at Universal. See if you can dig a little deeper into their files, Abs. I just know you're going to find something we can use."

I didn't share her enthusiasm, mostly because I dreaded going back to that place and its caustic atmosphere. Still, I managed to arrive on time, which was a good thing, because my walk had stiffened and it was slow going getting into the building. Darren was already at his desk when I entered the snake pit. "Hey," I said to him as I gingerly took my seat. "You're in early."

Darren gave me a quick glance. "Yeah, I had a deal blow up yesterday."

"Oh?" I said. "What happened?"

"The Schalubes left me a message that they got a better quote from some local bank in town. I'm working up a new estimate to see if I can't get them back."

"Ah," I said, working to look surprised at the news, "that's too bad. Well, I'll go sit with Bree again this morning and leave you to win your deal back."

Darren grunted as I got up and headed over to the processing area.

I met Bree at her cubicle. "Hey there," I said happily as I sat down next to her.

"Oh, hey!" she said, looking up. "I thought I'd lost you to the snake pit."

"Nope. I'm back," I said, holding in a sigh. "What's on the agenda for today?"

"Well, I'd toss you over to Stacey to train with a closer today, but she's out sick, so I'm covering for her, which means you can learn some of the closing stuff from me."

"You're a closer too?"

"Honey, I wear all the hats," Bree said with a laugh. "Here," she added, handing me a stack of files. "First, I need you to go through these and make sure the

title work is in the file and that we've got the right
mortgage amount and a clear title. While you're doing
that I can refill my coffee—you want some?"

"No," I said, holding up my own cup, "I'm good."

Bree headed off and I glanced at the first file in my
hand. Jacob was the name of the borrower on the file.
Curious, I opened the folder and was surprised to find
that the file was for Sheldon Jacob—that Good
Humor bar in the snake pit. "Huh," I said to myself
as I dug through the file. "Looks like he's buying a
rental property." I looked through the paperwork and
was puzzled by how little of it there was. Sheldon
wasn't supplying much information on how much he
earned or what his assets were. He did list about a
dozen other rental properties, however. "I'd hate to
have him as a landlord," I muttered to myself.

Quickly, I went to the appraisal at the back of the
file and glanced at the house Sheldon was purchasing.
"Cute," I whispered, then took a glance at the three
houses called "comps" that were used to set the value
of this house. My brow furrowed as I looked back to
Sheldon's house. The three up for comparison were
clearly much worse than the one up for sale. "That's
weird," I said.

"What's weird?" Bree asked as she took her seat.

"Look at these comps," I said, turning the folder
toward her. "Tell me they're not lower in value than
the subject property."

Bree's eyes got wide. "You weren't supposed to see
that!" she hissed. She yanked the file out of my hands
with such force that it knocked over the coffee cup
she'd just set down on her desk. Brown liquid went everywhere.

"Yikes!" I squealed as some of the hot coffee
spilled on my dress slacks.

"Shit!" she said, frantically moving things out of the way, then dabbing at the coffee with the Kleenex from her desk.

"Let me get some paper towels," I said and jogged painfully to the kitchen. I was back a minute later and helped to wipe up the mess.

"My pictures!" she said as she saw that a few of the framed photos on her desk had been splashed with coffee.

"I got it," I said and reached over to rescue them. As I was wiping off the third frame, my breath caught and I let out a gasp. "Oh, my God," I said as I stared at the face in the photograph.

"What?" Bree asked urgently. "Is it ruined?"

"No . . ." I said, still gaping at the photo. "It's just . . ."

"What?" she said as she took the photo from my hands to examine it. "This is my mom. She died when I was little. I'd scream if anything happened to this photo."

I nodded dumbly at her. "She's very pretty," I said. It was the same face I'd seen stare out at me from the cold case file Dutch had given to me. "It must have been hard to lose a parent so young." My radar was humming happily. No doubt my crew had set up this little coincidence. They'd done a wonderful job of catching me completely by surprise.

"It was." Bree sighed. "I'd give anything to talk to her just one more time," she added sadly. The crew chimed in with a special request. The minute we finished cleaning up the mess, I excused myself to the restroom and then detoured to the parking garage and the privacy of my car. After locking myself in, I dialed a number and got a very groggy "Hello?" on the line.

"Oh, man!" I said with a slap to my forehead. "Theresa, I am so sorry! I completely forgot the time difference. I'm so sorry I woke you!"

"No worries," my best friend said from California. "The cat's been doing circles on my stomach for the last ten minutes, so I suppose I should get up to feed her anyway."

"Really sorry!" I said again, feeling bad.

"Abs, don't worry about it. Now, what's so important that you have to call me at the crack of dawn?"

"I need a favor," I said. "And it's a doozy, but this one's been set up by some folks on the other side, so I don't really know that we have a choice in the matter . . ."

Later, after I'd arranged things with Theresa, I headed back to Bree's desk. She glanced up as I took my seat. "Man, I was about to check on you. You okay?"

"Huh?" I asked.

"You went to the restroom like a half hour ago," Bree reminded me.

"Oh!" I said with a laugh. "Yeah, too much starch, not enough fiber," I added with a pat to my abdomen.

"I know how that goes," she said, turning back to her computer.

"Listen," I began, trying to think of a way to broach the topic, "I have a thought about something you said earlier, and I'm not sure that you'd be open to the idea, but maybe I could run it past you and you could think about it?"

Bree looked at me curiously. "Of course," she said.

"You see, this isn't my only source of income."

"Uh-huh?"

"I'm also a professional psychic."

"Get out of here!" she said, giving me her full attention. "That is so cool!"

I smiled, grateful that she seemed receptive. "Yes, well, it can be. But what I wanted to approach you about was what you said earlier, about wanting to talk to your mother one last time."

Bree gasped. "You can do that?"

"Uh, no," I said. "But I have a best friend who can, and she's willing to read you today after work if you're up for it."

Bree's eyes widened, but then I saw a little concern there. "How much is a reading?"

"Normally a little over two hundred dollars, but this time it's free."

"Why is it free?" she asked. "I mean, don't get me wrong, that's awesome, but you barely know me."

"Like I said, my best friend is really good at this, and because she's my friend she's willing to do me this favor. And I want to do it because when I saw that picture of your mother, I just knew I needed to help you get some closure."

Bree's eyes welled up with emotion. "You are awesome," she whispered to me as she looked around at the other girls, who were pointedly giving us looks for talking and not working. "Just tell me where to go and I will so be there!"

At lunch I headed over to the title office for the closing on Fern. I had signing rights for both my sister and Dave, so neither of them needed to attend. The closing went smooth and easy, and I was given a big fat check for my trouble as I finally handed over the keys to what had been one nightmare of a real estate investment.

Back at Universal, Bree and I got through the rest

of the day, preparing closing packages and doing a flurry of paperwork. With every large envelope I stuffed I became more and more grateful for the fact that this gig was temporary.

At quarter to five I headed to my office, intent on getting there before Bree did so I could prepare the room. I'd told Theresa that I wanted to assist with the reading, something she was excited about. We'd teamed up for a client once or twice before, and the energy was usually pretty amazing. It was like our abilities intensified when we joined them together, and I knew that if Bree's mom was willing to talk, I might be able to get to the bottom of who murdered her.

Candice was just leaving the office when I came down the hallway. "Hey, there," she said to me with a wave and a wince. "Are you as sore as I am?"

"Probably," I said as I got close. "Any luck finding the Hummer-slash-battering ram?"

"Not yet," she said. "But I'm working on it. You plugging away on your client list?"

"Nope. Something better. I'm working on a case for Dutch and Theresa's helping me out."

"How's she doing in California?"

"Awesome," I said brightly. "I hear one of the cable channels wants to do a documentary on her."

"Good for her. Want to meet me for a drink after you're done?"

"Sorry, I got plans with the little Dutch boy," I said. "Methinks he's needing some attention from his girl-friend."

"Okay then. I'll call you tomorrow," Candice said and she headed out while I went in.

I had the place ready by five, and Bree arrived right on time. I placed her in one of the leather chairs and pulled the phone close—we would use the speaker function for the session. I also had the tape recorder ready to go so that I could record the details. At ten past five, the agreed-upon time, Theresa called in. I made the introductions and we started the session, with Theresa taking the lead.

"I'm getting an older male figure here," Theresa said. "He's showing me the initial R, like Rob or Robert."

Bree squirmed excitedly. "That's my grandfather! His name was Robert."

"Terrific. He's showing me a flag. Was he in the military?"

"Yes, he was. He was a lieutenant in the navy."

"He's also saying that he's got a female with him who has a name that begins with a G, like Gene or Gina."

"I think that's my grandmother," said Bree. "Her name was Virginia, but everyone called her Ginny."

"Perfect," said Theresa.

Just then I had several flashes in my head and I said, "Whose dog has spots all over him?"

Bree looked at me and laughed. "Our dog is named Spot!"

"You're kidding." I laughed. "You actually named your dog Spot?"

Bree nodded. "My four-year-old son wanted to name him, and that's what he chose."

"Now I'm getting another female . . ." Theresa said through the speaker, but then her voice trailed off. I closed my eyes for a moment and concentrated, working to build up the psychic energy and amplify it as much as I could. "Something awful happened to this woman," Theresa continued. "She says she died violently."

Bree didn't seem to respond, so I opened my eyes

and looked at her. She was sitting back in her chair, no longer excited but completely overcome with emotion as tears coursed down her cheeks. "What else are you getting, Theresa?" I asked gently.

"She is also pointing to a flag, but it's not the military. She says she was connected to the government in some way."

Bree nodded, and her mouth opened, but only a small sob came out. "That fits, Theresa," I said into the speakerphone.

"I think her name begins with an S or a C. . . ." There was a pause while Theresa worked at it. "Something like Cindy, or maybe Sandy."

"Cynthia," said Bree, her voice choked with emotion. "Her name was Cynthia."

Theresa went on. "She's very motherly to you," she said. "Is this your mother?"

Bree nodded and stared mutely at the speakerphone. I said, "Yes," so that Theresa could continue.

"She says she is very proud of you and she watches over someone with a T like Thomas or Timothy. He feels little—like your son."

"That's my son," said Bree. "His name is Tom."

I braced myself for the risk that I was about to take, but my reason for bringing this little meeting together was not just to help Bree get some closure. It was also to solve a murder. "Theresa," I said carefully, "is Cynthia willing to tell us any more about the night she died?"

Bree gave me a sharp look, but I ignored her and focused on amping up the wattage on my radar. Immediately the world around me disappeared and I was looking at a brightly lit kitchen with sunflower wallpaper and oak cabinets. At the table sat a man who was tall and extremely handsome, with jet-black hair and piercing hazel eyes. He was unshaven but wearing a suit and a tie pulled loose at the neck. I watched as he slammed his fist on the table, creating a sound so real I felt myself jump.

Across the table sat Cynthia. She appeared calm, but there was an icy coldness to her and a manila folder in front of her. As if her voice was coming from a tunnel, I heard her say, "Keep it down, Ray. My daughter's asleep."

"You think you're so clever," Ray said. "You think you've got it all figured out, don't you?" he said as he stood up, his eyes narrowing with rage. I turned my attention back to Cynthia. Her face instantly changed from confident to wary, and then, so quickly that it was startling, the man grabbed Cynthia by the shoulder and whipped her out of the chair. She had no time to react and I saw real fear in her eyes. In a move that stunned me with its precision and efficiency, he grabbed her by the chin and in one awful yank pulled up and back. There was a snapping noise and Cynthia slumped to the floor.

The man named Ray then grabbed the folder on the table and turned around to face me. My breath caught as our eyes seemed to lock, and I felt my blood go cold. And then I felt a horrible shaking, and the image in front of me vanished as I saw Bree above me tugging on my shoulders and heard Theresa shout, "Abby! Abby, come forward!"

I put my hand up to stop her shaking and took a moment to try and get rid of the weird disorientation I felt. "What happened?" I asked.

"I don't know," said Bree, looking frightened. "You asked about the night my mother died and Theresa said she felt my mom go quiet. And then I looked up at you and you were just staring straight ahead, and you wouldn't answer me when I called your name."

Theresa's voice sounded from the speakerphone. "Abs? How you feeling?"

"I'm good, Theresa," I said, running a shaky hand through my hair. "Just got sucked into the energy is all."

"What'd you get?" Theresa asked.

I glanced at Bree, unsure how much to divulge. "Not a lot," I said vaguely. "I think I saw the inside of your house or something.'

"Did my mother say anything to you?" Bree asked. "Did she tell you anything about who might have murdered her?"

I frowned. "No," I said, which was not quite a lie. Bree's mother hadn't actually *told* me anything—she'd shown me, a technicality that I would work on after I gave the info to Dutch. The last thing I wanted was for the name to mean something to Bree and for her to do something stupid, like confront her mother's killer.

"Well, she's gone," said Theresa. "The minute you went into your little trance her energy closed itself off to me."

"Can't you get it back?" asked Bree. "I mean, that wasn't enough time! I didn't even get a chance to tell her I love her!"

"Hey there," I said, reaching out to place a hand on Bree's arm as tears spilled down her cheeks. "She's just pulled her energy back a little. She's not gone for good. And trust me, she can hear every single word you say. So if you want to tell her you love her, then by all means, say it out loud or in your head. She'll hear it both ways."

Bree was again openly sobbing, and I felt like a real

shit for taking up the last of her mother's energy before she had to sever the connection. Theresa, ever the softy, said, "Bree, I have my appointment book right here. And I have a cancellation at the end of the month. Why don't I slot you in, and we can try again to reach out to your mom after she's had some rest, okay?"

Bree nodded at the speakerphone and said, "That'd be fantastic. Thank you."

"Good. Abby can give you my number, and you call me around this time on the thirtieth, okay?"

"Thanks, T," I said, trying to make a mental note to myself to send Theresa a big fat bouquet of flowers for being such a great friend.

"My pleasure. Now I've got to fly. Bree, you hang in there and we'll talk again in a couple of weeks, okay?"

After Theresa hung up, Bree collected herself with the help of several tissues and a sip of water. "I can't believe how emotional I am," she said.

"Sometimes we don't realize how much we miss someone until we're faced with hearing from them again."

Bree nodded. "I gotta get going," she said as she stood up and slung the strap of her purse over her shoulder. "Thank you so much for doing this, Abby. You and Theresa are amazing. I can't believe you need two jobs! If I had your talent, that's all I'd do."

I smiled but didn't comment on that one. "You drive home safe, okay?"

"I will, and if there's anything I can ever do to repay you, you just ask."

"I'll keep that in mind," I said slyly.

A little later that night there was a knock on my front door. "Come on in, Dutch," I called from the kitchen, where Eggy and I were snacking on some chips and salsa.

"Why are you eating?" he asked when he came in and found me happily munching away.

I slid a chip to Eggy, who crunched it loudly and wagged his tail at the same time. "I had to close on Fern Street this afternoon and I didn't have time to grab lunch."

"What do you mean you didn't have time? You have the whole day at your disposal," he said.

I took a long pull from the Coke I was drinking and tried to think up a quick answer to that. I decided changing the subject and putting Dutch on the defensive was the way to go. "Speaking of all day to get something done, I notice you haven't gotten your haircut yet."

Dutch ran a hand subconsciously through his hair. "I had to cancel my appointment. We were in briefings all day."

"I could cut it for you," I offered.

"You can cut hair?"

"Sure!" I said while I thought, *How hard can it be?*

"Okay. You want to do it now before we go to dinner?"

"Absolutely," I said, feeling giddy with the combination sugar/caffeine/salt high I was currently experiencing. "You wet your head down in the sink and I'll get the scissors."

I raced to the bathroom and dug around in my medicine cabinet for an old pair of haircutting scissors that I kept on hand to use whenever my extra-long locks needed a little trim and I didn't feel like paying fifty bucks for a haircut. I also grabbed a towel and comb, then headed back to the kitchen. Dutch was seated at the kitchen table with a head full of wet hair, looking a little nervous.

I flashed him an enthusiastic smile and wrapped the towel around his neck, tucking it into his collar, then began combing his hair. I was about to open with the big news that I knew the first name and physical description of the man who killed Cynthia Frost when the phone rang. Distracted, I glanced at the caller ID. It was Theresa. "Hey, chick," I said as I answered.

"How you feeling?" she asked me.

I tucked the phone between my ear and my shoulder and continued combing Dutch's hair. "I'm fine. Just got sucked into the ether for a minute is all."

"I'm assuming you saw more in that ether than you let on to Bree," Theresa said.

I picked up the scissors and pulled up a lock of Dutch's hair. "I did indeed," I said as I took a tentative snip. "It was pretty ugly," I added, pulling up another lock.

"I'll bet," Theresa said. "Listen, the other reason for my call is that Cynthia came back to me this afternoon."

"You're kidding," I said as my scissors snipped away.

"Not kidding," Theresa said seriously. "I was giving this guy a reading and in she popped. She basically took center stage and wouldn't leave until I promised her to deliver a message."

"To Bree?"

"No," Theresa said. "To you."

I frowned. "This doesn't sound like I'm going to like what she had to say."

"It's not all bad," Theresa said. "But she was insistent I get this to you. She wants you to watch over Bree, because she could be in real danger."

I felt goose bumps form on my arms. "That's why I didn't tell her what I saw in the ether," I said. "I was afraid she'd do something stupid."

"Yeah, well, you'll need to watch out for her, Abby. Her mother seemed extremely concerned." Just then my doorbell rang.

"Got it, T. Thanks again. I gotta fly." I hung up with Theresa and with a pat on Dutch's head I said, "Hold tight, cowboy. Let me see who's here."

I headed to the door and opened it to find Dave, covered in sawdust and looking frightful. "Wow, when you clean up you really go all out," I said with a smirk.

Dave looked down at himself and began to pat his shirt, which sent clouds of sawdust up in the air. "Sorry about that. I've been working on a new project and it's a little intense."

"You here for your check?" I asked as I turned away from Pigpen.

"Yep," he said. "I just cut your jeweler friend a check and I gotta make sure I have enough in the bank to cover it."

I looked over my shoulder as we crossed into the kitchen. "I'm proud of you, David. You're growing up so fast."

Dave rolled his eyes. "Yeah, well, at least she's been a good wife all these years."

"Just think how good she'll be with a big 'ol rock on her finger," I quipped. "Have a seat at the table and I'll get your check."

Dave stepped carefully over the hair on the floor as he walked around the table to sit across from Dutch. "Getting a haircut, buddy?" he said with a pat on Dutch's shoulder.

"Abby's idea," Dutch replied without much enthusiasm.

I grabbed my purse from the counter and was about to dig around inside of it for the certified bank check I'd had drawn up for Dave when I happened to catch the look he gave Dutch as he sat down.

"What's the matter?" Dutch asked, also catching the expression on Dave's face, which was a mixture of shock and horror.

"Uh . . ." Dave said with wide eyes.

"Oh, God," said Dutch, his hand going up to his hair. "How bad is it?"

Dave stood up abruptly. Looking nervously at me, he said, "You know what? You two are in the middle of this. Why don't I just stop by in the morning before the bank opens and pick up my check then?"

"Abby!" Dutch said as he swiveled around to face me. "Bring me a mirror!"

It was then that I noticed that he looked an awful lot like someone who'd just escaped a close call with a combine. "See ya!" Dave said and he bolted for the front door.

"I can fix it!" I said as Dutch stood up, his face turning a purplish hue.

"Bring . . . me . . . a . . . mirror," he growled. I gulped and shook my head no. "Fine," he said and yanked the towel from his neck as he moved to go around me.

I put two hands on his chest and said, "Wait! I swear I can fix it!"

"I can't believe I *let* you do this to me," he said, his expression a mixture of anger and dread.

"It's not that bad!" I said, then lunged for his waist, desperate to keep him from looking in the mirror.

Dutch dragged me to the bathroom. I didn't let go until he was a foot away from the mirror—and then I ran for it.

Chapter Nine

I hung out in my bedroom until the swearing stopped. Then I heard my front door open and close—okay, maybe it did slam a little. After waiting a few extra seconds, I opened the bedroom door a crack and peeked out. "Dutch?" I said tentatively. "Yo, Dutch!" I called a little louder. Eggy came to the door and sniffed at my feet. "Did he leave?" I asked Eggy, who replied by wagging his tail.

I sighed as I stepped out of the bedroom and picked him up. "I've really done it this time," I said to him. Eggy pumped his tail harder and gave me a slurpy kiss. He agreed.

Just then I heard the front door open again. I tightly gripped Eggy, preparing to bolt back into the bedroom. We both listened as the TV went on. We waited to see what would happen next. Nothing but the sounds of a ball game filled the silence.

Finally, I worked up the nerve to venture out into my living room. I found Dutch sitting on the couch with an FBI baseball cap pulled down low on his head.

Little tufts of hair poked out under the hat and I worked *very* hard not to giggle. "You want some dinner?" I said when he didn't look up as I entered the room.

"I called for Thai food from my cell," he said. "Should be here in twenty minutes." Dutch's tone was low and even, which meant he wasn't just pissed—he was super-pissed.

"Great," I said as I set Eggy down. "How about a beer?" When in doubt about how to proceed with a very pissed-off boyfriend, offer alcohol—*lots* of alcohol.

Dutch gave me one curt nod.

I hurried into the kitchen and pulled out two beers, and then I grabbed a frosted mug from the freezer. Uncapping the beers, I went back to the living room, set a coaster on the table in front of Dutch, and poured his beer into the frosted mug. When he failed to thank me, I went back to the kitchen and put the chips into a decorative bowl, carrying them and the salsa out to him. "Nothing goes better with beer than chips and salsa!" I said brightly.

Dutch grunted and switched the channel to CNN.

I sat down in the leather chair next to the sofa and Eggy jumped into my lap. We all sat in silence watching the television until the doorbell rang. "I got it!" I said, jumping to my feet and hurrying to my purse. "This one's on me," I said to Dutch, who continued to moodily stare out from under his cap at the flickering light of the set.

I paid for the Thai food and took it into the kitchen. There, I put a healthy portion onto a dinner plate and began to walk it out to him, then stopped and swiveled back to the fridge, where I grabbed another beer.

"Here you go," I said as I set the plate and beer down in front of him. I waited several seconds for Dutch to say "thank you," or "you're the best," or "I appreciate it," but I didn't get so much as a grunt.

With a heavy sigh I went back to the kitchen and got my own plate. Taking it back to my chair, I sat down and ate with Dutch in silence. Finally, after an hour, I got up the courage to say, "I solved your case today."

Dutch slid his eyes to me, then moved them back to the TV.

"I know who killed Cynthia Frost."

That was the ticket. Dutch clicked the MUTE button and turned his whole head to look at me. He didn't say anything; he just waited for me to continue.

"I tracked down Cynthia's daughter today," I said, nervous under his steely glare. "And I convinced her to let me try and contact her mother using Theresa. We were able to make a connection and Cynthia replayed her murder for me."

"Go on," Dutch said quietly when I paused.

"I got a really good look at the man who killed her. His first name is Ray and I never heard his last name, but I could work with a sketch artist and give you a good idea what he looked like."

Dutch unclipped the cell at his belt and flipped it open. Punching a few keys, he said, "Hey, Uli, it's Dutch. I know it's late on a Friday, but any chance you're free to come to Royal Oak and do a sketch? My girlfriend is a professional psychic, and she says she has a good description of the guy that murdered Cynthia Frost." There was a pause and Dutch said, "Great. Here's the address . . ."

I cleaned up the dishes while we waited for Uli to

show up. Dutch continued to ignore me in the living room, so I did a little tidying up around the house. After all, I didn't want Uli to think I was a slob.

The doorbell rang about the time I was putting the vacuum away. Dutch got up to answer it. He greeted a beautiful woman of about fifty with wavy brown hair and soft ebony eyes. She wore a gorgeous lavender pashmina over a white silk blouse, skinny jeans, and high heels. Her jewelry was large and chunky, and her hands had slender fingers and prominent veins. She looked every bit the artist and I instantly liked her.

"Welcome," I said as Dutch made the introductions.

"Lovely to meet you," she said in a thick German accent.

I'd noticed that Uli did a double take when she looked at Dutch. After coming in and setting down her bag and sketch pad she turned to him and said, waving to his head, "What has happened to you?"

Dutch's face turned a shade of pink as he replied, "My gal here decided to trim my hair while gabbing on the telephone."

Uli's hand flew to her mouth as she attempted to stifle a giggle. "I see," she said, clearing her throat. "After we are done with the sketch, I shall fix for you."

"Thanks, Uli, but I'd hate to put you out—"

"I shall fix for you," she interrupted firmly. "I was hairstylist back in Germany. I cut many heads. I do good job."

Dutch gave her a tight smile. "Why don't you and Abby get started? There's better lighting in the kitchen."

"Ja," she said and followed him into my kitchen.

She and I sat at the table while Dutch went back

out to smolder in the living room. While she was setting out her pencils and such, I whispered, "Can you really fix his hair?"

"Ja," she said. "I shall fix for him. Next time do not talk while you cut with the scissors."

"Believe me, that's the last time I'll be allowed anywhere near him with so much as a toenail clipper."

Uli started by asking me about the general shape of Ray's face, nose, lips, ears, and eyes. She offered several sketches of just those features so that I could pick the ones that looked similar.

She asked me to sit next to her as she drew so that I could guide her in the basic shapes and shading as she went along. A little into the process I noticed a frown form on her face, and she began to ask me a few questions about Dutch and me, like had I ever been to his office and met any of his coworkers or his boss. I hadn't, and I couldn't figure out why she seemed particularly troubled by that information. "So, you had a vision of this man and that is how you know he is the one who murdered Cynthia?"

I told her all about my session with Bree and Theresa and how I'd been sucked back into the energy of that event. I described what I'd seen, how Cynthia seemed to know her killer, and that his name was Ray and that he had snapped her neck like a twig. Uli's brow furrowed and there seemed to be deep concern in her eyes, but she continued to sketch per my instructions.

Within about an hour she had a really good sketch going, and after two it could have been a black-and-white photo of the guy. "That's him!" I said when I saw the final picture. "Man, Uli, you are really good at this!"

"Ja," she said, but there was a look on her face that was hard and firm. "Dutch," she called over her shoulder, "we are finished."

Dutch came into the kitchen looking like he was in a slightly better mood, but that could have been because of the third beer he'd sucked down. As he glanced at the sketch his face changed too, matching Uli's in its seriousness. He studied the sketch long and hard, then glanced at me and asked, "Are you positive this is the man you saw?"

"Yes," I said, giving him a curious look. "That's the guy who murdered Cynthia."

"What are you going to do?" Uli asked Dutch.

Dutch rubbed his face with his hand. "Damned if I know."

I scowled. I hate being left in the dark. "Can someone please explain to me what the heck is going on?"

Uli ripped off the page from the sketch pad and left it on the kitchen table. "I won't say a word until you decide what to do," she said to Dutch. He nodded and then she grabbed him by the arm and pushed him into the chair she'd been sitting in. Turning to me, she said, "I will need a towel and scissors."

I looked back at Dutch, who just kept staring at the sketch on the table. I threw my hands up in the air and muttered, "The scissors are right over here on the counter. I'll be right back with the towel."

Half an hour later Uli was finished with Dutch. His hair was a little shorter than he usually kept it, but I had to admit, he looked damn good. He'd insisted on holding a mirror while she cut his hair, to track her progress so as not to be caught by surprise, and when she was done he gave her a relieved nod of approval. "You did a great job," he said to her. "Even better than my barber."

Uli smiled as she packed up her pencils and her sketch pad. "If you want me to cut again for you, just ask. I have small salon in my house." She handed him a business card. "But don't tell anyone else. You know how the bureau frowns on these things."

"No worries," he said as he stuffed the card into his wallet. "And thanks again for coming by."

Before leaving she turned to him and placed a hand on his arm. "If you decide to do nothing with the sketch, then I will understand."

Dutch nodded. "Thanks, Uli, but there's no way I can let it go. I just have to figure out who I should trust with this intel." After Uli left, I stood in front of him with my arms crossed and my toe tapping. "What?" he asked.

"Who's the guy in the sketch?"

"It's better if you don't know," he said.

"Would you like me to turn on my radar and try a few guesses?"

Dutch narrowed his eyes at me and finally blew out a sigh. "The man in the sketch is a younger version of the ASAC, Raymond Robillard."

My jaw dropped. "He's your *boss*?"

"Yes," said Dutch. "And the fact that you've never seen him and couldn't have just pulled his face out of thin air gives that sketch a lot of validity in my book."

"What the heck was the FBI's ASAC doing with a CIA operative?" I asked. "I mean, how did they even know each other?"

"Ray is ex-CIA. He switched houses when his boss and the SAC, Dan Winston, came over too. Back in the eighties he was Cynthia's peer."

"Why the hell would he assign you to work a case where he murdered someone?"

Dutch smiled wryly. "Two reasons. One, who would

ever think of the guy ordering an ongoing investigation as having anything to do with it? And two, since I'm the rookie, he could rest assured that a seasoned agent wouldn't be assigned. It gives everyone the impression that Robillard is still trying to solve the case when in fact he's just blowing smoke."

"And if you did find something incriminating, he could redirect you or pull the case from you before it went too far."

"Bingo," Dutch said. "I'm absolutely positive that he never counted on Cynthia making contact with my girlfriend and giving an eyewitness account."

"You are so lucky to have me in your life," I said smugly.

Dutch rubbed his head. "And I'm even luckier to have a sketch artist for a barber." I swatted at him and he laughed, then grew sober again. "This is going to be a hell of a case to prove," he said to me. "Is there anything else that Cynthia said in the vision? Something that might help me nail Robillard?"

"She had something on him," I said as my radar began to hum. "There was a manila folder on the table right before he killed her. He took it after he broke her neck."

Dutch sat down heavily on the couch. He looked tired and troubled. "Any idea what she had on him?"

Before answering him I came over to the couch and sat down too. I focused hard on that folder and what it might contain. A tiny whisper of a thought floated to me. "There's a connection to Las Vegas. And somewhere in Asia—I think it's Thailand."

Dutch reached for the pen and paper on my side table and jotted a few notes. "Anything else?"

I nodded. "Oddly, there's also a connection to San Francisco here too."

"Got it."

Goose bumps formed on my arms. "Dutch," I said quietly.

"Yeah?"

"Be really careful, okay?"

He gave me a smile, then set the pen down and pulled me into his arms. "You got it, doll." And he kissed me long and deep.

The next morning I met Candice at the gym. We were both still very stiff and sore, so most of the paces she put me through involved light weights with lots of stretching in between. I had to admit that as we left the gym I felt a lot better.

"Feel like breakfast?" she asked as we got to our cars.

"I always feel like breakfast," I said to her. "I could go for an omelet at Spago's."

"Cool," she said. "I'll see you there."

Candice pulled out of the parking lot ahead of me and we traveled northbound on Woodward Avenue. As we approached Thirteen Mile I got a prickly sensation along my arms and my radar began to hum a warning. I glanced in the rearview mirror and saw something that made my breath catch. A black Hummer with some front end damage was weaving through traffic, accelerating in our direction. "Shit!" I said as I noticed the scratches and dents to the Hummer's grill.

I grabbed my gym bag and with one hand on the steering wheel, I tried to open the zipper to get my purse and cell phone out. I glanced again in the rearview mirror and saw that the Hummer was gaining ground. "Dammit!" I swore when the zipper on my bag wouldn't easily open. I glanced back up to the road in front of me and jumped on the brakes. I'd nearly rear-ended the car in front of me. My heart was pounding hard in my chest, so I inhaled and exhaled deeply.

Glancing back up, I noticed that the Hummer had disappeared. I almost breathed a sigh of relief when I watched it whiz by me. Candice was several car lengths in front of me and she ducked under a yellow light just as it turned red. The Hummer accelerated and bolted through the intersection. "No!" I shouted as I braked in front of another car at the light. To my horror I noticed that I was blocked in on all sides.

Reaching over to my gym bag, I used both hands to get it open and haul out my purse. With trembling fingers I rummaged around, trying to locate my tiny cell phone. When I glanced back up, I could see Candice's rental car and the Hummer gaining ground on her. I looked back to my purse and finally found the cell. I quickly flipped it open and dialed Candice. Her phone went straight to voice mail. "Candice! Look in your rearview mirror! The Hummer! It's right on your tail!" I yelled as much into the phone as into my windshield.

In front of me the light turned green and cars began to move. I dropped the cell phone in my lap and concentrated on driving. I could see the Hummer and Candice, about half a mile up the road. Spago's was off to the left, and as I wove through traffic, punching the accelerator, I could see Candice's car make the turn, followed by the Hummer. I picked up my cell again and hit redial. Again, Candice's phone went straight to voice mail. She must have turned it off when we were working out.

I tore up the street at increasing speeds, both hands on the wheel as I focused on getting to Spago's. Finally I was at the turn, but I had to wait for four lanes

of oncoming traffic to clear before I could go. I kept
looking into the parking lot, trying to catch a glimpse
of Candice or the Hummer, but Spago's parking lot is
in the rear of the building and I couldn't get a good
view of it.

Just then a break in traffic opened up and I punched
the accelerator hard. Behind me I heard a horn—the
hole had been a wee bit tight—but I didn't look back
as I zoomed into the parking lot and took the sharp
corner with a squeal of my tires. I spotted Candice's
blond head right away. She was over in the corner of
the lot, her car blocked in by the Hummer. A gargantuan man was towering over her, shaking his finger.

I headed straight for them, and for a moment I had
the lovely idea of ramming my Mazda into his Hummer. Granted, my SUV was decidedly smaller, but I
might at least distract him enough for Candice to get
away. Still, as I approached it was clear that Candice
was too close for me to risk it.

The gargantuan must have heard my car coming,
because he turned slightly as I approached. I stamped
on the brakes and skidded to a halt not five feet from
him. He grabbed Candice roughly and jerked her over
to the side with him.

Jumping out of my car, full of adrenaline and bravado, I yelled, "Let her go!"

Gargantuan looked somewhat confused, but then he
said, "Stay outta this!"

It was then that I noticed he had a gun pointed at
Candice's chest. The look on her face pleaded with
me not to push it. I raised my hands into the air and
said, "Don't hurt her!"

"Get back in your car and drive away," said Gargantuan. "Now."

I glanced at Candice. She gave me a curt nod, but

I found it hard to breathe and even more difficult to move. "Let her go," I pleaded.

"I said get outta here!" yelled Gargantuan, pulling the gun away from her and pointing it at me.

Then I saw Candice's hands move in a blur of speed and precision. With a maneuver far too fast for me to track, she had the man's hand twisted back and his gun flying skyward. A second later she was holding the gun and he was on the ground, writhing in agony. His palm was facing up and bent back at an angle that had to be painful.

Next, she kneed him right in the nose, but didn't let go of his palm. He recoiled and she pulled up on the arm as he let out a howl of pain. Pointing the gun at his face with her free hand, she said to me, "You got your cell phone, Abby?"

"Yes," I said, stunned at the quick turn of events.

"Call the cavalry and let's put this slime behind bars for a while."

Two patrol cars and one unmarked car arrived at the scene. Milo, dressed in a gorgeous black suit and a crisp white shirt offset by a metallic pink tie, got out of the unmarked car and walked up to us just as they were putting Gargantuan into the patrol car. "Why is it that when there's trouble in this town, Abby, I always find you in the middle of it?" he asked with a grin.

"Animal magnetism," I deadpanned.

"Miss Fusco," he said to Candice with a nod.

"Mr. Johnson," she said back. "Abby and I were rammed by another car when we were upstate the day before yesterday, and this is the guy who did it."

Milo turned to me. "Does Dutch know you were rammed by another vehicle the other day?"

I pumped my head vigorously. "Of course. I told him we'd been in a car accident."

Milo scratched his chin thoughtfully. "I seem to remember him telling me that you said it was a 'fender bender.'"

"Absolutely," I said, still nodding my head. "Our fender was most definitely bent."

Milo grinned and gave a wheezy little laugh. Turning to Candice, he said, "Is there any way I can get a *straight* answer out of you?"

"Depends on what the question is," she said easily.

"Great," he said, removing a small notebook and a pen from his pocket. "Taking a statement from two wise guys is just how I like to start my mornings."

Candice and I cooperated fully with Milo, except about questions pertaining to the case that we were working. Candice did most of the talking, and when it came to filling Milo in on the details of who we were visiting up in Jackson and why, she wouldn't divulge a word. "That's confidential, detective," she said when he asked.

"Why?" Milo wanted to know.

"Because I don't need the police butting in on a case brought to me by a private citizen. I have my client's confidence and privacy to protect." I shot Candice a grateful look.

Milo scratched his head, then eyed me, thinking perhaps I might crack and give up a name. "Abby?" he said. "Want to elaborate on who you spoke with upstate and why?"

"Can't," I said, doing my best to look apologetic. "Candice has hired me to assist with her investigation, which makes her my boss. And if my boss won't give it up, then I'm sure not going to."

"I see," he said. Behind us we heard a loud rumble and we all turned as a huge tow truck pulled into the lot.

"Did he have any ID on him?" I asked, curious about who this guy was.

"Oh, yeah," Milo said as he tugged on his chin thoughtfully. "He had plenty of ID. We found three different driver's licenses in his wallet, and one in the car. I figure all four are fake, and the fact that he's carrying so many probably means his prints are in the system. We'll take him back to the station, fingerprint him, identify him, then book him on assault with a deadly weapon. And once we tow in the Hummer and collect the forensics to match the damage done to your car, Candice, we'll get him on attempted murder too."

"Awesome," I said happily. I could rest easier knowing the guy who wanted to kill us was off the streets.

"Not so much," said Milo seriously. "This guy stands a chance at posting bond, and he'll probably be out within a day or so. I would recommend that you two call your client to tell them this case is too dangerous and you're dropping out."

Candice flashed him a sardonic smile. "I appreciate that, detective. However, I'd rather not change the name of my agency to Candice Fusco, Chickenshit PI, just yet."

I stifled a giggle. When Milo shot me a look, I pushed out my chin and said, "Yeah. What she said."

"Is that the way it's going to be, Abby?"

His steely glare made me a bit nervous. "You're not going to tell Dutch about this, are you, Milo?"

Milo gave me a sly smile, obviously smelling a weak spot. "Oh, I'm gonna tell him all right, and you *know* how he loves hearing about the antics of his girlfriend from the Royal Oak PD. That's a phone call I can't *wait* to make, Abby."

Damn. "Fine," I said, flipping open my cell phone again. Dialing some numbers, I put the phone to my ear and began speaking after the beep. "Hey, Dutch, it's me. Listen, Milo's got this really funny story to tell you about that fender bender Candice and I were in the other day, and he may feed you a big fat lie about some guy in Spago's parking lot trying to shoot Candice, but I want you to know that Candice handled it, no problemo, and Milo's just a big fat fibber. Any-hoozel, we should have dinner again soon. That Thai food last night was da bomb. Oh, and I love the new haircut—it suits you. Okay, gotta go, love-ya-mean-it, buh-bye."

I stuck my tongue out at Milo as I pocketed the cell phone.

He shook his head at me and gave another wheezy laugh. "You know," he said, "Dutch has handled some serious trouble in all the years he's been in law enforcement, but you, Abby . . . well, you just take the cake."

Once we'd finished with Milo, or he'd finished with us, Candice and I regrouped by her car. "You still feel like an omelet?"

"Now I feel more like a Coney Dog," I said, looking at my watch.

"Let's get it to go," she said, "and we can take it over to your place. I'd rather talk to you in private."

We ordered two dogs, extra chili and extra mustard, along with two orders of chili cheese fries and two large Cokes, then headed back to my house. When we got inside, Eggy jumped off the couch and hurried over to Candice to sniff the bags. "Does he like Coney Dogs?"

"Eggy's not one to discriminate. If I'll eat it, he'll eat it, and the worse it is for you, the more we both like it."

We sat down in the living room and unloaded the bags. There is no better scent than a steamy-hot Coney Dog and chili cheese fries. Spago's has some of the best in town, with a sweet, soft bun and extra-spicy mustard. Candice and I chowed down first, not really saying much other than the occasional "Mmmf, this is good!" Afterward we both reclined on the couch, thankful for elastic waistbands.

"So what'd you want to talk to me about?" I asked lazily.

"Oh, yeah," she said, straightening up. "It's about the guy in Spago's parking lot. I think our friend Bruce might have sent him."

I sat up a little straighter and looked at her. "You do? Why?"

"Because when he boxed me in with his Hummer and pointed the gun at me, he said, 'I got a message from Lutz. He wants you to stay the hell outta his business.' "

I thought about that for a minute. "I'm not buying it," I said.

"Me neither," said Candice. "It just seems too easy."

"So, what do we do?"

"We call Lutz to see if we got the message right."

"Good thinkin'," I said. Candice dialed information on her cell phone and got the number for Jackson prison. She dialed the directory and asked how to go about getting an inmate on the phone. She was told that a message would be sent to the inmate and that he could call her from a prison pay phone, and all she'd have to do was accept the charges when he called. Candice left her number and hung up.

Both of us were feeling the effects of heavy carbs and full stomachs, so I clicked on the telly and we made small talk. "I really like your house," Candice said as she looked around.

"Thanks," I said. "It's coming together, even though I haven't spent a lot of time here."

"Man, if I had a house like this, I'd never leave," she commented. Just then her cell rang and she answered it. I waited while she took the call, which was short and to the point. When she hung up, she looked at me and said, with eyebrows bouncing, "Feel like another road trip?"

"You can't mean back up to Jackson?"

"I can and I do," she said. "Lutz claims that he didn't have anything to do with that gorilla attack today. In fact, he's asking to speak to us. He says he's got some information that he wants to exchange for some help with his hearing, and he insisted we come today."

"I'm in," I said, getting to my feet. "We taking your rental?"

"Nope," Candice said as she also got up. "I've got a better idea."

Half an hour later we were on the road. Candice had returned her rented sedan and traded up for a Hummer, which was a lot more expensive to rent, but she wasn't flinching. "I got the idea from the guy who rammed us," she said as we pulled out of the rental lot. "Fight fire with fire, right?"

"We are up *high*," I said, looking out my window at the pavement passing by below us.

"Yep," Candice said, grinning from ear to ear. She

was having a blast in her big badass car. "I *love* this thing!"

I laughed. "It's like I'm driving with Moses," I said as I looked at all the cars moving to other lanes in front of us and giving us a clear road ahead.

"Now that's what I'm talkin' 'bout," said Candice with a head bob. "Remind me when we get back to the office to shop prices. I think I might take my insurance money and invest in one of these babies."

My right side felt light and airy. "I don't think there's any 'might' about it," I said to her. "And if it's a choice between a dark color or one in white, go with white."

Candice gave me a double take. "I was *just* thinking that I'd like one in white!" she exclaimed.

I gave her a smug smile and tilted the leather seat back. "I'm napping for a bit," I said. "Wake me when we're close."

It felt like I'd been out for only a few minutes when my shoulders began to shake and I heard, "Yo, Abs . . . Come on, sugar, rise and shine."

I snapped my eyes open and sat straight up. "We're here?" I said, blinking rapidly.

"We're here," she replied. "This baby can fly," she added with a caress to the steering wheel.

"Thanks for driving," I said as I unbuckled the seat belt. "I can drive on the way home if you want."

"That's okay," Candice said quickly as she got out of the car. "I'm fine to drive home."

I smiled sideways at her. "Awww, it's true love," I said. "Your gym guy, Simon, is going to be jealous."

She gave me a roll of her eyes and we moseyed up to the lobby. Candice moved ahead to the guard at the desk and displayed her driver's license and PI badge. The guard asked her who she was there to see and she gave Bruce Lutz's name. The guard wrote down the name and turned to me. I followed suit with the driver's license and said I was there to see Lutz as well.

We were told to wait in the seating area while Lutz was contacted and told he had visitors. I yawned as we sat down, but my lazy mood was interrupted with a distinct jingle from the old radar. "We're not going to be able to see him," I said.

"Who? Lutz?" Candice asked.

"Yeah," I said, knowing I was right.

Candice scowled. "But he requested that we come up."

I nodded. "I know, but the radar's telling me he won't see us." There was a heavy feeling to the intuitive thought I was having, and I didn't know what it could mean. I found out about fifteen minutes later when the guard at the desk called us up front and said, "No luck, ladies. Lutz is in the infirmary and isn't taking visitors."

"But he was in the infirmary the last time we came and he saw us," said Candice. "This is really important," she insisted. "He even requested our visit. We've driven two hours to get here."

"You don't get it, lady," said the guard. "Lutz is in a coma. He's being moved to County General as soon as the ambulance gets here."

I gasped. "What happened?"

"Don't know," said the guard. "I just screen the people that come in here and send a request for visitation down to central. Any information I get back is minimal."

Candice turned to me. "Come on," she said. "There's nothing more we can do here."

We got back on the road and headed due east, Candice alone with her thoughts, while I chewed on mine. Finally she said, "Maybe it would help to talk this thing through."

"You mean, what we know and what we don't?"

"Exactly."

"Fine. Let's go with the basics. According to my vision and my trusty inboard lie detector, we know that Lutz did not murder Walter McDaniel."

"As someone who has been on the receiving end of that radar of yours, I'm willing to accept that theory as true."

I beamed at Candice. "Next, we know that Dick Wolfe is one nasty dude, who ordered the hit on Walter because Walter was sticking his nose into Wolfe's business."

Candice cocked her head slightly. "Actually, we don't know that," she said.

"Remember my vision?" I said. "My crew says Wolfe did it."

"No, that's not what I'm talking about. I mean, I'm willing to support you on the theory that Wolfe ordered the hit and may actually have been present for it, but what I'm questioning is the why."

That got me. "You think he killed Walter for another reason?"

"Anything's possible," said Candice.

"Okay, I'll give that one to you."

Candice turned her head and winked at me. "I'll turn you into a PI yet," she said.

I rolled my eyes a little and got back to the checklist. "We know that Lutz was attacked with a knife—we don't know why. We know that he's confessed to a crime he didn't commit and that he's spent the last nine years in jail for it, but we don't know why. We know that some gorilla tried to smash us off a bridge—and we *think* it's because we're looking into Lutz's case, but we don't really know why. And finally, we know that after requesting to see us, Lutz somehow ended up in a coma, and we don't know why that happened or if it has a connection to us."

"You getting the feeling there are a *lot* of unanswered questions here?"

"Think you and me better try and start finding out a few of the why's before we work on any more of the who's or what's."

Candice gave a firm nod of her head. "We need to start from the beginning," she said. "We need to look into Walter's past. Remember I told you he had all those rental properties?"

"Yeah," I said as I thought about it.

"Have you been able to find anything in Universal's computer records?" she asked.

I frowned. "Naw. You need a password, and I haven't been given clearance. . . ." My voice trailed off as I thought of something. "But you know what? I think I know someone who could get me into the system and help me find out exactly what I need to know."

"Who?"

"One of the girls who works as a processor at Universal now owes me a great big favor. I'm thinking I can cash that puppy in."

"Can you trust her?"

My right side felt light. "Yeah," I said, "I think I can. Maybe all we need is to look into a few records and some of these pieces will fall into place."

"Let's hope so," said Candice. " 'Cuz I sure don't like having a gun in my face."

I turned to her. "You know, I gotta tell you, I was really impressed with how you took that bad boy down. Where'd you learn to do that?"

· Candice slid me a grin. "I've got some moves," she said confidently.

"Can you teach me a few?"

She laughed at that. "Sure, but if you decide to practice on that hunky boyfriend of yours, you did not learn them from me. *Capisce?*"

"Yeah, yeah. And thanks for keeping mum today with Milo. He'd have a cow if he knew I was working on freeing Lutz."

"Abby, at this point, Lutz will be lucky to survive."

"You think?"

"Someone wants him dead," she said flatly. "I think that what we need is a new goal, and that goal should be finding out who wants Bruce Lutz out of the way and why."

"I'm with ya," I said. I turned back to the window and watched the scenery flash by. Things looked a lot different from the other day when it had been raining so hard. I settled into the seat and reclined it again.

"You taking another nap?" Candice asked me.

I yawned. "I still get wiped out pretty easily, and this week's been a doozy."

Candice nodded. "Fine, girlfriend. Go ahead. I'll wake you when we get back to your place."

Chapter Ten

Candice shook me a little while later and I snapped my eyes open again and sat up straight. "We're here?" I asked sleepily.

"We're on your street," she said, "but Dutch's car was in the driveway, so I thought it might be best to drive around the block for a minute and let you think up a good story."

I looked at her, a little confused. "Story? Why do I need a story?"

"Remember that snappy voice mail you left him this morning?"

"Oh," I said, slapping my forehead. "You're right. He's definitely going to want an explanation. Maybe we should go hang out at your place?"

Candice gave me a warm smile. "Even I don't want to hang out at my place," she said. "Besides, I have a date with Simon tonight and I need to go home and get ready for it."

"Crap," I said as we turned the corner and my house came back into view. "I guess there's no avoiding it. Okay, drop me off here and I'll get this over with."

Candice stopped, and I jumped out of the car and headed up my driveway. The door opened before I'd made it to the front step. "Hey there," Dutch said.

"Hi," I said brightly. "This is a surprise. I didn't think I'd get to see you again so soon."

"Voice mails that include a rambling message about men with guns usually make me to want to check up on my girl," he said as he held the screen door open for me.

"Awww," I said. I gave him a pat on his incredibly flat stomach. "You're so good to me."

"Have a seat and tell me all about it," he said.

I sniffed the air. "Is that lasagna?"

"It is."

"Oh, man! I love lasagna!"

"Like I said, have a seat and I'll feed you while you tell me all about it."

"Is that your mother's recipe?"

Dutch answered by sweeping me up into his arms, carrying me over to the couch, and depositing me on one of the cushions. "Sit. I'll be right back with food," he said and trotted off to the kitchen.

A moment later he came back with two steaming plates loaded with layers of pasta, mozzarella, and meat sauce. My mouth watered as he set my plate down and took the seat next to me. I dove in and started chowing down in earnest. "Mmmm," I said with a head nod to him.

Dutch dangled his fork above his meal and asked, "I hear that Candice is pretty good in hand-to-hand combat." Quickly, I took another huge bite of food, pointing to my mouth to indicate that it was full and I couldn't comment. Dutch continued, "I also understand that the little fender bender you two were in the other day was more like a demolition derby and that Candice's car had to be hauled up from a ravine."

I swallowed but immediately took another enormous bite. Munching furiously, I shook my head. Dutch eyed my dinner plate. I'd already eaten almost half of my lasagna to his one little bite. "Better slow down there, Edgar. You'll get heartburn."

I smiled as I chewed, trying to think up a diversion, but all I could manage was, "It's so good!" and I dove again into the pasta.

Dutch smiled politely. He knew that eventually I'd run out of dinner and have no choice but to talk to him. "I buzzed your cell phone this afternoon," he said. "It went to voice mail but I was able to track the ring. What were you guys doing up near Jackson today?"

Shit! I thought. I hadn't even heard my phone go off. Then again, I'd been deep in slumber until we'd hit the prison. Stalling, I took another huge bite, noticing that I was down to the last little bit. I'd have to think fast if I was going to come up with something believable. I chewed very slowly, holding up my finger to indicate that I couldn't talk quite yet.

"No problem," Dutch said to me as he took a nice-sized bite. "I've got all night to do nothing but listen to my gal."

Just then the phone rang. I leaped to my feet and shouted, "I got it!" and hurried to the phone in the kitchen.

"Guess where I am," said my sister when I answered.

Automatically my radar flipped to the On position. In my mind's eye I saw a man in a lab coat. "You're at the doctor's?" I said.

Light laughter sounded through the phone. "Damn, you're good," said Cat. "Actually, I'm in the emergency room."

I gripped the phone. "What's happened?"

Cat sighed. "I was running around trying to get the kids ready for a birthday party and I fell down the stairs."

"Ohmigod! Cat, are you okay?"

"I'm fine," she said. "But my foot isn't so hot."

"You hurt your foot?"

"More like broke it."

"Get out of here! Is Tommy there?" I asked, referring to her husband.

"He's at a golf thing. I was actually alone with the kids when it happened, and it took a while to call for help."

"Why?"

"I sent Mathew to call for an ambulance while Michael got me some pillows to prop up my leg. Turns out Mathew kept dialing nine-nine-one into the phone instead of nine-one-one."

I suppressed a giggle. Mathew took after me in so many ways. He also had a radar that rivaled my own. Intuitive types like us tend to struggle with numerical sequences. "Did they eventually send an ambulance?"

Cat sighed. "Yes, and didn't the boys love that experience. I think they're plotting to push me down the stairs so that they can go for another ride."

"Where are they now?"

"Tommy's mom is here with them. I'm waiting to hear the results from the X-ray."

"Are you in pain?"

"I am, but I don't really care."

I smiled. "They've got you on some good drugs, huh?"

Cat giggled. "Yes indeedy!"

"Do you need me to do anything? Can I call anyone for you?"

"No, sweetheart. Tommy is on a flight back home and he should be here in a few hours."

"Okay, but call me if you do need anything."

"I will."

I hung up the phone and headed back into the living room. "Everything all right?"

"Cat's been taken to the emergency room. She fell down the stairs," I said as I sat down.

"Is she all right?"

Suddenly I thought of something, and I managed to get my eyes to water. "Yes," I sniffed. "I think so," and then I buried my head in my hands and shook my shoulders a bit.

Big strong arms encircled me. "Honey," Dutch said as he pulled me to him. I gave a few more shudders and managed to make a sound like a sob. Dutch patted me on the back and whispered, "It'll be okay. She was able to talk to you, right?" I nodded slightly but kept up the shoulder shaking and sobbing sounds. "See? She'll be okay. Plus she's exactly where she needs to be—in the emergency room where doctors can look after her."

I sniffed loudly and gave a hoarse "I know."

Dutch continued to hold me tight and pat my back. "Listen, why don't you go and take a bath while I clean up down here?"

I gave that a few more loud sniffles and said in a whiny voice, "But I thought you wanted to grill me about the case."

Dutch kissed my cheek. "Oh, babe," he said gently, "that can wait until tomorrow. You go upstairs and run your bath. I'll clean up and we can watch a movie to get your mind off your worries. Okay?"

I nodded and wiped my eyes. "Thanks," I said as I got up and trudged down the hall. Once I got into the bathroom and began my bath, I took a serious look in the mirror and held up my hairbrush like a microphone. "I'd like to thank the academy," I said to the mirror, then sighed at my reflection as I thought about how great Dutch had just been. I scowled at my image. "It was necessary," I said. The face staring back didn't look convinced. I stuck my tongue out and turned toward the tub, hoping the guilt would wash off with a few bubbles.

The next morning, just as Dutch was waking up, I pounced. "Hey there," he said with a smirk as my fingers went places they couldn't go in public.

"Morning, sexy," I purred.

"You're frisky this morning," he said, blinking the sleep out of his eyes.

"Mmmhmm . . ." I said and shimmied closer. Twenty minutes later, I was bright-eyed and bushy-tailed, and Mr. Sexy was drifting back to sleep, just like I'd planned it. Carefully I crept out of bed, grabbed jeans and a shirt, and headed to the kitchen. As Eggy snuggled in his doggy bed I quickly made him his fried-egg breakfast, then headed out the door before Dutch could wake up and pester me with questions.

I knew that eventually he'd corner me, and I really hated hiding the truth of what I was up to from him, especially when he'd been so great about comforting my fake meltdown the night before. But the longer I could put him off my trail, the more time I'd have to figure out who really killed Walter McDaniel and why.

Not knowing where else to hide out until Dutch cleared out of my house, I went to my office. As I walked through my door, I was surprised to find Candice at her computer with a big cup of Starbucks coffee by her side.

"Hey," I said, closing the lobby door.

"Hey, Abs," she said, looking up. "You avoiding Dutch?"

I nodded. "You avoiding grandma?"

Candice nodded. "She's driving me crazy. Simon picked me up last night and I introduced him to Nan, and before I know it, she starts talking about what a good wife I'd make and how she thinks we should have lots of babies together."

"That's a mood killer," I said.

Candice groaned. "I've got to move out of that house."

"You thinking of getting a place?"

"Yeah, but I hate the thought of living in an apartment, and until my business takes off, I'm reluctant to sink my savings into a house."

"Maybe you could rent a house," I suggested, feeling my radar begin to hum.

"Yeah, but I'd have to sign a lease, so I'd still be committed for a year."

"I think you'll find a compromise," I said to her. "There's a place out there for you, Candice. You just have to wait for it to materialize."

Candice sighed and leaned back in her chair. "I hope you're right, 'cuz there is only so much of Nana I can take. Anyway, you ready to tag along and do some digging on Walter McDaniel?"

My eyebrows lifted. "Today? But it's Sunday."

"All the better. People tend to be home on a Sunday, so they're easier to find."

"Ah," I said. "Good point. And by that, I mean let's go. The longer I can avoid Dutch, the better."

Candice and I made it out to her car and I had to smile. "Still driving the Hummer, huh?"

"The insurance check for my SUV should be along soon. The moment it gets to me, I'm cashing it in on one of these babies."

"Kind of hard to find a parking space," I said, eyeing the two spaces she was occupying.

"They have midsize ones," Candice said easily. "Still, I really like the bigger model. I'll have to weigh it all out."

We hopped in and headed out as Candice put a small gadget on the dashboard and pushed a button. The screen on the gadget lit up and a little voice said, "Exit the parking structure and turn left onto Washington Avenue."

"That's cool," I said.

"Comes in handy," she said, patting the gadget. "I've already programmed all the addresses. We'll start with Dillon McDaniel."

"Walter's son?" I guessed.

"Yeah. Walter's wife passed away a few years ago. Dillon's in his mid-thirties. He's got a house in Bloomfield Hills, and as far as I can tell, with all the property he inherited, he doesn't do much except collect the rent from his tenants."

As we drove, I noticed a little box next to my feet. "What's this?" I asked.

Candice grinned. "My spy box," she said. "Go ahead. You can open it."

Inside I found all sorts of cool gadgets like a tiny digital recorder, night-vision goggles, and something that looked like a mini bullhorn. "What's this thingy?" I asked, holding it up.

"That little gizmo allows me to listen to people inside a building or their house. I just drive by and I can hear all sorts of stuff."

"Very cool!"

"I stopped by my favorite spy shop on the way home yesterday and picked up a few things. I had to replace the kit I had in my SUV when it crashed."

"The next time you go to that store, can I come?" I asked.

Candice grinned at me. "Yep. You are going to make one great private eye, Abs."

We drove up Woodward to Sixteen Mile and made a left. From there, we traveled a mile or so past my old junior high and made a right onto Cranberry Cross. From here, the sizes of the houses we passed went from large to supersize. I scowled as we moved into the opulent neighborhood. I wasn't comfortable around anyone else's wealth except my sister's, mostly because my sister wasn't a snob about it.

Candice's little navigating gizmo chirped and said, "At the next house turn right into the driveway." Candice did just that and the gizmo said, "Destination complete."

"Wow," said Candice, looking up, and up . . . and up. "Nice digs."

"He's got an affinity for British palaces," I remarked as I took in the castle in front of us.

Dillon's palace had a gray masonry exterior and had been designed to resemble a castle, complete with turrets, parapets, crenellations, round towers, and what looked to be a small moat circling the house and running under the driveway.

Candice and I parked and walked to the front door, where a large brass knocker hung. "Is there a doorbell?" she asked, looking over the arched frame of the doorway.

"I think you need to use the knocker," I said.

Candice sighed and picked up the heavy handle, clanking it three times against the brass knob. "That's obnoxious," she whispered after the last loud clang had sounded.

"At least there's no mistaking that someone's at the door," I said quietly.

We heard footsteps echoing from beyond the door, and after a moment a small window flipped open and a set of brown eyes stared out at us. "Yes?" asked a male voice.

"Mr. McDaniel?" Candice asked.

"This neighborhood is off-limits to solicitors," the voice responded.

"We're not solicitors," Candice said, pulling her PI badge out of her purse and holding it up to the window. "We're here to talk to you about the man who murdered your father."

The small window closed with a small *thwack* and a moment later the door opened and a man about five-ten stood there in a paisley silk robe, a white shirt, and yes, an ascot. "You may come in," he said.

Candice and I glanced at each other, then walked across the threshold. Once we were inside, I had to work hard not to gape. Surrounding us in the circular front hallway were a dozen or so suits of armor, propped up like a small army guarding the castle. Some were holding swords, others battle-axes, and one or two wielded those metal ball things with spikes on the end. "Charming," I heard Candice say as she looked around.

I had to hold my breath to keep from laughing, because the last thing this place had was charm. "Very unique," I said with a convincing nod.

"Thank you," said the man, extending his hand to me. "I'm Dillon," he said warmly.

I smiled and said, "Nice to meet you, Dillon, I'm Abby Cooper."

Dillon shook my hand and swiveled to Candice, who also introduced herself. Once we'd all gotten acquainted, Dillon gave a light wave of his hand and said, "We can talk on the patio. This way, ladies."

He led us through the rather dark interior of his castle, which seemed to be decorated entirely with things from merry old England. We reached the patio and again I tried not to gape. The patio was covered and overlooked the pool. In the center of it was a large round wooden table, and each chair around it was decorated like a throne. Dillon headed to the largest throne chair and pulled it out for himself. Before sitting, he pointed to the other chairs at the table, indicating that Candice and I should take seats.

We sat down and Dillon pulled a pipe and a lighter out of his robe pocket. Putting the pipe in his mouth, he squinted while he lit the tobacco and asked, "So what's this about, exactly?"

Candice discreetly put a hand on my leg under the table, letting me know that she would do all the talking. "We've been hired to gather evidence for Bruce Lutz's parole hearing," she said.

Dillon cut her a quick look as he took a puff on his pipe. "Who hired you?" he asked.

"I apologize, Mr. McDaniel, but that's confidential."

Dillon gave a grunt and pulled the pipe out of his mouth. "In other words, you could be here on behalf of Lutz, or against him."

Candice gave him a winning smile. "I assure you, our intentions are that the man who killed your father serves the maximum sentence allowed." Of course, I knew that she wasn't referring to Lutz, but the way she said it made it sound like we were intent on socking it to Lutz at his parole hearing.

Dillon gave her a nod of approval. "I'd kill Lutz with my bare hands if it were legal," he said, and my lie detector went off.

Candice gave him a look of deep sympathy. "I never met your father," she said, "but everything that I've heard about him suggests he was an amazing man."

Dillon looked down at the tabletop. "He was," he said quietly. "And to be shot like that—execution style—was such an insult to his legacy."

After a moment of silence, Candice said, "We're so sorry for your loss."

Dillon snapped his head up, and the wave of sadness that had flashed across his face was gone. "It's been a long time, but it still feels like yesterday. How exactly can I help you, ladies? The police have all the evidence against Lutz. I'm afraid I'm not the one to tell you anything new about my dad's murder."

Again my lie detector went off, and I worked hard to keep my face from showing any emotion. I looked down at my arms and saw goose bumps popping out on my skin. Something was off here, really, really off. Candice wasn't aware of what I was sensing, and she asked Dillon a few rudimentary questions before going for the gusto when she said, "The one thing that puzzles me, Dillon, is that when I looked into your dad's records, I noticed something peculiar."

"Oh?" Dillon said as he took another puff from his pipe.

"Yes," said Candice, and I could tell she was choosing her next words carefully. "It appeared as if right around the time that your father was murdered, many of the rental properties that were in his name were being financed through Dick Wolfe's mortgage company, the very man he was investigating."

Dillon gave Candice a soft smile. "Ironic, isn't it?" he said.

"Can you elaborate on that?"

Dillon blew out a sigh and pulled a package of tobacco from his pocket. "My best friend and college roommate got his first job with Wolfe's mortgage company. This was before we knew how corrupt the son of a bitch was," he said with a trace of malice. "The rental property idea was actually mine. I'd been in a car accident just out of college and I'd won a tidy settlement. My dad had suggested that I invest the money in something that could produce a return and give me some income, because I couldn't work after the accident. I decided to purchase several rental properties, but I had poor credit and couldn't borrow the money on my own. My dad offered to cosign on the loans, and my old roommate did the paperwork."

"Did your dad realize who your roommate worked for?" Candice asked.

"He had no idea. Artie, my buddy, came over with the application papers, and my father just signed without asking a lot of questions. About a month later, we closed, and that was at the title company, so I don't think my dad ever knew of the connection. It wasn't until I spoke with the two detectives on my dad's case that I learned about Wolfe, and then I quickly refinanced my loans and told my old roommate that he needed to look for a new boss. He no longer works at the mortgage company."

Again my lie detector went off. "You're right. That is ironic," I said somewhat sarcastically into the silence that followed Dillon's speech. This was the first time

I'd spoken, and both Candice and Dillon cut me a look of surprise. I didn't care. I didn't like Dillon. I wasn't sure *why* I didn't like him, but my radar was never wrong about such things, and it was screaming that he was a big fat liar, liar, pants on fire.

Candice stared hard at me, then turned back to Dillon and said, "I assume you didn't stop with just those few properties," she said, giving a nod to the extravagant—and somewhat eccentric—surroundings.

Dillon smiled. "I've got thirty-six rental properties," he said smugly. "And I'm always on the lookout for more."

Candice discreetly looked at her watch and said, "Thank you so much for your time, Mr. McDaniel."

The three of us got up and trooped back through the castle. As we passed into the front hall, my radar buzzed and I turned to an enormous portrait of a kingly-looking man dressed in royal robes and a gold crown. What intrigued me was the likeness the portrait had to Dillon. I squinted at the brass plate under the painting and saw that it read, KING EDWARD VII. I didn't know why my radar had pointed me to it, but there wasn't time for much reflection as we reached the entrance and Dillon shook Candice's hand good-bye. "If you need any additional information, please call on me again."

Candice thanked Dillon and we left. When we got into the Hummer, she turned to me and asked, "So what was it that the old radar was hitting on?"

"It was that obvious, huh?" I said.

"Only to someone who knows you well," she reassured me. "You did pretty good with the poker face until you said that bit about it being ironic."

I sighed. "Couldn't help it. I don't like Dillon. His energy sucks. And he's a liar."

"Which part was he lying about?" she asked curiously as we got back on the road.

"A lot of it. For starters, I think he's hiding something about Lutz. Or the truth about Lutz. When he said that the police had all the evidence against Bruce, my lie detector went haywire."

"What could he know that the police don't?" Candice wondered.

"I'm not sure," I said. "And I don't even know where to begin to find out."

"What we need is more information," said Candice, looking pointedly at me. "And you, my friend, are the key to that."

I was about to reassure her that I was doing my best at the mortgage company; then I thought about Bree, and the danger she might be in now that I knew who'd really killed her mom. "I think I have an idea," I said as we turned back onto Woodward Avenue.

"I'm all ears," she said.

An hour later, we were parked in front of a well-tended little bungalow in the heart of Berkley, a neighboring town to Royal Oak. "This is cute," Candice said as she parked in front of the house.

"Yeah," I said. I got out on my side and headed up the walk. Candice fell into step behind me and I said quietly to her, "This time, let me do all the talking, okay?"

She nodded and I pressed the doorbell, taking a quick glance at the driveway, where two cars were parked. There was some noise that sounded like a television from inside and a woman's voice called out, "Coming!" A moment later the door opened and Bree gave me a look of surprise, then said, "Hey, Abby! What are you doing here?"

"Hi, Bree, sorry to intrude on a Sunday, but can I talk to you for a quick minute?"

Bree gave me a quizzical look as a male voice from behind her asked, "Who is it?"

Bree turned her head to say, "It's a friend of mine from work. I'll be right back." She stepped out onto the porch with us, closing the door behind her. "Let's go across the street to the park," she said, motioning to a nice-sized playground and a group of picnic tables.

We all crossed the street and made our way over to the tables. As we sat, I could see that Bree was looking intently at me, probably thinking I had some message from her mother. I did indeed, but it wasn't one that she would probably welcome. "Thanks for talking with us," I began.

"No problem. How'd you find out where I lived, anyway?" she asked. "Our number and our address are unlisted."

Candice hid a grin and I was quick to say, "I'll tell you about it someday. What I'm here for is to pass on some information, and collect something from you."

"Okay," said Bree, swiveling her head over to Candice, probably wondering who she was.

"By the way, this is my friend Candice. She's also a psychic and she's been working with Theresa and me on your mom's murder."

Candice smiled confidently and extended a hand. "Nice to meet you," she said to Bree. "And may I just say that you have a fabulous aura!" She waved her hand around Bree's head and Bree blushed slightly.

"Wow, you sure know a lot of psychics, Abby," Bree said.

I laughed. "Yeah, well, birds of a feather. So as I

was saying, the message I have to pass on is that I've given the police a physical description of who killed your mother."

Bree looked at me grimly. "She showed you what happened, didn't she?" she said simply.

"Yes," I said, meeting her gaze. "It wasn't more than a few seconds, but it was enough to have a sketch artist draw a portrait."

"Can I see it?" Bree wanted to know.

I felt my left side grow thick and heavy. "I'm sorry, Bree, but your mother feels that would put you in danger. And that's the main reason I wanted to come by today. I want you to be on alert that if your mom's case opens back up, her killer may believe the source of the information was you."

"No one would believe a psychic could hit the mark, huh?" she said bluntly.

"That's right. The good news is that the law enforcement officer I spoke with seemed to think that the sketch was good enough to narrow the list of suspects. He has to go slowly and gather his evidence carefully, and while he's doing that, you need to be wary of strangers at your door, or of being followed and being alone in unfamiliar places."

Bree glanced nervously at her house. "Do you think my family's in danger?"

My left side again felt thick and heavy. "No, my radar says they're going to be okay. It's you who could be at risk, though, so it's important that you take precautions. Okay?"

Bree wrung her hands. "How long do you think it will be before they catch the guy who killed her?" she asked.

I shrugged. "I'm not sure. But as I get updated, I'll pass that along to you."

"Good. Thanks again, Abby, for all of this. I mean, I'll definitely keep my eyes open and be careful, but I'm really grateful to you for connecting me to my mom again, and for shining some light on her murderer."

I grimaced, because the next thing that I had to ask played right into her sense of gratitude. "You're welcome," I said and paused as I thought how to broach the subject. "Now I need a favor from you."

"Sure," she said enthusiastically. "You name it."

"It's big."

"I figured it might be," she said with a laugh.

"I need your log-in and password at Universal."

Bree tilted her head curiously at me. "Why?"

I looked her dead in the eye. "I can't tell you, but it's important."

"Is it illegal?" she asked.

I smiled. "No. I need it to look up something. The information will not be used illegally, I swear." For emphasis I held up my hand, scout's honor style.

Bree hesitated. "They guard those passwords pretty closely, you know," she said to me. "I mean, they've fired processors before for giving out their passwords to loan officers."

Crap. I was putting her in a really sticky position. "Bree, I swear, I need to look up this information one time, and then I will never use that password again. In fact, how about if I tell you that I only need it tomorrow morning, say, before eight a.m. Then you can go to the IT department and tell them that you've forgotten it and need it reset. Okay?"

The look of worry on Bree's face brightened at the suggestion. "That's cool," she said. "I can live with that."

"Great," I said, pulling out a piece of paper and a pen from my purse. "Write it down on this, and after I'm done in the morning I'll flush it down the toilet."

Bree actually laughed as she took the paper and pen. "It's not like it's the code to Fort Knox or anything."

While Bree was writing down her log-in and password, my eye caught a silver sedan making its way slowly down the street. It paused ever so slightly in front of Bree's house, then continued to the end of the block and turned the corner. "Here," she said, pushing the paper in front of me.

I took the paper and folded it several times as the three of us stood up. Thinking about the suspicious behavior of the car I'd just seen, I said, "Remember, if there's a stranger at the door, don't answer and stick close to your husband for a while, okay?"

"You really think I'm in danger, don't you?" she asked earnestly.

"I think that you can go a long way toward making sure you keep safe. I'll talk to that law enforcement officer again, and hopefully he can have someone keep you under surveillance or something."

We headed back across the street and waved good-bye to her as we got into the Hummer. "Want to fill me in on the mother-murder thing?" Candice asked while she buckled her seat belt.

"Can't," I said flatly. "It's official FBI business and Dutch would kill me if I said anything," I added, feeling a bit guilty about keeping something from her.

"Okay," she said, holding up a hand in surrender. "Don't want to know too much and make myself all vulnerable."

"I know what you mean," I said moodily.

We drove in silence back to the office and parked in the garage. "What now?" I asked her, noting that it was still fairly early in the afternoon.

"Now I do some digging," said Candice. "I want to check out Dillon's story and find out what he's lying about."

"Good idea," I said. "While you're doing that I can get back to my mailing list."

We headed up to our suite and as we came down the hallway we saw a tall figure pacing in front of the door. "Uh-oh," I whispered as we approached.

"I'll let you do the talking," Candice whispered back, then said, "Good afternoon, Detective Johnson."

"Candice," Milo said evenly. "Abby," he said without a hint of warmth in my direction.

"Hey there, Milo," I said with a brilliant smile. "What're you doing here on a Sunday?" I asked as I opened the door to the suite.

Milo followed us in and said, "The question is, what are you doing talking to Dillon McDaniel about his dad's murder?"

Crap. "He called you, huh?" I asked, as my mind worked feverishly to come up with a plausible story that didn't involve telling Milo I thought Lutz was innocent.

"Yes, he called me. He wanted me to find out who'd hired you and Candice to dig up dirt on Lutz. Trouble is, you two never asked him a question about Lutz. Instead you drilled him on his personal business. He seems to think you might be trying to cast some doubt on the case, and he's worried that Lutz is the one who hired you."

Milo was giving me the hard stare. Typically, he played good cop to Dutch's bad. But when he was alone, like now, he could really do the bad cop thing well. "Lutz did not hire us," I said, hoping I could leave it at that.

Milo gave me a look of contempt—he wasn't buying it. He turned his attention to Candice. "What do you have to say about this?"

"I have to say that in the brief time we've been looking into the murder of your former partner, the evidence is really beginning to turn us in a new direction," was all she said, but it was enough to incense Milo.

He started breathing hard through his nose, and his jaw clenched and unclenched a few times before he said, "This isn't a case you want to continue to work on, Candice. You're new in town, and at some point you'll need the full cooperation of the police on some other investigation you're working. I'd hate for you to get stonewalled because you've got a reputation for being friendly toward cop killers. And I'd also hate it if, say, a complaint ended up at the private investigators' licensing bureau. You know how they hate to renew licenses to PIs who rack up a lot of complaints."

My mouth fell open and I inhaled sharply. Milo was playing *really* dirty pool here. He was such a straight shooter—this just wasn't like him. "Hold on a second," I said.

"I'm sorry, detective, I must have misunderstood you, because I thought I just heard you threaten to hamper any future investigation I might conduct," said Candice evenly. Her eyes were narrowed and she was standing ramrod straight. I got the feeling she didn't cotton to being pushed around.

"Oh, I didn't threaten so much as promise you that if you proceed to try and muddy the waters at Lutz's parole hearing by introducing some bullshit about a hero's family and his financial affairs, I will make sure you go broke in this town."

"That's enough!" I yelled and stuck my face right into Milo's. He was still glaring at Candice, who was glaring right back. I took him by the shoulders and said, "*Listen* to me!"

Milo blinked and his eyes looked straight into mine. I'd never gotten up in his face like I was doing right now. "Let go of me, Abby," he said quietly, but I could tell he was one breath away from twisting me around and slapping handcuffs on me.

I let go of his shoulders and held up my hands, but I wouldn't back away from him. "Lutz didn't hire Candice," I said. "*I* hired her."

Again Milo blinked several times in rapid succession. "You?" he asked. "Why would you hire her?"

I sighed, trying to figure out where to begin. I decided I might as well start from the beginning. "Remember that night you came over with Lutz's file, and Dutch told you he'd asked me to look at those three cases of his?"

"Yeah?"

"Well, when he left the next morning I went to his study to work on them, but the case I ended up getting the most info on was Walter's. His file got mixed in with the others and my radar wouldn't let it go."

Milo's expression softened. Unlike my boyfriend, Milo had always believed in my intuitive abilities one hundred percent. "And?" he asked after a short silence.

I continued. "The very first impression I had was that Lutz didn't do it."

Milo rolled his eyes. "Abby, he confessed to it. He had details only the killer would know."

"He had details *fed* to him by the killer, Milo!" I insisted. "I swear to you, Lutz did not kill Walter!"

Milo folded his arms. "Then who did?"

"Wolfe was there," I said, trying to remember the images that had flashed into my mind. "And someone else. But I'm not sure who actually pulled the trigger."

"Wolfe has an alibi," Milo said with a sigh. "He was playing poker at a friend's house. Five separate witnesses have all given sworn testimony that he was there all night."

It was my turn to roll my eyes. "And I bet all five of those witnesses work for Wolfe," I said.

Milo looked a little uncomfortable and I knew I'd hit the nail right on the head. "Whatever," he said with a wave of his hand. "We have a guy in jail who has *confessed* to the crime. We have another guy who has five witnesses who place him well away from the scene and no other evidence against him. Someone's going to pay for Walter's death, Abby, and if it's the guy who confessed, then that's okay with me."

I shook my head sadly. "You know," I said after a long moment, "I really used to think you were one of the good guys, Milo. That you were a cop worth looking up to."

Milo's jaw set and his lips formed a thin line. I'd stung him. "Don't even *think* about lecturing me on this, Abby."

"Oh, I'll think about it," I snapped. "What would Walter say if he were here and he knew this was your attitude? Do you think he'd be proud?"

Milo's complexion darkened and his face turned so fierce that I knew I'd gone too far. "You have no idea what you're saying," he said, his voice barely above a whisper. "I'm gonna leave now, and it would be a pretty good idea if we didn't talk to each other for a while." With that, he stormed out of the office and slammed the door behind him.

"Wow," Candice said when he'd gone. "Think we hit a few nerves there."

I had tears in my eyes and I fought hard to pull them back before I answered. "Guilt can blind you to a lot of things," I finally said.

"Do you want to drop the case?"

"No," I said firmly. "I need to solve it now more than ever."

Chapter Eleven

Candice and I hung out at the office until dinnertime, when we decided to grab a bite to eat. I told her that I needed to swing by my place first and take care of Eggy. As we came down my street, I spotted Dutch's car in my driveway. "Abort! Abort!" I said and made a circular motion with my finger.

"You and the boyfriend fighting?" she asked as she pulled into a nearby driveway and turned around.

"No. But five seconds after I walk through that door we will be," I said. "If I know Milo, he's gone straight to Dutch, and Dutch is going to tear me a new one about sticking my nose where he doesn't think it belongs."

"Supportive," Candice said sarcastically.

I sighed. "That's the problem. He usually is, but he helped put Lutz away, so he's not going to let go of all that hard work so easily."

"Men," Candice said with a sigh.

Over dinner she and I discussed strategy. Candice planned to find out what had happened to Lutz and continue checking into Dillon's background. There was only so much she could do on a Sunday, though; she felt she'd have better luck on a weekday.

I was going to get to Universal as early as possible the next morning and use Bree's password to look up anything that might give us a clue in the old loan files around the time of Walter's murder. We planned to regroup at lunch, exchange information, and decide what to do next.

"Whatever you find," said Candice as she pushed her dinner plate away, "I think it's best if tomorrow is your last day at the mortgage company."

I let out a sigh of relief. "I'm so glad you think so," I said. "I hate that place."

Candice smiled. "The nine-to-five grind isn't your thing, huh?"

I shook my head vigorously. "At least it served its purpose. Now I *know* I need to get that mailer done and work on building my business back up. There is no way I ever want to work for corporate America again."

"I feel ya," she said. "I may be poor right now, with slim prospects, but I'd almost rather starve than go back to working for someone else's PI firm."

Candice and I paid, then cruised back to my place. Dutch's car was gone from my driveway, and I felt both relieved and disappointed. "Coast is clear," said Candice as she spun us around again and headed back to the parking garage to pick up my car.

When I got home, there was a note from Dutch on the kitchen table:

> Abby,
>   Call me in the morning. We need to talk. And don't even think about dodging me on this.
> Dutch

I sighed and wadded up the note before pitching it into the waste can. No sense saving that love note. I picked up Eggy, who looked very tired. No doubt my boyfriend had been passing the time by tossing a ball around with him. I carried my pup to bed and watched the telly until I fell asleep. Sometime in the night I woke with a start. My heart was racing and my sheets were soaked with sweat. Eggy had moved to the other side of the bed and he yawned sleepily at me.

I flipped on my light and grabbed a pen and pad of paper from the drawer in my nightstand, then began scribbling furiously about the dream I'd just had.

Sometimes my very best intuitive information comes when I'm asleep, and I've always been one to pay attention to my dreams. The one I'd had tonight was particularly intriguing, albeit a bit on the terrifying side.

From what I remembered, it had started out simply enough. I was a shepherd on a hill overlooking a flock of sheep. The day was sunny and warm, and I remember feeling the heat of the sun on my skin. The sheep were all grazing peacefully, until a cloud moved over the sun and cast a shadow on one section of the herd.

I don't remember what pulled my attention to one group of sheep in particular, but a song had seemed to fill the air around me. A man's voice had been singing, "Who's afraid of the big bad wolf? The big bad wolf? The big bad wolf?" As I looked to a small clump of sheep, there were cries of alarm from them, and they scattered. Right on their tail was a monstrous wolf, with bared fangs and black fur, chasing a sheep along the fence line.

I tried to stand, but I felt weighed down by gravity. When I finally struggled to my feet, my eyes had trouble focusing. It was as if my lids were too heavy and my eyes kept closing. Running was out of the question—I could barely stand, let alone walk, and all around me the frantic bleating of the sheep rang out along the hillside.

Then suddenly the sheep made a sharp turn and one of them headed up the hill toward me with the wolf right on its heels. I struggled to keep focused and with all my might I lifted one leg and was able to take a small step. The sheep bleated and ran as the wolf gained speed and was almost on top of it. I cried out, "Nooooo!" just as a gunshot rang out. The sheep fell over and turned into Walter McDaniel. And it was just then that I got a clear image of the face of the wolf, which had suddenly taken on human characteristics. I had a vague recollection of the face, but what made it click in my head was the crown on the wolf's head. It was King Edward VII.

I could remember being terribly confused by the whole scene and then I felt two sets of hands grab me roughly under the arms and pull me back and away from the scene. "Where are you taking me?" I asked, trying to twist around so that I could see the face of my kidnappers.

"To jail!" said one of the men.

"But why?" I wailed.

"You're guilty of murder," said my captor. "You let that wolf kill your sheep!"

I fought against them, but it was no use. I was dragged into a building, which I instantly recognized as Universal Mortgage. In the next moment, I was thrown into a large cage filled with snakes. I moved to the door of the cage and began pulling on it. That was when Dick Wolfe appeared and laughed as I struggled with the barred door.

"Look out," he said with a chuckle. "Snakes are going to eat you!"

I looked down at my feet and saw dozens of snakes slithering all over my shoes and up my legs. "Let me out!" I screamed.

Dick laughed and was joined by Darren Cox.

"Let me out now!" I demanded as I felt more snakes crawl up to my middle.

Dick and Darren just laughed harder, taking turns pointing at me as they whooped it up and slapped each other on the back.

I felt a snake encircle my neck, and dozens more wound around my legs, and up to my torso. I screamed and pulled on the door to the cage with all my might, and just in time I woke up.

After writing out the dream I got out of bed and wriggled out of my shirt. It felt damp and uncomfortable. Slipping on a fresh one, I crawled back into bed and scooted over a bit to be closer to Eggy. I grabbed the paper I'd written the dream on and read back through it, pausing to circle a few phrases and make a note or two in the margins. When I was done, I felt sleepy again, so I set the pad down and turned out the light. The next sound I heard was my alarm.

I slapped it off and quickly got out of bed. I had to be at Universal right when the doors opened, which Bree had told me was around seven thirty.

I made it with about five minutes to spare and paced in front of the door, glancing at my watch. Seven thirty came and went, as did seven forty. Finally, at seven fifty, a receptionist stepped off the elevator and came up to the locked door. "You're here early," she said to me as she took a key out of her pocket.

"Just want to get a jump on the day," I said with

a big smile, trying to hide my irritation about her being late.

She opened the door and we both entered the lobby. I walked briskly back to the snake pit and sat down at Darren's desk. I flipped his computer on and waited, tapping my foot impatiently while it warmed up. Finally the screen welcomed me and I clicked the icon that would allow me to enter Universal's software system. Punching in Bree's log-in name and password, I smiled as a menu displayed several choices. I ran a quick search using Dillon McDaniel's name, and scowled as I saw that there were a good dozen or so properties listed. "So much for not using Universal to write your mortgage paper," I muttered. Clicking through a few of them, I noticed that most were fairly recent purchases, none older than five years, and none of the applications had his father's name as the co-borrower.

Going back to the search function, I typed in "Walter McDaniel" and waited nervously while the computer processed my request. An error message popped up, saying that the record I was looking for could be found in Version III. I frowned and stared at the computer screen for a minute. Minimizing the window, I scanned the screen for other icons. I found another icon that looked similar to the logo I'd opened, but was a different color. Double-clicking that, I opened it and let out a sigh of relief as the software welcomed me to Universal Mortgage Version III. Again I typed in Bree's log-in and password and waited until the menu screen displayed. Pulling up the search function, I typed in Walter's name, once more. Five loan applications appeared.

My crew gave me a nudge to hurry and my heart

began to race. I glanced up at the clock and saw that it was ten past eight. Processors would be getting their morning coffee and clicking their computers on, and in a few more minutes some of the loan officers would likely arrive. I focused on the screen again and clicked on the first application. Again my crew sent me a warning. "Two seconds," I whispered as I hit the print icon and watched the hourglass spin in the middle of the screen. I got one more buzz from my crew before I logged out of that program, and I hurried to exit the other.

Just as I got up to go over to the printer, I saw the door to the snake pit open and in walked Sheldon Jacob. He paused ever so slightly when he spotted me and glanced at his watch as he sat down. "You're here early," he grunted.

I flashed him my biggest smile. "Just anxious to learn how you guys make so much money!"

Sheldon squinted his beady eyes at me as he unloaded his briefcase. "Most of the women don't last," he said.

"Excuse me?"

"They can't take the heat that we boys bring. You might be better off in processing," he added.

"I see," I said, trying not to bolt to the printer, which, very unfortunately for me, was located right behind Sheldon.

"The last girl we had in here only lasted two weeks," he continued.

"I wouldn't have taken this job if I wasn't up to the challenge," I lied.

Sheldon grunted and looked at me as he sat down, his chair squeaking in protest. "I give you ten days—tops," he said, then flashed me his own winning smile.

I lifted my chin and moseyed over to him. "Believe me," I said as I got close, "I'm not to be underestimated."

"Yeah, okay," he said and snickered in earnest. Then he picked up the phone and started dialing. I had apparently been dismissed.

I moved discreetly over to the printer and carefully picked up the application I'd printed out. Without turning around, I pushed through the door and out into the hallway, then walked swiftly to the ladies' room. Once inside the stall I scanned the application, bemoaning the fact that I hadn't had more time to look through the records. Everything about the application seemed in order. Nothing seemed inflated or falsified. Walter had been the primary borrower and his son, Dillon, had been the co-borrower.

Walter's assets had been considerably more than his son's, with a nice 401(k) balance and healthy sums in his checking and savings. His cars were paid for, he had relatively little debt, and the mortgage on his primary residence was nearly paid off.

Dillon had only his settlement money as an asset, some sixty thousand dollars. He didn't list any other assets. He planned to put ten thousand down on the house he was purchasing. I glanced at his address; according to the application, at the time he'd been living at home with his mom and dad.

Yet something nagged at me, and I wasn't sure what. I scanned back through the application, but couldn't put my finger on what my radar kept insisting was something I needed to take note of. With a sigh I tucked the application into my pocket and went back to the snake pit. I didn't know if I would be put back with Bree again, so I decided just to wait for Darren to come in and tell me what to do. While I was wait-

ing, Darren's phone rang and I glanced at the readout.
It indicated that Andrea LaChance from human resources was calling. Shrugging my shoulders, I picked
up the phone. "Hi, Andrea, Darren isn't in yet," I
said.

"Is this Abigail?" she asked.

"Yes, it is."

"You're the one I wanted to reach anyway. Mr.
Wolfe has requested you in his office this morning at
ten a.m."

My mouth went dry. "Oh?" I said and cursed the
little squeak in my voice.

"Yes. Please be punctual. Mr. Wolfe hates tar-
diness."

"Do you know what this is about?" I asked, but
Andrea had already hung up. I slid the phone back
into the cradle and looked around the room. The
snake pit was filling up, as it was very nearly nine a.m.
No one was paying attention to me, so I discreetly
hooked the strap of my purse over my shoulder and
got up, intending to walk ever so calmly to the door.
I was stopped by a voice behind me. "Leaving
already?"

I turned around and saw Sheldon, looking very
much like a cobra with his beady little eyes and round
head. "Actually, I'm supposed to be training with a
closer this morning. If Darren comes in, will you tell
him I'm down the hall?"

Sheldon didn't answer me; he just swiveled back
around in his squeaky chair and picked up his phone
again. I took that as a positive sign and walked out
the door and into the corridor. I wasted no time heading to the lobby and aiming for the exit to the parking
garage. There was no way I was meeting with Wolfe.
I had no idea what he wanted, but my thinking was

it wasn't anything good, and I'd gotten pretty much all the information I was able to at this point anyway. It was better just to cut my losses and run.

I made my way to the parking garage and was on my way to my car when I saw an extremely pregnant woman walking toward me. She looked very familiar and I knew we'd met before because when our eyes met, her face registered surprise. "I can't believe I'm running into you!" she exclaimed.

"Hey there," I said, smiling back while my brain worked frantically to recall her name. I assumed she must be a client, as I have a lot of them around the area and I'm always getting waved at or said hello to by people I think are total strangers.

"Remember me?" she asked as she drew even with me.

I gave her an apologetic shrug. "I'm sorry. I think you're a client of mine, but I'm terrible with names. Can you remind me?"

Her smile broadened. "I never gave you my name, and I'm not really a client." My face must have registered confusion, because she went on to explain, "We met at Jackson Prison. I was there visiting my brother. I'm Selena," she said and offered me her hand.

"Oh, yeah!" I said, shaking hands. "I remember now. Wow, you're a long way from there. What brings you to this neck of the woods?"

"I live in Hazel Park," she said, pointing south. "And I'm here to close on my loan."

My radar buzzed and I automatically tuned in. "You're heading into Universal?" I asked. After she nodded I said, "Why do I get the feeling you're not happy about signing the mortgage docs?"

"Because of what you said," she explained. "You

told me to be very cautious about signing any legal paperwork, but it's for my brother. I have to do this."

A car came up the ramp and headed in our direction. I was getting jumpy in the parking garage, and didn't want to hang out there a moment longer than I needed to, but Selena looked scared and overwhelmed, and my heart went out to her. "Do you maybe have time for a cup of coffee?" I asked. "I know a place about two blocks over."

Selena looked at her watch. "Maybe a quick one. I gotta be back here by ten."

Each of us drove our car over to the coffee shop, parked, then went inside and took a seat in a booth. After we ordered I said, "Tell me about what's going on with your brother, Selena."

She gave a heavy sigh and rubbed her large belly protectively. "If I tell you he could die," she said.

"Fine," I said as I spooned some sugar into my coffee. "Then let me tell you. There is some connection between the closing on your loan and your brother's well-being. I get the impression you're being forced into it, but it's for the right reasons. It's to keep your brother safe."

Selena's eyes began to water. "He's my brother," she said. "If I don't help him and something happened to him, it would kill my mother. If I do help him, I don't know how I'm going to make the payments."

"Tell me what's really going on, and I promise I'll try and help you," I said.

She took a long moment to answer me, but finally she said, "A few weeks ago, my mother went to visit my brother and he was banged up pretty good. He said that he couldn't talk about what happened, but my mother was so upset when she got home. And then a few days later a letter arrived. There were pictures of my brother. He looked really bad. They must have been taken right after he was beaten up. And there was a letter with the pictures. It said that we had to come up with ten thousand dollars or my brother would end up a lot worse."

"And by a lot worse, I'm assuming they'd kill him?"

Selena nodded and her lip quivered. "I went up to see him the very next day, and he said that there was a man in the jail that had threatened him. He said that he knew my brother's family had money and that he expected payment of ten thousand dollars or Nero was going to be tortured and killed."

"Why didn't your brother just go to the prison authorities?"

Selena looked at me like I was an idiot. "Because he's trying to stay alive, not get killed faster."

"Ah," I said. Prison sounded like a real fun place. "So what did you do?"

"There was a card in the letter that came to the house. The letter instructed me to call the number on the card and I could arrange for payment to keep my brother alive."

My heart began to race. "Whose name was on the card?"

"Sheldon Jacob," she said. "He's a loan officer at Universal. He said he could get me the cash out of my house to save my brother plus a little extra for me. I told him I couldn't make the payments—I'm barely getting by as it is. He said that he could find me a renter for the house and get me into a house that's cheaper, but the place he has in mind for me is a lot closer to Detroit and the neighborhood is bad. There are gangs and drugs and shit I don't want my kids seeing." Selena rubbed her belly in earnest now.

I could tell she'd sacrificed a lot to own her home and try and put her children and her mother in a safe neighborhood. Now she was on the verge of taking a huge step backward, all to save her brother.

At that moment, so many images flooded my mind that I blinked several times in rapid succession and I knew what I had to do. "Selena," I said, reaching across the table to grab her hand, "you can't sign those papers."

"I have to!" she said earnestly. "Otherwise Nero will be killed!"

My brain worked frantically. If Selena hadn't gone to the authorities the last time, then there'd be little chance getting her to go now. "Fine," I said, letting go of her hand. "Sign the papers today and give me two days."

She cocked her head to the side, confused. "What?" she asked.

"In Michigan you have a three-day right to rescind on a refinance. You won't receive a penny until that rescindment period is over. We've got until Wednesday at midnight to get your brother to safety. If I can do that, will you rescind the loan?"

"You mean if you can help Nero, and I say I don't want the loan by Wednesday night, then the loan is no good?"

I smiled. "Exactly. I have friends who I think can help your brother. Just give me two days to do it, okay? Don't say anything to anyone, and especially don't say anything to your brother or your mother."

There was a small glimmer of hope in Selena's eyes as she looked at me. "I'm really sorry," she said at last.

"For what, honey?" I asked her.

"I was such a bitch to you at the prison, and here

you are the only person that's really trying to help me."

I patted her hand reassuringly. "We girls have to stick together," I said and glanced at my watch. "You've got fifteen minutes to get back over to Universal. This is my number," I added. I fished around inside my purse and withdrew my business card. "Call me tomorrow night and I'll give you a status report."

"Thank you," she said and took my card and pulled out one of her own. "My last name is Rivera," she said, pointing to her card. "My brother is Nero Rivera."

"Got it," I said with a wink to her. "Don't worry. We'll straighten this whole thing out."

After Selena left, I pulled out my cell and made two calls. The first was to Candice, and I told her I needed to meet with her right away. "How about we meet up at the office?" she asked. "I'm on my way there now."

"Perfect. See you in five." The next call was to Dutch. I got his voice mail and left him an urgent message to call me as soon as possible, told him that I was headed to my office and that I'd have my cell on all day.

Candice and I met in the lobby of our office building. As we waited for the elevator, we could hear a parade of sirens somewhere out on the streets. "Sounds like a three-alarmer," I said as we got into the elevator.

Candice smiled. "That is one thing I don't miss about downtown Kalamazoo," she said. "There's always a siren in the background."

"Dicey neighborhood?" I asked as I pressed the button for the second floor.

"Can be."

When the elevator dinged and the doors opened we walked down the hallway making small talk. As I pulled out my key to unlock the door, the sirens stopped screeching from outside. "Thank God that's stopped," Candice said. "They must have been responding to something close by."

"Well, we are only a few blocks over from the police station," I informed her as I turned the handle and pushed at the door. It opened about two inches and seemed to bump into something. "What the . . . ?" I said, pressing my hip against the door.

"What's the matter?" Candice asked.

"I don't know. Something seems to be blocking the door," I said. This time I put my shoulder into it.

The door gave way grudgingly and we could hear something sliding on the floor behind it. Candice pushed as well and we finally had enough room to wedge through the opening to see what had fallen against the door. I gave a shriek when I got into my lobby. Candice poked her head in and saw me pointing at the ground. "Ohmigod!" she yelled as she pushed hard on the door and came in behind me.

There on the floor lay Darren Cox. Encircling him was a giant pool of dark red blood. I stumbled backward, breathing heavily, and leaned against the wall. Candice bent down and felt for a pulse. Then she got up and drew her gun. She mouthed, "Stay here" at me and moved into the other rooms.

I stood there and just stared at Darren, unable to move and unable to think as I clutched dizzily at the wall. When Candice joined me again, a shadow appeared in the doorway and Candice stepped in front of me, raising her gun. A second later a police officer pushed his way into the lobby and took one look at Candice's raised gun and Darren's body.

"Drop your weapon!" he shouted, his own gun coming up to point right at her chest.

Candice wasted no time in complying. Her gun fell to the ground with a loud thud and she turned to me as more police officers crowded into the small lobby. "We are *so* dead," she said, right before she was jerked roughly by the arm and whipped around to be pressed up against the wall.

I was grabbed and hauled around too, and I squeezed my eyes shut at the click of handcuffs encircling my wrists. "What's going on?" I yelled.

"You're under arrest," said the officer who had put the cuffs on me.

"We didn't do anything!" I shouted.

"You have the right to remain silent," he said and continued to drone my Miranda rights in a monotone. Out of the corner of my eye I could see two officers leaning over Darren. One of them checked for a pulse and shook his head at the other officer. I felt all the breath go out of me as the edges of my vision began to darken. My knees buckled and I went down to the floor, struggling to breathe, but I couldn't seem to fill my lungs with enough oxygen. Two sets of arms grabbed me under the shoulders and pulled me out of the office just as I blacked out for good.

Several hours later, I was sitting across from Milo at the Royal Oak PD in an interrogation room. "Feeling better?" he asked me as I sipped at some water.

"No," I said hoarsely. "Milo, this is crazy. Candice and I had nothing to do with Darren's murder!"

Milo gave me a hard look. "Abby, you need to understand something here. Today I am not your friend. Today I am a detective assigned to a murder that took place in your office, and I'm the one who has to rely on the evidence, not my friendship with you."

I shook my head, perplexed. How had this happened? "Go easy on her, buddy," I heard a baritone voice say from across the room.

Milo glared at Dutch. "Go *easy* on her? Dutch, I've got a nine-one-one call of shots fired in an office building not three blocks from here. My guys respond in a minute thirty and they find your girlfriend in the room where the shots were fired, a dead guy on the floor, and your girlfriend's partner standing over said dead guy with a gun. You tell me how I can justify *going easy* on her!"

Dutch came over to the small table where Milo and I were sitting and took a chair himself. "Start from the beginning, Abby," he said gently. "Just tell us what you know."

I closed my eyes, but the image of Darren lying in his own blood wouldn't leave my mind's eye. "We didn't kill him," I whispered.

"Then tell us who did," said Milo. "Abby, you guys had to have seen it go down. The timing is just too close."

I shook my head again. "I swear to you, Milo, what I told you earlier is the truth! I called Candice right before I called Dutch and told her to meet me at the office. We met in the lobby and that's when we heard the sirens. We didn't hear any shots. We weren't in the suite when Darren was killed, and I may have my suspicions about who killed him, but I can't be certain at this point."

"Who are you suspicious of?" asked Milo.

I sighed heavily. "Dick Wolfe comes to mind," I said, rubbing my temples.

"It's funny you should mention him," Milo said. "He just left the station after giving a statement to another detective."

My head snapped up. "He what?"

"He heard Darren had been shot, and he called in to say that he and Darren had met early this morning. Darren said he had some suspicions about a new recruit to the company. He said this recruit was turning over loan applications to a competitor, and he meant to confront the recruit about it. Wolfe said that you were the only new recruit to the company and that he had assigned Darren to train you. Wolfe said that he called you to his office to discuss the matter, but you bailed on him. He thinks Darren hunted you down, and the two of you got into an argument and that may be how he died."

"That's ridiculous!" I snapped. *I didn't kill him!*

"What the hell were you doing working for Wolfe?" Dutch demanded. This was clearly the first he'd heard of my undercover stint.

"I was trying to clear Lutz," I said lamely.

Milo gave Dutch a look that said, "Told you so."

I scowled at Milo and continued. "Remember back when you gave me those folders to tune in on?" I asked.

Dutch nodded, and I could tell that he was working really hard not to yell at me. "Yes," he said through clenched teeth.

"Well, by mistake I tuned in on Walter's folder, and the vision I had said that Lutz didn't do it. He was the fall guy. Someone else pulled the trigger."

Dutch's eyebrows raised. "Who?"

"Wolfe, but he wasn't alone. There was another guy who is equally responsible, and I'm working on identifying who that is, but I'm not there yet."

"Is that why Walter's loan application was found in your purse?" asked Milo.

I nodded. "Yes," I said. "That's why I was working

undercover at Universal. Candice suggested that the only way we could get info on Wolfe was to get close to him, so I went to work there, posing as a new loan officer."

"So you discovered that Walter's son had put some loans through Universal," said Milo. "But he didn't know about the connection to Wolfe until after Walter died, so why did you go back to work this morning?"

"Because it's bigger than Walter's murder!" I shouted. "There's something much bigger going on, Milo! And people are suffering and losing their homes and getting beat up and *dying*!" I was breathing hard, getting worked up, and Dutch put a calming hand on my arm.

"Hey," he said. "Slow down, Edgar. Tell us what you know."

So I did. I told them about Darren's scam with the county clerk, about the poor Schalubes, about a loan officer who handed lists over to another crooked loan officer named Sheldon Jacob, and about Selena and her brother and how everything seemed to tie back to Universal.

Both Dutch and Milo took notes and eyed each other occasionally. When I was finished Dutch said, "Okay. Let me check a few of these things out. Milo, put a rush on the forensics on Cox's shooting. I'll call you in a couple of hours."

With that he got up and walked out. I looked at Milo expectantly. "Can I go?" I asked.

Milo shook his head. "No," he said.

"Why not?" I demanded. "I've told you everything I know!"

"And yet we still have a dead guy in your office and you standing over the body."

"*I didn't kill him!*" I shouted again, on the verge of a complete meltdown.

"So let me prove it," he said bluntly. "Until then, you and Candice are going to sit where we can keep an eye on you. There's a nice little five-by-ten room downstairs. You might not like all the bars, but at least the food isn't bad."

"I want a phone call," I said. "I'm calling my sister to bail me out."

"Not a problem," said Milo as he stood up. "Your bail hearing is set for tomorrow afternoon. You can waste your call now, or after bail has been set."

I was escorted down the stairs to be fingerprinted and photographed. I was then shown into a cell where Candice was already lying on a bunk with her hands under her head. "Afternoon, roomie," she said when she saw me.

"This sucks," I said moodily as I was pushed through the opening and the cell door closed with a loud clang behind me.

"Don't worry about it," she said, sitting up. "We didn't kill Darren. From the way the blood was starting to cake around his body and the rigor that looked like it was setting in, I'd say he'd been dead a while before we got there. Plus, I have an alibi. I was at the gym until just before you called. And I'm assuming you were someplace public as well?"

I nodded. "I have a receipt for coffee in my purse," I said. "And a witness I had coffee with."

"We're good," said Candice, lying back down on the bunk. "They'll arraign us tomorrow, we'll post bond, and my attorney will get us off."

I sighed and headed over to the opposite bunk. "I can't believe they killed him," I said softly.

"Just be grateful it wasn't us," said Candice.

"But why?" I asked. "What did Darren have to do with this whole thing? I mean, I'm assuming that

Wolfe is the one who pulled the trigger, and that he figured out I was working with you on trying to clear Lutz, but what does that have to do with Darren?"

Candice shrugged her shoulders. "Don't know, Abs. He could have just been in the wrong place at the wrong time."

I frowned. "So what do we do now?"

"We wait," said Candice.

"For what?"

"For something else to happen," she said ominously. But as it turned out we didn't have to wait very long at all.

Around seven Dutch came to the cell, his look grave. "I need to speak with you," he said to me through the bars.

"Great. Let me get my coat and we can go for pizza," I snapped from the bunk. By now, my own mood had darkened.

Dutch waved at someone off to his right and a police officer came and unlocked the door. I got up and walked over, praying that he was really taking me for pizza. "We can use one of the rooms upstairs," he said and I followed him up to the room we'd sat in before.

"So what's up?" I asked wearily as I sat down.

"Bree's missing," he said, getting right to the point.

I sat up in my chair and looked at him in horror. "What do you mean, Bree's missing?"

"I made contact with her yesterday evening," he said. "I understand you also had a little chat with her?"

I nodded. "I wanted to make sure she was on the lookout for anyone suspicious. I didn't want her mother's killer to think Bree was the one who tipped you off."

"You beat me to the punch," he said, and I could tell he was a little miffed.

"Sorry," I said and looked at the table.

"Anyway, I told both her and her husband to be cautious, and to call me about anything that felt weird or strange or scary. I got a call from the husband an hour ago. Bree was due to pick up her kid from day care. When she didn't show, they called the husband. He said he's called her at work and on her cell, but she doesn't answer. He said he called a friend of hers who also works with her, and she said that Bree went to lunch today and never came back."

"Oh, God," I said. I felt my insides go cold. "You don't think . . . ." I couldn't finish the thought. All I could think about was Bree's little boy and how much she adored him.

"I don't know, Abby," Dutch said. "I mean, I've been very careful, very discreet about doing some background checks on Robillard. But the guy's been very good about covering his tracks."

"You're sure she's really missing?" I asked, even though I knew the answer. "I mean, maybe she went to a friend's house, or a relative's? Maybe she forgot that it was her turn to pick up her son?"

Dutch shook his head. "Her husband has already called everyone he can think of. And she didn't forget. Her husband also told me that she called him in the morning to say that their son had a doctor's appointment and she was going to leave work a little early to make it to the doctor on time."

"Damn it," I said.

Dutch pulled out a picture from his coat pocket and gave it to me. It was of Bree and her son. "I asked her husband for a photo," he said and waited for me to say something as I took a tentative look.

I breathed a sigh of relief. "She's alive," I said,

seeing the somewhat three-dimensional image of Bree staring back at me. If she were dead, her image would've appeared flatter and slightly more transparent.

Dutch sat back in his chair and ran a hand through his short hair. "Can you tune in on a location or a clue as to where Robillard might have taken her?"

"You're sure he knows someone is pointing to him as the murderer?" I asked.

"The man's gotten away with it for twenty years, Abs. If anyone would be watching the investigation closely, it would be him. And . . ." he hesitated.

"And?"

Dutch gave me a guilty look. "And, before I went to see Bree and her husband, I went to Robillard's boss, the SAC, with my suspicions."

My jaw dropped. "Didn't you say that Robillard's boss was also ex-CIA?"

Dutch glowered at me. "I know it was risky," he snapped. "But I had to start somewhere. And I needed clearance to do the digging. I mean, I had to have access to Robillard's old bank records and his old itineraries. His boss was the only guy that had worked with Robillard long enough to give some insight and give me clearance."

"But you didn't tell him where you got that it was Robillard who killed Cynthia, did you?" I asked him nervously.

"No," Dutch said and hung his head. "He would never have taken me seriously if I'd mentioned I got the ID from a psychic."

The look on Dutch's face was really guilty, and I knew there was a little more to the story. "So how did you explain where the information came from?"

"I pointed to Bree. I said she had been meeting with a hypnotherapist and it had triggered a memory of who was in the house that night."

"Oh, my God," I whispered.

Dutch got up and began pacing the floor. "I know, I know!" he said, his fists clenched by his sides. "I blew it!"

I got up and went over to him, putting my hands on his chest to stop him from pacing. "This isn't your fault, Dutch," I said.

"It is absolutely my fault, Abby," he said and his face registered so much emotion that it broke my heart.

I smiled sadly at him. "You did it to protect me," I said. He gave me a funny look, so I elaborated. "You know Robillard is dangerous, and I think you pointed him away from me subconsciously to make sure I wasn't in anyone's line of fire."

"I'm an ass," he said. "I put an innocent woman in danger when I knew better. I should have just worked quietly behind the scenes for a while and assessed the situation differently."

"So now what?" I asked him. I wanted him to focus on the solution, not placing blame for the situation.

"We need to find her," he said, "and quick."

I went back to the table and sat down. I then closed my eyes and focused all of my concentration on Bree, but it was no good. All I kept seeing was my own jail cell. Finally I opened my eyes and gave an apologetic shrug of my shoulders to Dutch. "Can you get me out of here?" I asked him. "I can't focus in here."

Dutch gave me a sad look. "Sweetheart, there's nothing I can do on that front, and you know it. But Milo's working the guys in forensics overtime to clear you two. With any luck he'll be able to drop the charges before your arraignment."

"Fine," I said, feeling so weary I could barely think straight. Still, I closed my eyes again and tried my damnedest to get a bead on Bree. Nothing more came to me, so with a sigh I said, "Dutch, the radar's not working tonight. I'll need to wait until I get some rest. Come back after the arraignment and I'll try again. Okay?"

Dutch nodded solemnly. "I understand. I'll keep working on it tonight, and I'll be here in the morning for the arraignment."

Dutch walked me back downstairs and turned me over to the officer who had retrieved me earlier. Before leaving me, he gave me a tremendous hug and whispered in my ear, "Be good, okay? And don't worry, we'll figure all this out."

I hated letting go of him, but when the officer cleared his throat, Dutch stepped back and with a final squeeze of my hand he was gone. I trudged back to my cell and saw that Candice had already dozed off. The door clanged behind me and I looked at her to see if she'd woken up, but the noise only made her roll over and face the wall.

With an exhausted whimper I went over to my bunk and lay down, waiting for sleep to take me away. Still, tired as I was, it was late into the night before I closed my eyes.

Chapter Twelve

As it turned out, the charges against Candice and me were dropped by seven a.m. and there was no need for an arraignment hearing. The forensic results, along with the coroner's report—which Milo had also rushed through—showed that Candice's gun had not been the one that killed Darren and that he had been dead for no less than ninety minutes before either one of us showed up. That gave us both solid alibis, as I'd been at Universal until nine and Candice had been at the gym.

Further, the 911 call that came in reporting shots fired was traced to a disposable cell phone found in a trash can right in front of where Candice and I had parked our cars. Someone had to have watched us park and go into the building before making the call. Unfortunately, there were no prints on the phone, but it didn't matter. Milo knew we had been set up and so did the DA.

Dutch picked us up and drove us over to get our cars, then split to work on finding Bree. I promised him that after a shower and a little breakfast, I would do my best to tune in on any clue about her whereabouts. I also invited Candice over to my place, which she accepted gratefully. "There's no way I want to explain this to Nana," she said, holding up her fingers and showing me the ink marks from having her fingerprints taken.

"Cool. I have plenty of hot water and I can whip us up some breakfast."

While Candice was taking her shower, Eggy hovered close to my leg and I cooked up some scrambled eggs. My mind kept going back to Bree. My crew gave a tug on my energy and I turned my head to look at my purse, hanging on its hook by the door. I turned off the burner and grabbed the purse, knowing there was some kind of clue inside. I dug around and came up with Selena's card. That didn't fit with anything logical, but my intuition wouldn't let go of it.

At that point Candice came into the kitchen. "Mmmm!" she said happily. "Those eggs smell great, and I am famished!"

It was then that I got another clue from my crew. With a gasp, I rushed to the kitchen table and dumped out the entire contents of my purse.

"What's going on?" Candice asked, coming over to the table to see what was wrong.

"Ohmigod," I said breathlessly as I found the paper I was looking for. "It was right under my nose this whole time."

"What was?" she asked, hovering over my shoulder.

I didn't answer her right away. Instead I scanned the loan application's front page, then turned to the back page, then yelled, "Holy shit!"

"What?" Candice asked gripping my shoulder. "Tell me what's going on!"

I grabbed her hand as much for support as for my sense of urgency. "Look at the name on the bottom of this loan application!" I said and shoved the paper at her.

"Dillon McDaniel," she said.

"No!" I practically shouted. "Here!" I said, pointing to the small print by the loan officer's signature. "Sound familiar?"

Candice squinted at the page and sucked in a breath. "No friggin' *way*!"

"Way!" I said, scooping up the contents of my purse. "We have to go there!"

"Wait! What?" she asked as I hurried around the kitchen, dumping eggs into Eggy's doggy dish, then grabbing my sneakers.

"Candice, get your things. Bring your laptop and your spy kit. We can't waste another second. It already might be too late!"

"Abby, why do we have to rush—"

"Bree's there!" I shouted, interrupting her. "And I promised Selena! There's no time to talk about it, Candice! My radar says we've got to go. *Now!*"

"Abby," she said calmly as I shoved my feet into my sneakers. "Shouldn't we just turn this over to your boyfriend?"

"Yes," I said, grabbing her hand and her purse and shuffling us to the door. "On the way there, we will definitely call in the cavalry. *Now move!*"

I called Dutch as soon as we got in the car, but I got his voice mail. I left him an urgent and lengthy message and told him that we were already on our way. I hoped that it was enough for him to send a legion of FBI agents after us. I also left my cell phone on so that if he needed to track my whereabouts he could.

What I didn't know was that at the time I left him that voice mail, he was in the SAC's office getting his butt chewed out but good.

"So what's the plan?" Candice asked me as she sped through traffic on the way to the highway.

"I have no idea," I said. "I just know that Bree's in serious trouble, that it's all my fault, and that if we don't hurry, both she and Lutz could definitely be goners."

Candice drove like a madwoman and I held on tight and prayed a lot. She's a good driver, but she'd be better on the actual NASCAR circuit, where speeding and swerving in and out of traffic is less of a hazard. When we were almost to our destination I knew I had turned a lovely shade of green, but there was no way I was going to attempt to slow her down.

What worried me was the lack of sirens and the fact that Dutch hadn't called me back. I tried him again, but his line went straight to voice mail. I tried the central line to the Bureau and was told that he was in a meeting and could not be disturbed. I begged the receptionist to sneak a message to him if at all possible, telling him that his girlfriend really needed to talk to him and that it was a true emergency. She promised to try, but the moment she heard the word "girlfriend," her tone changed and I knew she wasn't going to interrupt his meeting.

"What's going on?" Candice asked me as I growled and threw my cell into my purse.

"I can't get him," I said.

"You can't *get* him?" she said. "Abby, how the hell do you expect to pull this off without the FBI?"

"I'm not sure," I admitted. "But when we get in there, just follow my lead."

Candice swiveled her head my way and gave me an

exasperated look. "*Follow your lead?* Do you understand what you are having us walk into?"

"I'm aware!" I snapped. "Just give me a second to think." I closed my eyes and called out frantically to my crew, who'd sent me on this wild-goose chase in the first place. When they gave me the answer, clear as day, I just smiled, then whipped my phone back out and began dialing.

Two hours later, as I was nervously pacing in the lobby and Candice was looking for all the world like she'd rather be anywhere but there, the guard at the desk said, "The warden will see you now."

Candice got up and I asked her for the tenth time, "What time is it?" I'd left my cell phone with its inboard clock in the Hummer, as Candice had pointed out that the GPS locator might work better from outside the prison walls.

"Ten minutes later than the last time you asked me," she said as we crossed to the guard.

"We're going to be cutting this close," I whispered.

"Don't I know it," she replied nervously.

We followed the guard through the labyrinth of metal and barred doors, down long corridors, and up the flight of stairs to the double doors that led into the warden's office. We were greeted by the matronly Evelyn again and told to have a seat. We waited another ten minutes and my foot began to tap anxiously. "No time for small talk," I mumbled to Candice. "I'll have to get right to the point in there."

Candice also glanced at the clock, her mouth set in a grim line. "If we don't get to see him soon, you can forget about talking and focus on running."

Finally the phone on Evelyn's desk rang and after setting it back down she showed us into the warden's office.

"Thank you, Evelyn," the warden said to her as we entered. "Could you please run an errand or two for me?" he asked before she left.

She looked surprised at his request, but recovered and said, "Of course, sir."

"Wonderful. Here is a list," he said, handing her a piece of paper. "After you complete it, you may take the rest of the afternoon off."

When the doors had closed behind Evelyn, the warden sat down behind his desk and looked at us thoughtfully. "Ladies," he said warmly, "I assume you're here to find out what happened to Mr. Lutz?"

I opened my mouth to say "No," but instead nodded as my right side felt light and airy.

The warden shook his head. "It's really very sad," he said. "We see this type of behavior all the time, unfortunately. An inmate gets very close to parole and he begins acting out violently. Psychologists believe this is due to inmates' subconscious belief that they truly belong in prison and against their better judgment they ensure that's exactly where they'll remain."

"Are you saying Lutz got into some kind of fight and was hurt again?" I asked.

"Exactly. He began an argument with another inmate and before my staff could get to him, he was beaten to within an inch of his life. When he recovers, and it looks like he will, I'll have to report the incident, as several of my staff clearly saw Mr. Lutz provoke the fight. It will have a very negative effect on his parole hearing, I'm afraid."

Candice kicked me and motioned discreetly to the clock above the warden's head. I gave an imperceptible nod and got on with it. "That's too bad, but what we're really here to discuss, Warden Sinclair, is how someone goes from being a loan officer at Universal

Mortgage to being the warden of a maximum-security prison. Quite a career change, wouldn't you say?"

To his credit, the warden didn't look surprised. Instead he gave me a smile—of the crocodile variety. "I had no doubt you two would eventually make the connection," he said smoothly.

"Oh, we've made that and more," I replied. "We know that you and Dick Wolfe are quite chummy. We know all about your early days in his organization, and how you and Dillon McDaniel were college roomies and best buddies. We know that with your degree in criminal justice and the fact that your father was also the warden here, that you were tailor-made to rise through the ranks here in Jackson and take your scheme to a level no one anticipated."

Warden Sinclair looked bored, staring at me with droopy eyelids. He lazily waved his hand and said, "Go on, finish it."

"First I'd have to start it," I snapped, my adrenaline kicking in. "Let me see if I've got this story straight. You find out that Dillon's received a large settlement after his car accident and you convince him to sink it into some rental properties. His credit is for shit, but that's no problem. His dad's credit is fine and he's willing to sign on as co-borrower.

"Next you tell Dillon about this wonderful insurance, called private mortgage insurance, that for very low monthly premiums, ensures that should either the borrower or the co-borrower die, the loan would be paid in full."

The warden chuckled. "Stroke of genius talking him into that, wouldn't you say?"

My hands clenched into fists, but I went on coolly. "And you had that little lightbulb because when big bad Dick Wolfe came to you and said he had a problem, that he was being investigated by a detective who had a personal connection to you, he asked you for help and information. He asked you for a time and place when this cop would be vulnerable."

Sinclair snickered evilly. "And Dillon was only too willing to cough up that info. 'My dad's going on a stakeout!'" he mimicked in a high, squeaky voice that turned my stomach.

"But Dick wanted you to show your loyalty, didn't he, Warden Sinclair? He wanted you to pull that trigger."

"We do what we must," the warden said with a sigh. "It was too easy, really. He was sitting there in his unmarked car, staring down the street at Wolfe's girlfriend's house as Dick pulled into the driveway and I drove up and parked right next to him. He got out of his car to come over and warn me that it was dangerous to be there. I told him he didn't know the half of it!" Sinclair smiled like he was recalling Christmas morning. "As I said, it was really too easy. He went down without even flinching."

I wanted badly to leap across the desk and punch him into next week. Instead, I kept going. "So, after you shoot McDaniel, Dick realizes you're too much of a liability, but you've been loyal and he sees the opportunity your degree and your connections can offer him. He has Lutz take the fall for McDaniel's murder and while Lutz is here, he's to continue working as Wolfe's muscle, with the promise of riches once he gets out of prison.

"Through a bondsman or two, Wolfe identifies people willing to put up their homes as collateral on the bond. When their family member ends up in prison, namely here, Lutz gives them a beating they won't soon forget. Word gets back to the family member that they need to supply some dough—fast—and lo and behold, Universal makes it possible by giving them high-interest loans with ridiculous closing costs that they can't possibly afford, turning the cash they get out of the refinance over to you."

The warden beamed at me. "Very good—Ms. Cooper, is it? Now finish it."

"When the family begins to default on the mortgage, Universal suggests they rent one of the other properties in the cache, thus keeping Dillon quiet, as he's got renters for life and a steady stream of properties for sale while these families default on their loans and are foreclosed upon. Dillon gets a discount on the appraised value and buys the houses for cheap. Everyone's hands get greased, everybody's happy except one person, and that's Lutz."

"He was doing so well up until it came time for his parole hearing."

"He wanted out," I said flatly. "He wanted to get his parole and get out of the business, but his problem was that he was too good at roughing up the targets and you guys didn't have anyone else in place to do his dirty work. So you gave him a taste of his own medicine. You gave him a good beating, and when it was clear that he meant to come clean to us, you beat him into a coma."

"The man refuses to die," Sinclair said as he looked at his nails.

"And then when Wolfe discovered that Bree had been in your old loan applications, he had her brought here."

"Did you know there are older sections of this prison that are no longer usable? Many of the cells in the basement area, for example. They were used for solitary confinement, but the state has deemed them too unsanitary for use. These old buildings are fascinating, really. No one ever goes down there, and you can scream for days with no one to hear your cries for help," said the warden. "It is a gloomy place without much light, but I'm sure Bree will be delighted to see you two," he added with a big, toothy grin.

"I'm sure she will be," I said. "And I'm sure she'll feel a whole lot better once we get her the hell out of here."

The warden laughed like I'd said something really funny. "And just how do you suppose *that* is going to happen? You're in the middle of a maximum-security prison and completely at my mercy, ladies."

I glanced at the clock again. I had only seconds. "Do you believe in magic, Warden?" I asked, as out of the corner of my eye I caught Candice reaching up to her lapel to pinch the fabric.

"Magic?" he asked me, still looking amused.

"Yes," I said. "You see, I'm a magician, and with one snap of my fingers I can make the impossible occur." And with that I held up my fingers so that he could see, counted down from three, and gave a loud "snap!"

The room was silent for five whole seconds. The warden gave me a look that said I was off my nutty, and began, "That was *some* magic trick, but I'm afraid I don't have time—" when all hell broke loose. Alarms went off inside his office and his phone lit up with incoming calls as shouting rang out from the grounds outside.

The warden jumped up from behind his desk and ran to the window, and just as he turned his back to us, I grabbed Candice's hand and boogied to the door.

We were out in a flash and bolting down the stairs when a shot rang out behind us. "Shit!" I said as I ducked low.

"This way!" she said and pulled me down a corridor.

"How are we going to get through the gates?" I asked as we ran headlong down the corridor toward the first set of security gates.

"Leave it to me!" she said.

The guard was already wearing a look of panic as he saw us running toward him. The alarms were ringing so loud that it was hard to think, let alone speak. Candice pounded on the door as the guard began to raise his walkie-talkie to his ear. She screamed, "Fire! There's fire up in the warden's office!" The guard's eyes became huge and he hit the buzzer to let us through. When we cleared the other side, she worked herself into hysterics and said, "The warden! He's trapped in the fire! You've got to rescue him! He'll *die,* man!"

"Get down that hall and take a left!" he shouted to us as he hit a button on his console, then reached for his phone and punched in three digits. "It will lead you to an emergency exit and I've just unlocked that door!"

With that, the guard bolted through the door and ran down the hallway toward the warden's office. The moment he was a yard or two down the corridor, Candice pulled her purse off her shoulder and ran the straps through the loop in the door handle, knotting them so that the door could be opened only about six inches.

We took off running as hard and fast as we could and just as we'd covered about a hundred yards we heard, "Halt!" behind us. I looked back and saw the guard and the warden struggling to open the door.

"Go!" Candice commanded, pulling at my sweatshirt and forcing me to run faster. I could see the emergency exit fifty yards ahead. I dug in hard and put on some speed as I matched her stride for stride. We were closing the distance when another shot rang out behind us and a window splintered off to my right. I ducked low but kept going. We were twenty yards away, then ten, then five, and that's when the door opened and a huge, beefy guard stepped through, blocking our escape.

I put on the brakes, but Candice made a kind of growling sound and charged ahead. The guard barely had time to reach for his Mace before Candice was suddenly airborne. In a move that would have put Jet Li to shame, she karate-kicked him in the nose, which sent him spinning to the floor. We dashed through the emergency exit and out into the open, gaining ten more yards before a dozen rifles cocked and a booming voice yelled, "Halt! Get down on the ground. Now!"

Candice grabbed my arm and pulled me to a stop. We dropped facedown in the dirt, our hands over our heads. I was panting so hard and my heart was racing so fast I thought I was going to pass out, but something leaked through the fog of my exhaustion that made my skin crawl. I heard uproarious laughter.

I wanted to turn my head to Candice, but I was truly too scared to move. The laughing continued. And then it sank in that I knew that laugh and knew it well. It was thick and throaty and oh-so-sexy. Very slowly I turned my head and looked up. Standing over me were six feet two inches of solid Greek god.

"Dutch!" I yelped and got to my knees. "Ohmigod! Thank God it's you!"

"Did you start all this?" he asked, pointing up to the sky, and I slowly took in the three helicopters circling the prison and an entire squadron of state and local police emptying out of police cars, not to mention the SWAT teams and FBI filing around the perimeter.

"Me?" I said innocently and forced a laugh. Candice also got to her knees and looked up at Dutch. Turning to her, I said, "Can you believe this guy?"

She forced a giggle. "I know!" she said. "Thinking we had anything to do with a prison riot—that's just *crazy!*'

Dutch helped us both to our feet and gave a signal for the other FBI agents with their big scary guns to stand down.

"Want to tell me what you're doing here?" he asked.

"Candice?" I said to her. "Show the man."

Candice reached up to her lapel, turned it back to the tiny pocket, and pulled out her itty-bitty recorder. "It's all on this microchip, Agent Rivers," she said. "I'm pretty sure you'll be delighted to hear that Warden Sinclair has confessed to killing Walter McDaniel, and you'll also have enough there to put Dick Wolfe away for a very long time."

Several days later Dutch and I were sitting on my couch and he was pumping me for information. "You *promise* me this is off the record?" I asked.

"Scout's honor," he said, holding up his hand pledge-style.

"Fine," I said after checking my lie detector. "Right before we made it to the prison, I had Candice pull over and check a few things on her computer so I could put the final pieces of the puzzle together."

"What things?"

"Well, first I had her look back into Dillon's financial records, because the box on the loan applications was checked for private mortgage insurance and I wanted to see when the balances of the loans were paid off."

"When were they paid off?"

"They were paid in full about two months after his father's death."

"So he knew going into it that his father was a target?"

"That I can't say for sure, but I do know he had a lot of guilt over it."

"How do you know that?"

"In his house is this huge portrait of King Edward the Seventh. I did a quick Google search on Edward and it turns out that one of the biggest stories about him was that when his father, Prince Albert, died, Edward's mother, Queen Victoria, accused her son of patricide. She said that it was the stress he'd caused by being such a deviant from the family that had killed his father."

"That boy's in need of some serious therapy," Dutch said, shaking his head.

I nodded. "Anyway, the next call I made was to Selena. I told her that it was imperative that she contact her brother, Nero—he's that inmate at Jackson I told you was being beaten up—immediately and have him call us."

"Why do I think I'm not going to like where this is headed?"

I smiled. "Remember," I sang, "we're still off the record."

Dutch sighed and looked like he was bracing himself. "Go on."

"So we talked to Nero, and he's a really nice guy, it turns out—"

"If you like criminals," Dutch interrupted sarcastically.

I rolled my eyes. "Anyway, he was more than willing to help us with a little, er . . . distraction, if that meant it would stop the blackmail against his family and bring the guys who were doing it to justice."

Dutch tapped me on the head and said, "You are just damn lucky no one was seriously hurt by your 'little distraction.' "

I gave him a big grin. "All part of the plan," I said. "I knew the warden would agree to meet with us. He's that type of guy, very egocentric."

"*Was* that type of guy," Dutch corrected, and that caught me off guard.

"What?" I asked.

"He hanged himself late last night. I didn't know if I should tell you or not."

I blinked at him a few times, but I honestly couldn't feel sad. Sinclair was one bad dude. "Probably took the easy way out," I said. "As a former prison warden, he would probably have been doomed to much worse in prison."

"Exactly," said Dutch. "So I'm assuming that when the tape ends at the part about you asking the warden if he believes in magic, that's when the riot broke out?"

I smiled again. "Nice timing, don't you think?"

Dutch shook his head. "I'm taking you to Vegas, Edgar. You're too lucky for words."

I snuggled closer to him and changed the subject slightly. "How's Bree?"

"She's good," he said. "I stopped by her house on the way here to check in on her. She's even found a new job that pays better money, if you can believe it."

"Really?" I asked, my tongue firmly in my cheek.

"Yeah," he said as he squeezed me tight and gave the top of my head a kiss. "Turns out someone put in a really good reference for her at that bank you used to work at."

"You don't say," I said.

"And she's got a pipeline of loans to refinance too," Dutch added. "She'd been taking the top page of every loan application home with her for the past two years, just in case she was ever cut loose."

I giggled. "Good for her," I said. "My radar says that she and her hubby won't be worrying about their finances for much longer." Then I thought of something else and asked, "What happens now with your boss?"

Dutch gave a sigh that blew wisps of my hair around. "As you know, when I walked in and accused the SAC of misconduct, I got my ass handed to me."

I gulped. "You may have mentioned that."

"But in a way it was good, because now I know the SAC's on my side. He's going to be overseeing the investigation, making sure that I'm given clearance on my end to come up with proof, while leading Robillard in the opposite direction."

"But Robillard's still going to be working at the Bureau?"

Dutch nodded and his chin rubbed my head. "Yep. For the time being, I've got to pretend like nothing has changed. I'll still be reporting to him, but when I give him a status on Frost's murder it will be the same as all the other investigators, bubkes."

"I don't like that you have to work for such a dangerous man," I said, twisting around to face him. "What if he finds out you're investigating him?"

Dutch smiled confidently. "He won't, babycakes. Trust me."

The worry in my heart only increased. "Please be careful, Dutch. Okay?"

Dutch stroked my cheek. "Always," he said. "And speaking of investigating, have you gotten any other feelings on those two college kids who disappeared?"

I frowned. "You know, I looked at that file again yesterday, and there's just nothing new. The creepy thing is that I know we're not done with it. Something else is coming. It just hasn't happened yet, but trust me, when it does we'll know."

"Sounds ominous," Dutch said with a smile that didn't quite touch his eyes.

I nodded. "Tell me about it."

We fell silent for a moment and then he said, "Hey, you feel like coming for a drive with me?"

"Where're we going?" I asked.

"I have a surprise," he said coyly. "And no tuning in on it before I show it to you!" he demanded sternly.

My eyes widened and I let out a laugh. "Okay, okay!" I said, holding up my hands in surrender. "I promise. If the radar buzzes I will not tune in."

Dutch pulled me up off the couch and Eggy followed us to the door. I looked from my dog, whose tail was wagging furiously, back to Dutch. "Bring him," Dutch said with a grin.

We piled into Dutch's SUV and had driven only a short distance when Dutch reached into the glove box and pulled something out. "Here," he said, handing me a sleeping mask.

"You're kidding me," I said, looking at him like he was crazy.

"Come on," he replied with a big grin. "I want you to be surprised."

"Fine," I said. I donned the mask. "But it's messing up my good-hair day."

We drove for a little longer. Then I felt the SUV come to a stop. I heard Dutch's door open and he said, "Hang tight. I'll come around and get you." I waited for another couple of seconds and heard my own door open. "Here we are," he said as he reached in and picked me up by the waist to help me down.

"Can I take off the mask now?" I asked.

"Almost," he said. He swiveled me around and had me walk awkwardly forward for a few steps. "Okay, you can take it off now."

I whipped off the mask and opened my eyes. We were at Dutch's house, but the structure was almost unrecognizable. Construction had completely overtaken the bungalow and there was a huge addition where the bedroom window used to be. "What are you doing to your house?" I asked.

Just then the front door opened and Dave stepped out onto the front porch. "Afternoon, boss," he said jovially to Dutch.

"Dave." Dutch nodded and grabbed my hand to take me up the rest of the walkway. "Congratulations, by the way," he added, indicating the shiny new band of gold on Dave's left ring finger.

I gasped and looked down at Dave's hand. "You did it?" I said.

"I did," he grumbled, working hard to conceal a grin. "My old lady and I are officially hitched."

"Dave, that's fantastic!" I squealed. "Tell me all about it!"

"I will, but first I'm supposed to show you around," he said and waved us in.

Dutch's living room and dining room remained untouched, but that was about the only space that wasn't currently under construction. "Over here is the new kitchen," Dave was saying as we stepped over several pieces of lumber.

I did the appropriate "ooohing" and "ahhhing," admiring the increased size and the new cabinetry. "It's amazing, guys."

"But wait! There's more," said Dave happily. "This way, lady and gentleman."

We followed him back through the living room and up the stairs and I stopped in my tracks as I saw the huge master suite open up in front of me. "Ohmigod!" I exclaimed. "This is huge!"

"Yep," said Dave. "We pushed out several feet to create room for a walk-in closet and, over on that side, a new bathroom."

I walked into the closet and said, "This is bigger than my study!"

"And speaking of studies," said Dave, wagging a finger at us to follow him back down the stairs and around to a new room just off Dutch's study, "in here is the room that I've just finished." He opened a door.

As I passed him, I noticed he gave a big wink to Dutch, and the minute I was inside I knew why. In a little doggy bed on the floor was a cute little dachshund puppy, who struggled off the bed on chubby legs and over to us. "A puppy!" I yelled and clapped my hands as I squatted down. "Dutch, when did you get it?"

"Yesterday," he said. He came over and sat on the floor next to me. "I'm calling her Tuttle."

"Unusual name," I said as Eggy sniffed the puppy and happily wagged his tail. "I think Eggy likes her."

"He better," said Dutch and looked up nervously at Dave. "Can you give us a minute?"

Dave nodded and closed the door behind him. "So what's going on?" I asked. I let Tuttle go and she and Eggy began to chase each other around the room. "I mean, I don't think Virgil's going to take kindly to you getting a puppy."

"He doesn't have to worry about it," Dutch said.

I reached out and grabbed his arm in alarm. "What have you done with Virgil?" I demanded.

Dutch laughed. "He's with my mother," he said. "She's always loved that damn cat, and her own kitty, Moppet, died last year. I could tell she was ready for another one and I thought it was a good solution."

"You gave away your cat?" I said.

"I gave my mom a loving companion and solved the issue of space for my girlfriend."

"So this is why you're doing all the construction?" I gasped. "You did this all so that when I came over I wouldn't feel cramped?"

Dutch reached into his pocket and pulled something out. He opened my hand and placed a beautiful Tiffany key ring and a shiny new key in the palm of my hand. "No, Abby. I did this so that when I asked you to move in with me, we wouldn't have space or cats or anything else between us."

Tears welled in my eyes as I looked down at my palm. "Oh, Dutch," was all I could manage.

"I miss you when you're not around," he said. "I can't sleep when you're not next to me, and I worry a lot about what you're up to."

I laughed and reached up to cup his face in my hands. "I can't believe you did all this for me," I said to him.

"So say yes," he said.

"Yes," I said. "As soon as I find a renter for my place, I will move in with you."

Dutch smiled and wiggled his eyebrows. "I may know someone who's a little tired of their living arrangement and is looking for a house to rent."

"You do?" I asked.

"And you do too," he said. "Why don't you call Candice and see if she's had enough of living in a Pepto-Bismol bottle?"

As I leaned forward to kiss his socks off, I said, "You think of everything."

Winking at me and using his best Humphrey Bogart voice, he said, "That's why you got the radar and I got the brains, sweethot."

Read on for a sneak peek
at another Psychic Eye adventure
from Victoria Laurie

Death Perception

Available from Signet

Death has an energy.

It is thick as sludge, heavy as iron, and pulls you down into yourself like an imploding building. And as I sat across from the concerned mother of a very sick young woman and tuned in, it was the last thing I wanted to feel. "Please tell me my daughter will be all right," she whispered, her voice filled with fear. She'd obviously read the look on my face after she had asked about her daughter.

I had two choices here: I could tell her the truth or I could avoid telling her that her daughter had no hope—no chance at all. I looked up, prepared to meet those pleading eyes and be straight with her, but when I did . . .

I.

Just.

Couldn't.

"Marion," I said softly, "the energy I'm feeling here isn't good." A tear slid down Marion's cheek, yet her eyes remained fixed on mine, unblinking and welling with moisture. "I believe you and the doctors are doing absolutely everything you can to save her," I added. "And I don't think there is one thing more you can do to change the outcome. You have done everything humanly possible to help her fight for her life, and if she survives, it will be because of all the efforts you've made. The rest is up to her."

Marion swallowed a sob as I fought to hold my own emotions in check. "I can't lose her," she said. "She's my only daughter, Abby. I simply cannot face life without her!"

I took a deep breath. Breaking down in front of this woman would only add to her fear. "I know you're scared out of your mind right now, Marion. But your daughter needs you to be okay with whatever her outcome is. She needs to know that if she loses the battle against her illness, you'll be able to go on. That's the one gift you have left to give her, Marion. The one thing you can still do for her is to reassure her that you are strong enough to live your life to the fullest, even if she's not around."

Marion buried her face in her hands and I reached forward to rub her shoulder. "It's my fault," she sobbed. "It's all my fault."

"How could this possibly be your fault?" I asked.

Marion's body shuddered as she tried to pull herself together. "Julie called me from college. She said she found a bump on the side of her neck. She said it was about the size of a pea. I told her that it was probably a cyst. I had them when I was her age and didn't think anything of it. I told her that if the bump was still there when the semester ended, we'd get it checked out. The cancer had six more weeks to spread to the rest of her lymph nodes."

I bit my lip. Oh, man, that was rough. "Marion," I

whispered to her. "My crew is saying that there was no way you could have known. You didn't do this, and even if you had rushed her to a doctor right away, the end results would likely be the same." This was another lie, but at this point the only thing I could do for this woman was allow her the chance to forgive herself. Marion lifted her chin and stared me in the eyes, and I willed myself to look back without blinking. "It wasn't your fault, sweetheart," I said firmly. "You couldn't have known."

She nodded just as my appointment timer gave a small *ting*! We were out of time. Marion stood and I handed her several tissues to go with the one in her hand. "You're very kind," she said to me as she took the tissues.

"So are you," I replied, leaning in to give her a long, hard hug. "Now go and be with your daughter," I said, stepping back. "I'll keep Julie in my thoughts and prayers, and you call me anytime you need someone to talk to, okay?"

Marion sniffled and handed me some bills. "I will," she said hoarsely.

After she'd gone I went back into my office and sat down heavily. Turning my chair to the window I put my feet up on the sill, leaned my head back, and let the tears flow.

Sometimes, my job really sucked.

"Hey," said a voice behind me.

I swiveled my chair around and looked up at my business partner, Candice Fusco, standing just outside the door. "Hey," I said, my voice shaky.

"You okay?"

I inhaled deeply and wiped my cheeks. "Tough session."

Candice came into the room and sat down on the other side of my desk. "Want to tell me about it?"

I attempted a smile. "Just the psychic blues," I said. "I'll be okay."

Candice gave me a sympathetic look. "Must be hard to see what you see sometimes, huh?"

I cleared my throat. "Can be. Is that a file you need me to look at?" I asked, changing the subject and pointing to a folder in her lap.

She nodded. "It's our latest assignment. Family wants to see if we can hunt down the missing father. He disappeared six months ago."

I sighed. I didn't want to look at the file just then. I'd seen enough death for one day, and I didn't think I could tune in on another family about to be torn apart by the worst-case scenario. "Any chance it can wait until tomorrow?"

Candice smiled. "Of course. You look like shit, anyway. Why don't you go home to that hunka-hunka-burnin' love and have him take your mind off things."

That got a giggle out of me. "Thanks for understanding, girl," I said as I stood up. "I'll see you at the gym bright and early, okay?" Candice and I were also workout buddies.

"Sounds good. You hang in there, Abs."

I left my office, which sits in an old but charming building in the heart of downtown Royal Oak, Michigan, and stopped at the liquor store, where I picked up a bottle of wine—okay, two bottles of wine—then boogied home. With relief, I noticed my boyfriend's SUV already parked in the driveway, but then I also spotted a beat-up blue pickup parked in the street. My handyman and business partner, Dave, was also in attendance. *Damn*, I thought. I was really hoping it would be just my honey and me.

As I breezed through the door, I was greeted by

the smell of fresh baking bread and a roast in the oven. My boyfriend Dutch can *hang* in the kitchen— hence the reason Dave was taking so long to finish the addition he'd started three months ago, since he kept getting invited to dinner. "Abs?" Dutch called when he heard the door open.

"Hey, babe," I said wearily as I flopped on the couch. I was immediately pounced on by my dog, Eggy, and Dutch's new puppy, Tuttle, who wriggled and fought each other for my attention.

Dutch poked his head out of the kitchen doorway, took one look at my face, and said, "You okay?"

I nodded. "Yeah," I said with a sigh. "Just a really long day."

Dutch brightened. "Your practice is back up and kickin', huh?" My professional psychic practice had suffered greatly when I'd had to take a three-month hiatus to recover from a bullet wound I had gotten in February.

I nodded again. "It is good to be earning my own keep again."

"Dinner will be on the table in two minutes. Can you let Dave know?"

I rolled my eyes. "Ah, yes, our foster child. I'll let him know."

Dutch grinned. "He's bound to be done sometime, Edgar," he said, using his nickname for me, after the famed psychic Edgar Cayce.

"Oh, trust me, if anyone can milk the clock, it's Dave." I pushed up off the couch and trudged to the stairwell.

"Be nice," Dutch called after me.

I headed into the bedroom and found Dave on a ladder with the world's smallest paintbrush. I rolled my eyes again and cleared my throat to get his attention. "Hey, Abby," he said as he swiveled around. "How was your day?"

"Productive," I said to him. "I got *so* much done!"

"Good for you," he said, turning back to painting the wall with itty-bitty strokes.

I scowled. He'd missed the hint. "Wouldn't that go on better with a roller?"

Dave swiveled back to me again. "Yeah, but you don't get the great texture results that you get with a brush. Trust me, when this is finished, you'll appreciate the attention to detail."

"*When* being the operative word here," I said with a grin.

"True craftsmanship takes time," Dave said and took a whiff. "Dinner smells like it's about ready."

"You mean you can smell something other than paint fumes?" I asked.

Dave smiled. "This snout smells all," he said, pointing to his slightly oversized nose.

"Yes, Dave, dinner is ready. Put the paintbrush down and come to the table."

Dave nodded and I headed back downstairs. As I walked into the kitchen Dutch handed me a glass of the wine I'd brought home. "Here," he said. "It'll take that edge off."

I smiled at him and leaned in to wrap my arms around him. "You're a really great boyfriend, you know?"

Dutch gave the top of my head a kiss. "So you *need* to keep telling me."

I laughed and sat down at the table. A moment later Dave joined us and Dutch handed out plates of food piled high with roast beef, mashed potatoes, green beans, and fresh bread. "Man!" Dave said as he ogled his plate. "All my old lady ever serves up are TV dinners!"

I gave Dutch a pointed look that said, "See? *This* is why he won't go home!"

Dutch hid a smile and pulled a package from under his chair wrapped in plain pink paper with a matching bow. "Here," he said, passing it to me.

"What's this?" I asked, my mood lifting.

"For you," he said. "Open it."

"Is it your birthday?" Dave said with a note of panic and a mouth stuffed with food. " 'Cuz, no one told me!"

"It's not my birthday," I said to him, and eyed Dutch quizzically. "And it's not our anniversary . . ."

"It's a 'just because' present, Abs," Dutch said. "Now open it."

I ripped off the paper and realized it was a book. Turning it over, I read the title. *"Cooking for Dummies,"* I said, all the joy leaving me.

"Yeah!" Dutch said with enthusiasm. "You know, because you're always telling me you wish you could cook."

I scowled at him, because, for the record, I was *not* always telling him I wished I could cook. This was Dutch's not-so-subtle attempt to domesticate me, something I fought him tooth and nail on. "Ah," I said, a flicker of anger entering my voice. "So, all the copies of *Cooking for Absolute Idiots* were sold out?"

Dutch sighed. "Edgar . . ." he began.

I flipped open the book and pretended to read. "Ah! Here's something I can handle! Quick dinner suggestions: First, remove outer plastic wrapping from popcorn package . . ."

"Opened up a can of worms, there, buddy," Dave mumbled to Dutch.

"Abby," Dutch tried again. "I didn't mean—"

I dramatically flipped a few more pages. "Ooooh! A recipe for pizza! First, look up local delivery options in your neighborhood. Next, pick up phone and dial number . . ."

"If you need a place to crash tonight, you can bunk in my spare bedroom," Dave said to Dutch out of the corner of his mouth.

Just then the phone rang and my head snapped up, my radar on high alert as warning bells loudly shot off in my head. "You have to get that," I said to Dutch in all seriousness. Dutch gave me a quizzical look as the phone rang again. "Now!" I said as I closed the book and set it on the kitchen table.

Dutch stood and walked over to the phone. "It's my mom," he announced, looking at the caller ID. My stomach bunched as he picked up the line. I didn't know what had happened, but something awful was about to unfold here.

My assumptions were confirmed when we heard Dutch say, "Mom . . . Mom, it's okay. Don't cry. I'm here. Just tell me what's wrong."

Dave and I exchanged a look as Dutch walked out to the living room to sit down on the couch and talk to his mother. "What's your radar telling you?" Dave whispered to me.

"It's bad," I said. "I don't know what it is, but it's bad."

Dave ate the rest of his meal in silence and I pushed the food around on my plate, both of us straining to hear snatches of conversation from the living room. Finally Dutch came back, his face pale and his features tight. "It's Chad," he said.

"Your cousin?" I asked.

Dutch nodded. "He's been kidnapped."

I gasped. "Oh, God!" I hurried over to him. "What happened?"

"He was working security for some wealthy oil guy out in Vegas, and the last anyone saw of them was when they headed out to one of the casinos. Mom said they found the car pumped full of bullets, but with no sign of Chad or the guy he was guarding."

I squeezed my arms around Dutch. "When do we leave?" I asked him.

Dutch squeezed me back. "I'm going to catch the first flight I can, Abs. You should stay here."

"Not a chance in hell, cowboy," I said sternly. "You'll need my radar now more than ever."

There was a long pause and finally I felt Dutch kiss the top of my head and whisper, "Okay, Edgar. Have it your way. Now go upstairs and pack us some things while I book us a flight."

"What can I do?" Dave asked as he got up from the table.

"Look after the dogs while we're gone," Dutch said.

"You got it, partner," Dave said, and gave him a pat on the arm.

I left them to hurry up the stairs and pack. My radar had told me that today was going to bring something terrible. I figured it had been my reading session with Marion, though now I realized it was that awful phone call. But even as I pulled a large suitcase from the closet with trepidation, I had no real appreciation for the fact that my nightmare was only just beginning.